Reckless Encounters

Reckless Hearts Series
Book Three

L.A. SHAW

Copyright © 2024 by L.A. Shaw

All rights reserved. No part of this book may be reproduced, distributed, or transmitted in any form or by any means, without prior written permission from the publisher or author. Except for the use of brief quotations in a book review or as otherwise permitted by the U.S. Copyright Law.

This is a work of fiction. Names, characters, businesses, places, brands, media, events, and incidents are either the products of the author's imagination or are used fictitiously. Any resemblance to actual persons, living or deceased, or events is purely coincidence.

Reckless Encounters

Editor: Mackenzie at Nice Girl Naughty Edits

Cover Design: L.A. Shaw - Canva

Formatting: L.A. Shaw - Vellum

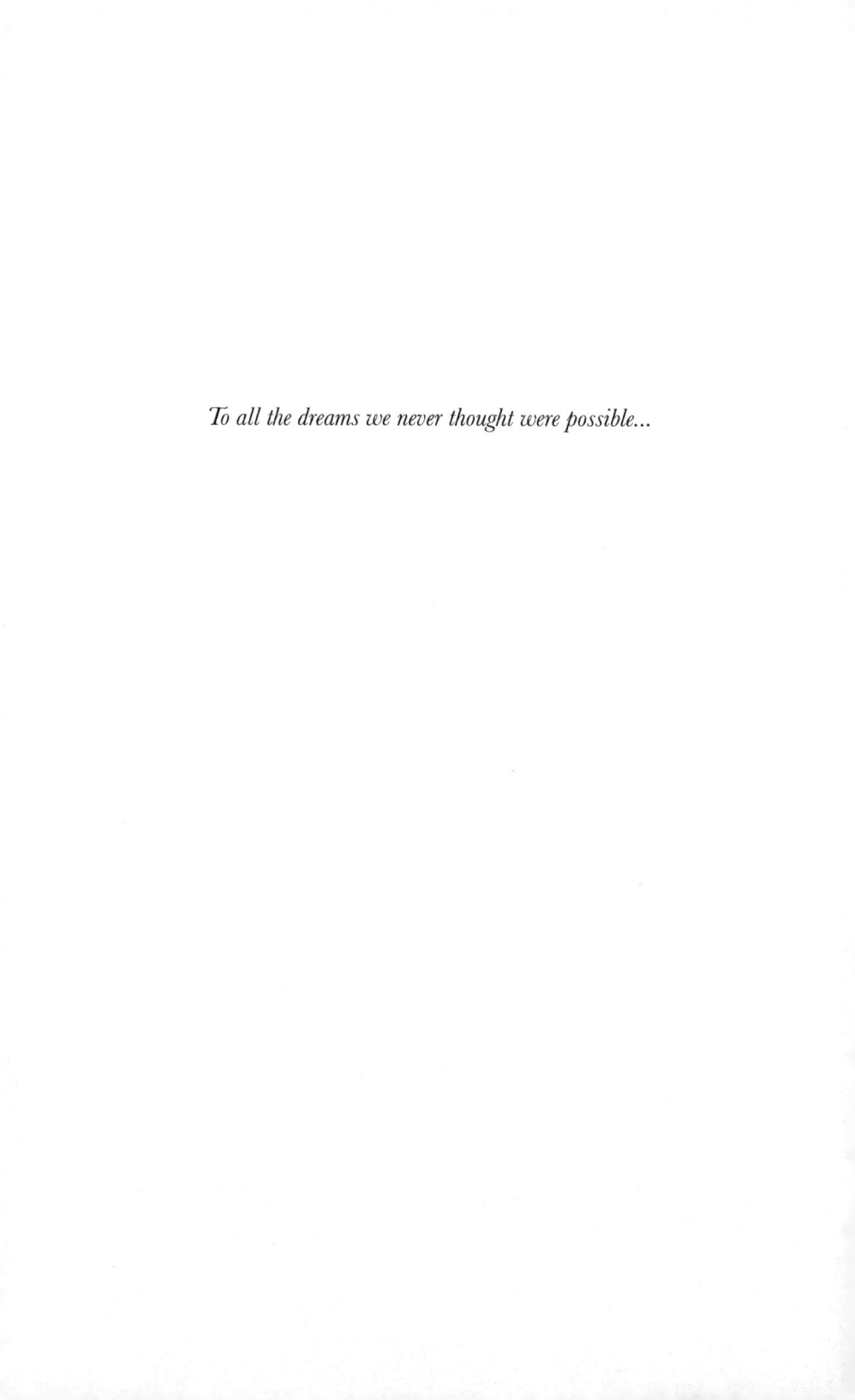

To all the dreams we never thought were possible...

Playlist

Music plays an important role in our writing process…
So, please enjoy our Reckless Encounters playlist.

Author's Note

Your reading experience is important to us.
Please scan the QR code for our
Content Warnings

Prologue

Parker

"Let's go, man, why aren't you dressed yet?" my buddy Eli asks as he strolls through the elevator door. Note to self: take away his keycard privileges. Now that he has a spot just a few blocks over, there's no need for him to have full access to my place.

"You told me nine o'clock," I say, peering up at him from my book, completely unphased by his annoyance.

"Uber will be here in fifteen minutes. I don't want to be late."

I casually slide a bookmark between the pages and place it on the coffee table.

"Be ready in ten. Beers are in the fridge," I say and make my way down the hall.

Honestly, I could probably be ready in five, but I want him to sweat it out a little. He's desperately hoping to see Quinn tonight, and I'm hoping for the distractions only opening night at an exclusive club can offer.

Eli's sister is the proud owner of New York's newest exclusive club, Masqued. Where its members have access to endless possibilities, most of which are of the…more risqué nature.

It's been a long week of countless meetings and dealing with people's bullshit. I could certainly use some distractions tonight, particularly one with long legs, a nice ass, and a gorgeous face.

A pounding fist on my bedroom door sounds as I'm finishing up the last few buttons on my signature black collared shirt. Grabbing my belt off the end of my bed, I stroll to the impatient Eli.

"Alright, you ready?" Eli asks with a huff.

I respond with a grin as I lace my belt through the loops of my black pants, fastening the blacked-out buckle.

Eli eyes my all-black outfit. "Have you ever considered adding some color to your wardrobe? Might make you more approachable."

"I'm good. Thanks, though." Smirking, I grab my wallet from the table in my entryway. Being approachable is the last thing I want to be.

I'VE ALREADY LOST Eli within a minute after the quick tour the Masqued hostess gave us. She pointed out the different areas within the club, and what to expect on each floor and down each hallway. To say my interest is piqued would be an understatement. I'm ready for anything and everything tonight might have in store for me.

With my black mask securely in place, I make my way to the bar and take in my surroundings in finer detail. I'm quite impressed by the design and finishes. Which is saying a lot coming from me, considering I eat, sleep, and breathe this shit. Unique lighting fixtures adorn the space, blanketing the main room in sensually dim light. Deep red velvet curtains line tall walls leading up to the two open upper, the color matching the bar seating and surrounding booths. The fixtures throughout are a blend of metal and wood, which only accentuate the overall vibe this place gives off. It's dark, seductive, and intriguing.

I'm greeted by a warm smile when I step up to the long bar top. The lace mask covering half of her face surrounds big brown eyes. "What can I get you?" she asks while placing down a cocktail napkin in preparation.

"Johnnie Walker Blue neat, please."

"Sure thing, be right back."

Turning around, I lean on the counter to see if I can spot Eli or anyone else I might know, for that matter. Eli and Wes tower over the crowd, and I spot them easily from across the room. Once I pay for my drink, I head their way.

Sloan is nestled in their little circle, and I lean in to kiss her cheek. Her velvet burgundy mask emphasizes her sparkling bright blue eyes.

"Place looks amazing, Lo. You did a great job."

"Thank you so much. I can't take all the credit. I had a vision, and Ava ran with it," she gushes.

"Ahh, yes. I should have assumed it was Ava behind this."

"Yes, you should've…" She smiles as her eyebrow quirks above her mask, but before she can continue, a male employee wearing a tailored suit pulls her attention. I must admit, the employees are all impeccably dressed and good-looking. Their uniforms match the feel of this place perfectly—the men in their suits and women in sheer backless dresses that exude sex appeal and exclusivity.

"How's it going, Wes?" I turn to him.

"Hey, man. Going great. Thanks for coming out tonight."

"You think I'd miss this?" I say with a smirk and raise my glass.

He chuckles and clinks his glass to mine. I look to Eli, who adds his already empty cup to our cheers.

My eyes dart back to Wes, who subtly shakes his head. *Well, shit.* I guess Quinn is not here like he had hoped.

"Enjoy yourselves, boys. The night is young," he says before walking away.

"You alright?" I ask Eli, knowing the answer I'll receive will be half-assed.

"Yeah, she already left... I'm going to get another drink."

While watching his retreating form stride across the room, a leggy blonde catches my eye. She's standing off to the side, entertaining quite a large group of people. She's stunning in a skin-tight, black, knee-length dress, showcasing her sculpted legs in high heels.

I continue sipping my whiskey as I watch her, gauging whether she's here with anyone. There's a break in their group conversation, and her eyes scan the room, eventually landing on me, who is blatantly staring. She raises her champagne glass in my direction, and I reciprocate from where I stand.

Eli rejoins me a second later, pulling my focus. He seems absolutely miserable, and I know him well enough to sense he's not sticking around for long.

Spotting an open circular booth that allows for a perfect view of my conquest, I nod in that direction. "Want to sit for a bit?" I ask him.

"Yeah, sure."

We remain silent as we sit, taking in the club from this position. Looking upward, you can see two more floors with glass railings. Allowing the patrons roaming the upper levels a clear view of the center stage.

"I think the burlesque show is starting," I say, noting the stage now being illuminated by soft spotlights.

"I'm probably heading out in a few," Eli says into his glass.

"You sure?"

"Yeah. There's nothing here for me," he murmurs, then throws back the rest of his drink.

A cute cocktail waitress comes to the opening of our circular booth. "Good evening. I'm Maggie, and I'll be your waitress. Can I get you guys anything?"

Eli doesn't even respond, just stares blankly at his hands, holding the empty glass.

"I'll have another Johnnie Blue neat, please. And he'll have a water and a beer."

Once the waitress leaves, my eyes search the crowd for the blonde. I find her in deep conversation with Sloan and Wesley across the room in a booth of their own. Her smile is radiant, one I can't seem to stop stealing glances of. So much so, I'm having a hard time pulling my focus to the half-naked woman walking out onto the stage.

Our drinks are delivered, and another bout of silence fills our booth as we watch the burlesque dancer move about. Not even ten minutes later, I can tell Eli is ready to go. He's restless and has no interest in being here. His face is void of any emotion other than disappointment.

The lights dim, and the stagehand collects the discarded clothes before scurrying off. With that, Eli stands, as I predicted. "I'm going to head out. I'll catch up with you tomorrow."

There's no point in asking him to stay, so instead I tell him to get home safely. He escapes just before the next dancer comes onto the stage, but this time, there's a chair in the middle.

The show continues for about an hour, with each performer bringing something different to the stage. Overall, it's hot as hell, and I'm thankful I get to experience it all.

My leggy blonde has since relocated to a small area behind the booths, where she is swaying her hips to the heavy beats streaming through the speakers. As her tight body leans against a pole, she's certainly using it to her advantage. I can't help but notice the small crowd forming around her, but there is no conversation involved—just pure lust. They're more interested in her than anything else in the room. Watching how she twists and glides her body teasingly. Well aware of the number of eyes she has on her. The way her pouty red lips curve into a small smirk when our eyes lock from across the space.

Without realizing, I have moved my position in my circular booth so I can have a better view of her and the show she's putting on. My dick aches, thinking about all the things I'd like to do to her. Picturing her long, toned thighs wrapped around my ears, the gasp I'd hear when I'm fully seated inside of her, the way that pretty mouth of hers would scream my name as I make her come all over my cock. *Fuck, I'm rock hard now.*

My concentration is broken when Wes's big fucking frame steps between me and my soon-to-be conquest.

I nod at him. "What's up, man?"

I clearly haven't been subtle in my admiration of the masked vixen across the way, because he glances over at her and then back at me. "You sure you know what you're doing?"

"I'm more than sure," I smirk, knowing no dumber words have ever been spoken.

I don't actually know what the fuck I'm doing or about to get myself into. But I don't seem to care, because my sight is set on her and it has been since the moment I saw her.

Shaking his head, he disappears up the stairs to where Sloan is waiting. I raise my glass to where she peers out over the club, a proud grin on her face. Good, she should be proud; tonight has been a huge success, and there is nothing I enjoy more than cheering on my friends and their accomplishments.

Next thing I know, a keycard is being placed on my table. Maggie smiles at me while setting another drink beside it.

"A member asked me to deliver this to you. She said she'll be in Room 8." She points in the direction of the hallway.

"Thank you, Maggie," I say, reaching for the tumbler, but leaving the golden beacon of a keycard where it lies on the table.

I glance over at the now-empty dance area. It appears my girl has taken matters into her own hands—well, at least it better be her.

There's only one way to find out.

Sipping my drink, I buy myself some time before heading to the room. I want her squirming with anticipation by the time I arrive, questioning whether I will show up. Wondering if she made the right decision to have this card delivered to my table.

Of course, the answer is yes to both. If she didn't make the first move, I sure as hell was going to. But there is something so fucking sexy about a woman initiating such an intimate thing.

I throw back the last of my glass and signal for Maggie to drop off my check. Then, before I know it, I'm striding down the wide hallway shrouded with the same burgundy velvet curtains and frosted glass windows. Eli explained to me earlier that the room's occupants can adjust the privacy screen on their door, ranging from completely opaque to full-on voyeur, enabling clear. Judging by the small gatherings scattered around several of the rooms, their occupants are putting on quite the show.

As I approach Room 8, I take note that the glass is partially hazy. *Interesting...my girl wants to put on a show but remain anonymous. I'm game, Legs, for any and all of it.*

The door's keypad flashes green with a wave of my card, and I step inside.

"Took you long enough." Her sassy voice sounds from across the room. She's fucking gorgeous, standing there all flustered and sipping from her champagne flute.

I'm unable to stop my smirk as I take her in. "Well, hello to you too, Ava."

One

Ava

A little over a year and a half later

Keep that head high, babe. I let my best friend Sloan's voice repeat over and over in my head.

The fresh cut to my sleek blonde bob, paired with the brand-new outfit I spent way too much on at Bloomingdale's this past weekend, is my warrior suit. I'm smiling because I know I'm good at what I do, and the nerves rumbling in my stomach are my reminder not to let the mask slip from my face. *Never let them see you sweat.*

Generally, I'm a self-assured person. I learned a long time ago that letting people see your weaknesses gets you nowhere. But today's different… Today, I'm walking into a den of wolves. Bryant & Co is one of the wealthiest investment firms in the city, and you'd have to be dead not to be nervous about an interview with them. Especially with the most arrogant asshole of them all leading the pack.

I walk past my favorite café in the West Village, taking deep breaths as I summon more confidence with every step. It's typically my first stop every morning before I am even fully functioning. But not today. I've seen way too many movies where the lead female character spills coffee all over her shirt before a big interview, and I am not about to let that be my luck.

Instead, I Doordashed a cup while I did my hair and makeup earlier this morning. The liquid gold is safely flowing through my veins and my cream blouse is perfectly intact. Win-Win.

A few blocks into SoHo, my heart thuds louder, knowing I am getting close.

This is my biggest bid yet, and it's a literal dream project for me. The only downfall is the six-foot-four tattooed suit that just so happens to be heading the project.

If I don't get it… *Nope*. Manifest good shit only.

When I get it, it's going to change my career and, honestly, my life. Interior design has been a dream of mine for as long as I can remember, but I quickly realized making a name for myself without using family connections wasn't going to be easy.

Two years ago, I left the design company I was working for and went out on my own. It was a huge chance to take starting my own business at twenty-six, but since then, I have had the opportunity to work on some really cool projects and be in complete control with my clients.

As I approach the front doors of Luxure, I take a second to admire the outside of the hotel's building. They are halfway through the construction phase of the revamp, and it's time to hire a designer that fits with the investor's style and desires.

The brick exterior may only be five stories tall, but my mind has already created so many ideas to pack into the inside of those five levels. Lucky for me, they have a French theme in mind, and thanks to my aunt who now lives there, I visit multiple times a year. If there was ever another place I would live besides New York City, it would be Paris, France.

My eyes lift to the sky, grounding myself between all the tall city buildings. Deep breath, smile in place. *Keep that head high, babe.*

"Good morning," an unfamiliar voice says from beside me as he reaches the handle and motions for me to enter. I say a quick "thank you" in response and walk through the open door.

"You must be Ava… I'm Logan." He holds out his hand, introducing himself.

"Hi, yes, that's me. How'd you know?"

Logan's stare lingers on my face. "Just a good guess. You are our first interview of the day." And then he's on the move again. "Follow me, I'll show you to our meeting room."

His welcoming demeanor calms my nerves slightly, but the thought of all the interviews to come after me has doubt stirring low in my belly.

As he leads me down a long corridor, I try taking in the changes from the pictures I've researched online of how the inside of the building used to look.

"This was one of the first rooms we had them finish so we could conduct meetings in here, just no paint or décor yet," he says, opening the door. "But that's why we are calling in the experts, like you."

Logan gives me one last reassuring smile as we walk into the room. Pulling the chair at one of the ends of the table out for me, he says, "Sit here so you can see everyone, as well as have easy access to the PowerPoint. The rest of the board should be in any minute."

I dig into my bag for my laptop and remind myself to thank Logan. I'm so overwhelmed, I've barely spoken to him. "Thanks for your help, Logan."

"Anytime." He smirks like there is more he wants to say.

In another setting, I would probably be flirting with a guy like Logan. He's handsome and well-dressed, plus he seems kind. No red flags yet… But right now, I need to focus.

Just as I get my pitch set up and turn back to look at the screen, *the* walking red flag himself waltzes into the room, causing a different type of feeling to stir inside me.

At the sight of one of his tattoos peeking out from under his suit jacket, I'm suddenly parched. From the very first time I met him, I knew he was an arrogant prick, but the way my thighs clench together whenever I see him is a testimony that the rest of my body doesn't care what my brain thinks about the man.

Apparently, ridiculously sexy combined with broody asshole speaks to my vagina in a way nothing else does.

My mind drifts back to that first night at Kings Hideaway over a year and a half ago…

Immediate desire ripples through me at the sight of the man approaching my end of the table. His black tailored shirt opens just enough to show off the sexy tattoos he's sporting under it.

Apparently liking what he sees by the sexy smirk that graces his mouth, his gaze peruses over me from head to toe.

When his tongue pokes out, licking over his bottom lip, a surge of tension forms between us. Like a string from his body to mine, connected in some unexplainable attraction to one another.

We continue staring, not speaking a word.

I try focusing my attention on Sloan, who was obviously not expecting to see the man she's been in love with for eight years here tonight. But by the way Wes is looking at her, there is no doubt in my mind he's head over heels for her too.

Eli, this man's friend, and my best friend's brother, breaks the spell.

"Parker, this is Ava, she went to college with the girls. You likely know her family, they are into investing as well. Pierce Corporation," *Eli says before turning his attention back to the other side of the table.*

I notice a look slide over Parker's face before he returns his gaze to me. "Ava Pierce?" *His demeanor has completely shifted from what it had been less than a minute ago.*

"Yep, that's me." *I try to sound cheery, wondering what his deal is.*

"An Upper East Side princess in my presence," *he sneers, then continues.* "And tell me what do you do? Go to events for Mommy and Daddy?"

Woah woah, shut the fucking front door. Who does this asshole think he is? It seems like my last name offended him, but it's not like he's slumming it in his perfectly fitted Tom Ford suit.

"First off, I'm no princess. And for your information, I just started my own interior design firm," *I snap back. I don't care how sexy he is; don't accuse me of things you know absolutely nothing about.*

His menacing glare bores into mine.

"Maybe not a princess, but a brat, nonetheless."

Parker doesn't acknowledge me as he walks into the room, but that doesn't surprise me. What does, though, is that I even got the interview if he had any say in it. We may have mutual friends, but based on our history, that doesn't mean shit to him. From the very first night we met, he treated me like a dumb socialite. And the one time I thought he saw more, he proved otherwise all too quickly.

The others who enter the room are friendly as they greet me, and shortly after, Logan speaks up and gives me the go-ahead to start.

I stand from my seat... *Confidence, baby.* Looking Parker directly in the eye to prove to him his asshole vibe isn't going to throw me off, I address the board. "Thank you all so much for having me. I have prepared a presentation for today. First, I would like to show you a few projects I have completed recently."

Along with the photos I click through, I explain what each project entailed, ending on my proudest venture. "Masqued is an exclusive club here in the city that I had the privilege of designing. I worked closely with the owner, who is a dear friend of mine, to make her vision come to life. This club is the epitome of sexy and mysterious, with privacy and hidden gems throughout the vicinity. Special details to make everyone's experience even more memorable."

Parker's deep voice rumbles through the room, cutting me off. "But this isn't an exclusive club... It's a hotel that people are going to be paying no less than a grand a night to stay at." The dickhead finally speaks, and I want to shove my heel down his throat.

I smile through gritted teeth, biting my tongue from saying, *"Well, as you know from experience, an elite membership to Masqued is over fifty thousand dollars a year."*

Instead, I go with, "Good point, Mr. Cole." Pressing the clicker, I flip to the next screen, showing the French designs and highlights I combined as inspiration for this hotel. "These are schemes I have pulled together for your hotel, specifically. Some are just ideas so I can see what you all like and don't like, which will allow me to design something uniquely curated for your desires. I also drew up my own visions for this place based off the things I knew you all wanted."

The board *oohs* and *ahhs* and I can tell they are impressed, which lights a fire inside me. One of pride and excitement.

"These are amazing and spot on with what we've discussed. Almost like you were involved in these conversations previously," Logan says with the same encouraging smile from earlier.

I notice Parker's eyes flit to Logan, narrowing from the way he's praising me.

Degradation is more of his thing.

Or come to think of it, maybe he saves his praises for something else.

His gaze moves back to where I stand, his grey eyes penetrating through me. With no emotion, he says, "Miss Pierce, do you have anything else you would like to show us? We have several more interviews this morning."

Without answering, I click to the next slide, displaying my hand drawing of the in-house spa. Everyone's faces—well, minus one—light up as they look over the display, and I let that reaction fill my chest with validation. *I'm damn good at my job.* Not wasting another second peeking in Parker's direction, I go into detail on the layout and different ideas for the overall feel in the spa area.

When I'm finished, I ask if anyone has any questions, preparing myself for battle again because no doubt Parker will have some smart-ass remark.

A female board member with a big smile responds first. "No question, I just wanted to say thank you. This is amazing. I'm Olivia, and I'm the co-project manager with Logan. To reiterate what he said, it feels like you are already in my brain on this project. I just want to commend you on your keen eye for detail, especially when you had minimal information." She gives me a wink, as if to say, *you got this in the bag, girlfriend*, and I instantly love her.

"Thank you so much, Olivia. It's an honor to be here. I know no matter what, this place will be magnificent." *But I'm surely hoping you all do a majority-wins type of voting system here and it's not just based on the head-dick-in-charge, then maybe I'll have a shot.*

"Any other questions?" Parker asks, barely giving anyone an opportunity to speak before he continues. "Thank you, Miss Pierce. Either way, we will be in touch within twenty-four hours."

I nod with a gracious smile, one I direct to the rest of the room. "Thank you all for having me," I say politely, then begin packing my things back into my bag.

"Ava, I can see you out," Logan says, pushing his chair back from the table. But before I can speak, Parker is heading my way. "No need, Logan… I have to use the men's room. I'll make sure she sees herself out."

Men's room, my ass.

With my heart picking up pace, I give one last wave and follow Parker out of the room into the hallway. I know I should tread lightly here, but I don't care how amazing of an opportunity this is, I'm not going to lie down and let someone walk all over me unless orgasms and consent are involved.

"Will you treat all your interviews today with the same kindness as you did me, Mr. Cole?" I ask, not bothering to contain my snark. Keeping my eyes ahead, we step down the corridor, his presence at my side putting me on edge.

"Well, Miss Pierce, it seemed to me that your fan club was already big enough. We wouldn't want you to get too comfortable now, would we?" His low, husky voice is full of sarcasm.

I stop short in my heels, grabbing his arm and stopping him in place. "Look…" I demand, and boy does he. For the first time today, he focuses on me, and I feel it *everywhere*. But I push those thoughts aside, needing to say my piece to this man.

"Put whatever vendetta you have against me to the side…and promise me today you will pick the best person for the job. No biases, no discriminations. Just whomever you think will help make this place what it deserves to be."

Parker surprises me and takes a step closer, and I have to tilt my head up to maintain eye contact.

Lifting his hand, he rubs his thumb over my bottom lip, slightly pulling it down. My breath halts in my chest, eyes unable to look away from his, frozen in the center of the storm darkening in his grey eyes.

"What you are implying would mean I would choose a vendetta over my company. There is only one person who would cause that reaction out of me, and I promise it's not you."

I instantly go from nearly pulling his thumb into my mouth and sucking on it to now wanting it between my teeth so I can inflict pain. Only, he's not done.

"Stop being a brat and making everything about you."

With a restrained huff, I shove his hand away from my face.

I'm not sure if it's a good thing or a bad thing, but why do his words sting? *And I promise it's not you.* I hate the way he gets in my fucking head.

One thing I do know is, "I'm not a brat…and you have no idea who I am, so don't act like you do."

Our eyes stay locked for a moment as I seethe, but I don't let him have the last word. Not that he cares anyway.

Turning on my heel, I strut toward the front doors, living on a prayer that I didn't just blow whatever chance I had at getting this job.

Babes Group Chat

QUINN

How did it go? Did Daddy Parker give you the job or not?

ME

The verdict's still out, and he was a dick per usual.

ME

Also, you are the only one of us with a "Daddy" in their life.

SLOAN

First, Eww... that's my brother. Second, I'm sure you did amazing Av.

ME

Thanks babe... and you know your brother does way worse things to Quinnie than make her call him Daddy.

QUINN

Nah... we aren't into the Daddy thing. It's so cute hearing Addy and Sophie say it, I don't think he'd be able to take me seriously if I called him that.

ME

Ugh I didn't think of that.

SLOAN

So truly how did it go?

ME

Everyone on the board seemed to love my ideas... except Parker

QUINN

I feel like Parker is the type of guy, even if he did love it, you would never know so don't get discouraged.

SLOAN

I agree... when do you find out?

ME

I think by the end of the day.

SLOAN

Perfect we can celebrate tonight... speak it to existence babe.

QUINN

Rub it in... another Friday girls' night missed =[

ME

Oh don't act like you aren't living out your teenage fantasy with your baseball daddy down in North Carolina.

SLOAN

Again, can we not with the calling my brother daddy...

SLOAN

And Q we will make up for it in the off season =]

QUINN

True... call me once you hear. Love you both

Two

Ava

"We'll take the top shelf margarita in a fishbowl with two straws and an order of the ultimate nachos, please." I order our usual as of lately. Sloan, Quinn, and I used to do this weekly, if not more often, and it usually consisted of a night full of shenanigans afterwards. But those are few and far between now.

"Wes loves when I come home extra frisky after fishbowl nights," Sloan says with that chummy smile she always gets when she mentions her husband.

"What's he up to tonight?" I ask, partially out of curiosity… but mostly because he has recently become closer friends with Parker. Wes originally met him through Eli like the rest of us, but with them both living in Tribeca over the past year, they seem to have developed more of a friendship of their own.

"He's actually up at King's Hideaway, finalizing plans for their big event next weekend." *Oh shit, I forgot about that.*

Wes's former agent's wife was recently diagnosed with breast cancer. So, Wes organized a fundraiser at the speakeasy he owns here in the city.

"I should have offered to help decorate. Is there anything I can do?" I ask, hating myself for being so wrapped up in my own things that I didn't think to recommend this before.

"No, no, he isn't even doing much decorating. More coordinating the food, seating, and that type of stuff." The vibe of Wes's bar is so cool the décor speaks for itself. The designer, Giselle Armistead, who helped him when he bought the bar, is someone I have always admired in the business.

"You're still able to come, right?"

"Yes, for sure, I'll be there." My mind scans my closet, thinking about which dress will show my legs off best.

"Awesome… Have you checked your emails lately?" she asks, lips pursed.

I lift my phone off the table. "Of course." Shaking my head, I tell her, "Nothing new."

"I'm sure it will come through soon. It's only seven, and knowing Parker, he's probably just finishing his workday."

That asshole's probably intentionally making me wait just to keep me sweating. He loves to torture me.

"Yeah, maybe. Oh well, distract me with something else."

Sloan chuckles. "How'd your latest Tinder date go?"

"I've moved on to Hinge now, and it was a disaster. Only wanted one thing…and ya know that wouldn't be so bad if he could have carried on a decent conversation prior to."

Sloan laughs, nodding along. "So what you are saying is, Hinge is full of fuck boys just like Tinder."

"Basically. I ended up walking myself home from the restaurant and hanging out with my neighbor the rest of the night."

"You mean, the twenty-three-year-old neighbor you occasionally hook up with?"

I pretend to clear my throat. "Twenty-two."

When she gives me a look of, *I love you, but really?* I feel like I need to justify myself a bit.

"Only six years younger than me. Plus, he's sweet and simple and wants absolutely nothing from me. Sometimes, we just take an edible and watch documentaries."

"So basically, he reminds you of our college days?"

I smile as a sense of longing falls over me. I met Sloan and Quinn in college, and they became the friends and, essentially, family that I had always wanted. We were inseparable. Of course, I'm beyond happy for both of them, and I dream of having what they have with their partners one day. But those days were some of the best times of my life, so I can't help but miss them.

The waitress comes back with our huge "fishbowl" full of tequila goodness. "Thank you."

"The nachos will be out soon. Let me know if I can get you ladies anything else."

Sloan and I both lean in from opposite sides of the table and each take a long pull from the straw.

"Gah, I needed that," I say, releasing a heavy sigh. I feel like I've been holding that all day.

"These never get old." Sloan smiles, giggling as she goes in for another taste.

We continue to sip and chat about life since the last time we saw each other until our nachos are delivered.

Mid-chew, the distinct tone of an iPhone ringing has my heart jumping into my throat. It's a local number. Fuck, what if they are calling to tell me I didn't get it?

"Answer it," Sloan insists, waving her hands at me.

"Hello," I say confidently, even though that's far from how I'm feeling.

"Hi, Ava! It's Olivia!" Her peppy voice reawakens the hope inside my chest. "You got the job…and I don't think I've ever been more excited to work with a designer before."

I cover the phone with my hand and mouth to Sloan, "I got it!"

She lets out an excited squeal, and I bite my lip to hold mine in.

"Ava, did you hear me?" Olivia's voice hums back through the phone.

I rush out, "Yes, yes…just trying to control my excitement and stay professional. I'm so thrilled to work with you, too. Honestly, I'm shocked right now."

"Well, leave your professionalism at the door for the night because we don't start till Monday. Come celebrate with me and Logan. We are going to Birdie Bar for a few drinks and we want to buy you one."

I think on it for a second, wondering if Parker will be there too, but you know what… Fuck it. I want to celebrate and get to know them more. The fact she is this excited to work with me puts me on cloud nine.

"That sounds fun! I'm finishing up girls' dinner with my best friend, but I'll head to you guys when we finish here."

I can hear the smile in her voice. "Okay perfect. This is my cell, so text me when you are on the way."

"Great, see you soon."

When I hang up, Sloan is out of her chair, wrapping me in a hug. "I knew you'd land it. I am so freaking proud of you, Av. You did this…all on your own. There is no denying your talent."

The waitress comes back to check in and Sloan orders us patron shots. Even a third one for Quinn—which we split in her honor as we FaceTime her with the good news.

If there is one piece of advice I could give teenage girls, it's to find your tribe. Find friends who are so much more than just that. They're your cheerleaders, confidants, therapists, bodyguards… They're your sisters.

Blood isn't always thicker than water.

"AVA!!" Olivia sing-songs through the crowd as I walk toward the cocktail table she's sitting at with Logan.

She hops down from her seat, greeting me with a hug. "I'm so damn happy to have another badass female working on this project with me." Embracing her, we rock back and forth. I finally allow my true giddiness to show. "Thank you so much. I don't think it's quite sunk in yet. This is a literal dream job for me."

"I knew you deserved it the minute I saw your pitch. I didn't even listen to anyone else's." She laughs, waving her hand in *good riddance* to the others before continuing. "We just had to make sure Parker was convinced of that."

"Yeah, same, but thankfully, he agreed...albeit reluctantly," Logan says, getting up to give me a congratulatory hug as well.

Ouch. But truly, what else do I expect from the asshole.

"Not that reluctantly," Olivia murmurs.

Logan's hand rests on my lower back as he pulls my chair out for me. "We just ordered a round of shots."

We chat about where we are from and the basic get-to-know-you questions. I find out Olivia is from Jersey and Logan was born and raised here in the city. Olivia is thirty-five and Logan is twenty-five. They both seem surprised to find out I grew up in the Upper East Side. Luckily, the shots are delivered just in time to avoid *that* conversation.

"Cheers to Ava...our newest teammate," Olivia says, and we all clink our glasses before throwing the shots back.

Olivia glances at Logan before asking me her next question. "So Ava, are you single?"

Ah, I see what's going on here.

"Single as a Pringle. How about you guys?"

"My boyfriend is actually on the way to meet us here now... but Logan's single."

Olivia's gaze falls behind me, and she speaks again before I can respond. "Well, that's the most interesting thing that's happened all year."

She moves toward whatever her eyes have landed on, and I hear Logan grumble, "What the fuck is he doing here?" just before I turn around to find a sexy-as-sin Parker talking to another guy.

Long gone is his suit jacket.

He's a walking, talking wet dream with the dark grey sleeves of his tailored shirt rolled up, showcasing his fully tattooed arms. The peach-colored rose peeks out of the top of his collar, crawling just slightly up his neck.

A memory of my tongue running along the rose petals flashes before my eyes.

Olivia slings her arms around the guy beside Parker and she steers them to the bar to grab a drink.

Parker's gaze moves up to meet mine, and I quickly turn back to Logan, realizing I've been staring for too long.

"So, I take it that's Olivia's boyfriend?" I ask quickly, hoping Logan didn't notice my perusal of the boss.

"Yep…he's Parker's friend and a tattoo artist here in the city, if that's your thing."

Unfortunately, it is absolutely my thing, especially when they come with a side of asshole.

Can we say, disaster waiting to happen?

"Do you want something else to drink?" Logan asks.

"I'm okay right now. I shared a huge fishbowl full of tequila, plus a celebratory shot with my best friend before coming here."

He chuckles. "Nice… Did you at least eat?"

"Yeah, we shared a delicious plate of nachos too."

"Fishbowls and nachos… Sounds like a place I need to try out. We should go sometime."

"Yes, for sure… It's over in Nolita, so it's easy to walk to from the office or the hotel one night." Logan is extremely attractive, but I haven't even started the job yet, so I don't want to give him the wrong idea. "Olivia looks like she'd be a margarita type of girl too… Maybe all three of us can go one day this week after work."

"Either way, I'm down. Wednesday night, I know I'm free, if that works for you," Logan says before taking a sip of the pint glass he's been working on.

"Where are we going?" Parker's deep voice interrupts as he takes Olivia's seat.

"Just planning a dinner one night this week after work," Logan answers.

"Isn't that cute, a Pierce and a Bryant? Two New York City legacies making immediate friends," Parker hums, sounding the opposite of amused and not looking my way.

"Wait, Bryant? As in, Bryant & Co.?" I question, confused at his insinuation.

A sheepish smile takes over Logan's face. "Dennis Bryant is my mom's father."

"Ah, cool, I had no idea."

I'm relieved when he doesn't pry into why I don't use my last name as clout.

Logan turns his attention to Parker, who has obviously pissed him off with his previous smartass comment. "Surprised you joined us tonight. You never come out."

He scoffs. "Well, after sitting through all those boring interviews, I needed a drink." Tipping his rocks glass toward us, he takes a swig of the brown liquid.

Whiskey… I can almost taste the memory.

His eyes find mine for the first time since he sat down. "Plus, I wanted to congratulate Ava here on landing the job."

What is he playing at?

"Thank you. I'm looking forward to working with you all on this." I force myself to act normal, just as I did with Logan and Olivia. But my body knows he's different.

"Well, you'll be working under me."

Under me.

My core tingles, and I quickly pull myself out of his dark stare. "Ya know, Logan, I think I may actually take you up on that drink."

He beams at me. "What do you want? I'll just go up to the bar and grab it," Logan says, pointing to the cocktail waitress dealing with a loud crowd in the corner.

"You pick…as long as it has tequila in it," I say, not wanting to mix my liquors and make a fool of myself tonight.

"Okay, beautiful." Logan nods before moving toward the bar.

"Beautiful…really? He's laying it on a little thick, isn't he?" Parker grumbles.

"It's called being nice. You should try it." Leaning in, I give him a saccharine smile.

"It's called *don't shit where you eat*, Legs."

"You are one to talk. From what I've heard, you've fucked half of Manhattan. I can't imagine none of them were colleagues." I roll my eyes.

"What I do is none of your business."

"Well then, same goes for you… I'm a grown woman, and I can do what I want and who I want," I say with a shrug, and he huffs a laugh that holds no humor.

"Not when I'm your boss. For fuck's sake, you just got the job. Are you already trying to get fired?"

He wouldn't, but the thought is sobering. "Again, none of your business… but Logan is just a new associate who I'll be working closely with, so I have no plans to take our friendship further at the moment."

"Or ever," Parker growls.

"Stop. You are pissing me off." I level him with a hard stare, watching as his nostrils flare. "I know you don't really know me, but believe me on this… If you are worried I am going to let something distract me from this project, you are certainly mistaken. This is huge for me."

He nods, taking another sip of his whiskey as Logan returns with our drinks.

Worried he will feel the tension in the air, I give him a bright smile. "Thanks so much."

Thankfully, Olivia and her boyfriend, who introduces himself as Braxton, rejoin the table, and the conversation turns toward baseball. We discuss Eli's recent game, as well as the Yankees' first month since opening day.

Logan notices my drink is empty. "Do you want anything else?"

"No, I'm actually going to head out. I have a dance class in the morning."

"Oooh, what kind of dance class? That sounds fun," Olivia chimes in.

"It's a combination class tomorrow. Hip hop and pole."

She gasps. "I've always wanted to try pole dancing, but I know it's hard. Takes a lot of leg strength."

"You should try out one of the beginner classes. I help teach that one sometimes, so I can get you a pass if you really want to check it out."

"Hell yes! Now that's a hobby I can get behind. I'll even buy a pole for the bedroom so you can practice," Braxton says, wiggling his eyebrows and making her laugh.

I chuckle. "Honestly, having one at home is helpful because you can practice a little each day and help build your strength, or if you really get into it, you can practice new moves you learn and keep them fresh in your head between classes."

"So, you have one in your place?" Logan asks, and I feel Parker's stare burning into me.

"Sure do!"

"Fuck," Logan says under his breath.

Feeling slightly awkward, I move the attention off me. "Olivia, they have morning and lunchtime classes during the week too. We can figure out a day that works with our schedule and I'll take you."

She does a little dance in her seat. "Okay, I'm excited! Can't wait to see you in action."

"Can I come?" Logan asks with a playful smirk, and Parker speaks for the first time since they all joined us.

"No."

Even though I know he's dead serious, we all laugh as I start to put on my lightweight jacket. "Where do you live Ava?" Logan asks.

"I'm in West Village."

"Nice… Well, I'm in Greenwich. Are you walking? We could head that way together."

"How convenient," Parker murmurs, and I see Olivia give him a quizzical look.

"Yeah, that sounds good. I like to walk, especially with this nice spring weather coming in."

"Ava, can I speak to you one second about next week?" Parker asks, but it doesn't quite sound like a question as much as it does a demand. Standing and walking in front of me, I follow him toward the door with an internal sigh once we say our goodbyes to Olivia and Braxton.

As soon as we're outside, he turns to me. "My assistant, Tasha, will send you all the information tomorrow about getting started on Monday," he says, and I look at him expectantly, questioning why he pulled me out here to tell me that.

Eyes on mine, void of emotion, he continues. "I just wanted to make you aware of the no fraternizing rule between an employee and the person they directly report to, which would be Logan and Olivia for you."

I narrow my gaze at him, wondering why he didn't just say this earlier during his whole *don't shit where you eat* speech.

"Yes, Sir," I say with a salute, just as Logan walks out, and I don't miss the way Parker's eyes flare at my words.

The way I love getting a reaction out of this man, both good and bad, is concerning.

He speaks again, nothing but business in his tone. "Logan, don't forget I need the project plan for next week typed out and sent to my email before I start work tomorrow morning."

Logan nods. "Yep... I'm planning to finish that up when I get home. Why are you working on Saturday anyway?"

"Because there is too much to do... I need to utilize some free time."

"Okay then, have a good night," Logan says with a wave, then places his hand on my lower back, guiding me down the sidewalk.

"Night," Parker says gruffly, and I turn my head slightly to peek at him. The city lights shine on his tightened jaw as he stares at where Logan's hand rests against me. My lips quirk at seeing that reaction.

And once again, my thighs clench.

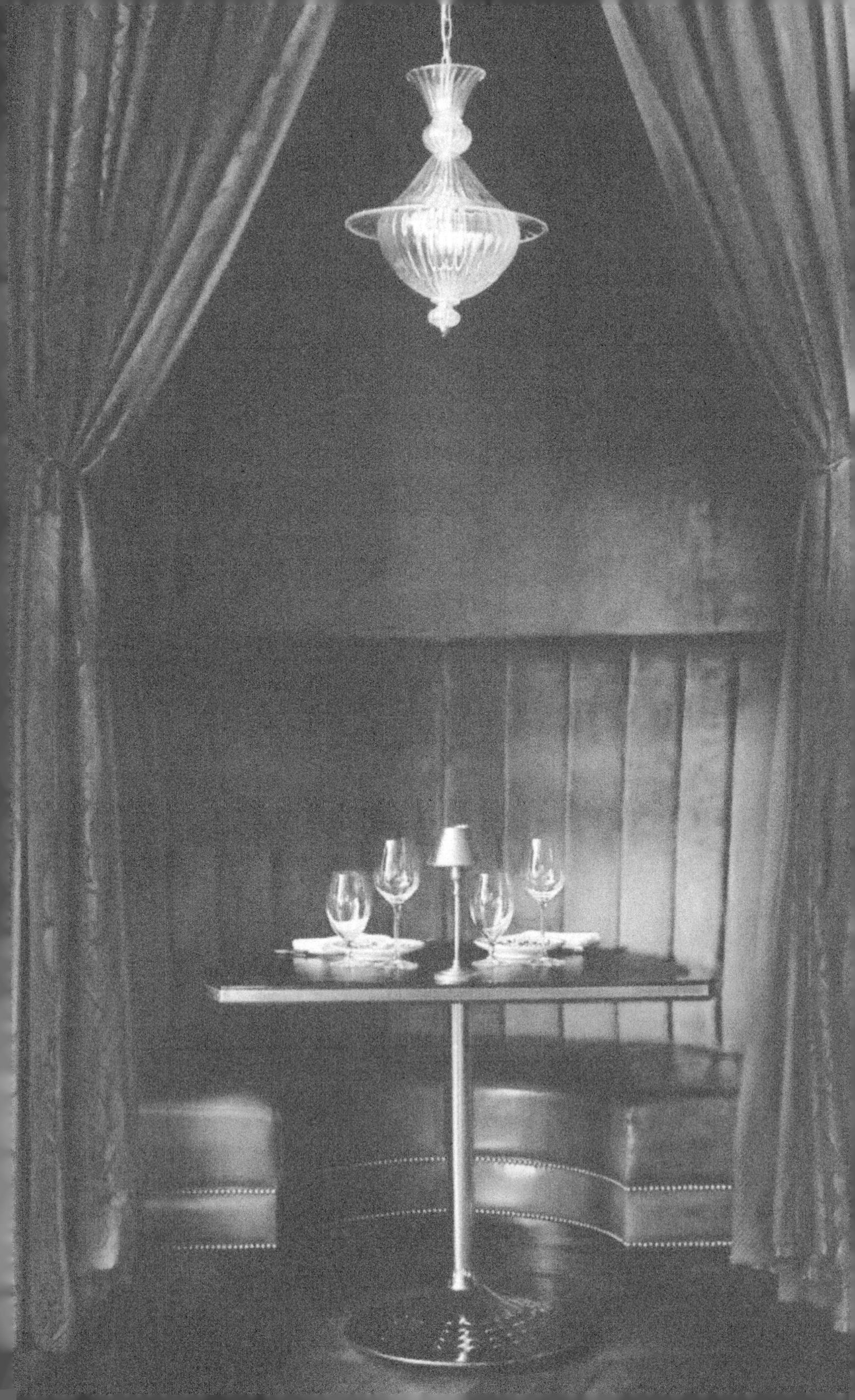

Three

Parker

"Yes, take a look at the revisions and have them sent back to me as soon as you can… Yup, not a problem. Talk to you soon. Have a good afternoon." I end the call with more force on the headset than necessary.

I'm in the process of acquiring two hundred acres of land nestled in the heart of the Catskill Mountains, a little over an hour north of Manhattan. It's set just outside a quaint college town and right in the heart of Hudson Valley, with the Hudson River visible from the property's edge. Zoning is approved for commercial use and there is an 1800s farmhouse already standing on the property. The opportunity was too good to pass up, but Mr. Harring is being quite difficult on what should have been an easy contract. It's been over two weeks of back-and-forth conversations and contract adjustments.

I get it, I do. He doesn't want to see his family's land turned into something that will strip the property of its charm. But I'd never do that. Hudson Valley holds a special place in my heart. It's where I used to vacation when I was young. We didn't have much growing up, but what we did have was our annual fall trip to the Catskills. We'd go hiking, apple picking, eat cider donuts from our favorite roadside farm stand, and just enjoy the beauty the mountains offered that time of year. It was my mom's happy place… well, that and her rose garden. After she died, the thought of vacationing there was too hard for my dad to face, and we never went back.

The idea of owning a piece of Hudson Valley and those memories sparked something deep inside of me, a passion project of sorts. Way out of the comfort zone of my usual city office buildings, hotels, and apartments. This will be a personal investment away from the Bryant & Co. name.

A knock on my door draws my attention away from my computer screen.

"Sorry to disrupt you, Mr. Cole. But I thought you'd like to know that Miss Pierce has arrived and is in the conference room."

"Thank you, Tasha."

It's been three days since Ava started working on the SoHo project, and I must say, I am impressed by her work ethic. She's overly prepared and has a smart-mouth response for every asinine question I throw her way. Getting her all riled up has become one of my favorite things to look forward to.

I take the stairs to the floor below my office to where the conference rooms and several other offices are. Bryant & Co. takes up two floors in a converted warehouse in the heart of Soho. The building itself is spectacular and is just a short walk away from our current project.

As soon as I'm near, I spot Ava's long legs in her hip-hugging knee-length skirt through the glass wall of the conference room. Her blonde hair is pulled back, leaving her slender neck exposed. I take a deep breath, preparing to spend the next few hours shoulder to shoulder with her. There's just something about her that makes me want to chew her head off one minute and fuck the brat out of her the next.

My mood instantly sours when I see Logan sitting across from her, blatantly staring down the front of her blouse. My jaw tics at the sight.

Being younger, Logan is still learning the ropes within his grandfather's company. I was skeptical of the newest member of my team, and assumed he was just another trust fund kid who landed a job at his family's company. And although he certainly is entitled, I do give him credit for being a hard worker who seems to care about his job. I guess he's not a bad guy, per say, just not someone I'd choose to be in my circle. Regardless of who he is to Mr. Bryant, I'm their boss, and I don't like to fuck around. I've been told I'm not the easiest to work for, but so far, Olivia and Logan have flourished as my project managers.

My reputation as a head real estate developer at Bryant & Co. means everything to me, and I've built my name from the ground up. Working under a Manhattan real estate legend such as Dennis Bryant has helped pave the way for who I am. He gave a no-name kid from Long Island a chance right out of college, and I'm more than grateful for the opportunities he's afforded me these past eight years.

Rapping my knuckles on the door frame, I enter the room, effectively disrupting the conversation Logan and Ava were having. "Oh, Park— Mr. Cole, perfect timing. I was just pulling up the main lobby and seating area designs." Her red-painted lips pull into a perfect smile. One, I get the feeling, she's more than used to pasting on her face.

I take a seat at the head of the table and make myself

comfortable. Ava looks at me cautiously, and then asks, "Will Olivia be joining us?"

"No," I answer.

I can hear Logan's exasperated sigh from where I sit, and then he adds, "She is at the job site overseeing a few things. She should be back in an hour or so."

Ava eyes me again, then steadies herself and pulls up her first slide. "Since you expressed your thoughts on Luxure having a more intimate lobby and check-in area, I drew up these options. In slide one, you'll see we have replaced the standard hotel counter with two sets of traditional-styled desks and chairs. This will ensure the clients feel comfortable in the space with fewer barriers between them and the staff. In slide two, we have continued the same color palette we've discussed throughout the lobby and seating area, making sure we highlight the architectural details throughout the main floor. I know, Mr. Cole, you had discussed the possibility of incorporating a small restaurant into the main area of the hotel. If you do go this route, I have a few alternate ideas that will incorporate that entrance as well. However, I believe having the restaurant on the rooftop would be better suited for the space."

"Why's that?" I ask, reclining in my seat.

"Well, for starters, the view from the roof is your moneymaker at this location. It could have floor-to-ceiling doors that open seamlessly to the Parisian-style garden I have planned for the rooftop bar. It'd become a must-see destination rather than just another New York City restaurant."

"But the building already has the commercial kitchen on the main floor. Moving it to the roof would be timely, and not to mention, costly," I challenge her. Though I already know from the look in her eyes that she's going to have a solution or a rebuttal.

"Ah, yes, that is true, but my plan doesn't involve moving the kitchen. As you're aware, Mr. Cole, your building has more than one elevator shaft. One of those being directly across from the pre-existing kitchen."

"So, you want the food runners to use the elevator to deliver food to our rooftop tables?" I clarify, staring directly at Ava and no longer at the screen with her projected slides.

"Yes, you wouldn't be the first hotel to perform this way." Her lip quirks, not breaking eye contact throughout our little back-and-forth. It fills me with satisfaction that shouldn't be there.

"Wow, that's such an interesting take on the restaurant addition. I wouldn't have thought of that," Logan says, a little too enthusiastically, if you ask me.

"Yes, definitely interesting. I will think on that. Thank you, Ava. Was there anything else we needed to discuss today?" I hate to admit it, but she's right about the rooftop.

Those hazel eyes meet mine again. "Yes, actually. I brought some sample boards with me that incorporate the color scheme. I laid them out over there under the window to get the best lighting." She gestures to the side of the room, and we follow.

About an hour into pouring over the five different sample boards, Olivia joins us. Around noon, our team has narrowed it down to two. Tasha delivers our catered lunch as we finalize the floor samples. By the time we're done, I feel like my head is about to explode. Not only from the ongoing back-and-forth, but from the way Logan constantly felt the need to inflate Ava's already robust ego.

The Pierce family name comes with its perks, especially in New York City. She carries herself with the presence and grace of a Manhattan socialite, yet when she opens her mouth, I get nothing of the sort. Ava is an anomaly. Just when you think she is going to act or do one thing, she surprises you and does the complete opposite. Her ability to challenge me at every turn makes her even more intriguing.

"Alright, I think we're about done here today. We've made great progress, and I can't wait to see the full samples next week," Olivia says as she shuts her laptop. "I need to get back to the hotel and check in."

"Oh, do you mind if I join you? I wanted to take some exterior photos so I can better plan for the awnings and railings," Ava chimes in, packing up her materials.

"Of course!" Olivia replies.

"Care if I accompany you ladies? I have some time before I need to be on a call," Logan asks, his voice filled with more charisma than usual. I can't help but roll my eyes.

His intentions are obvious, and I can't say I blame him. But Logan has been working for me for a little over two years now, and his track record of running through women is longer than most men I know. If he were to do the same to Ava, it could jeopardize our working relationship and my project. Besides, there is no way he could truly give her what she needs.

Olivia must notice my annoyance because she adds, "Was there anything else you needed us for this afternoon?" She's mistaking my displeasure for something she may have done.

"No, that will be all. Thank you for your work today," I say curtly, then stand and walk out before I do something stupid like follow their trio to the job site.

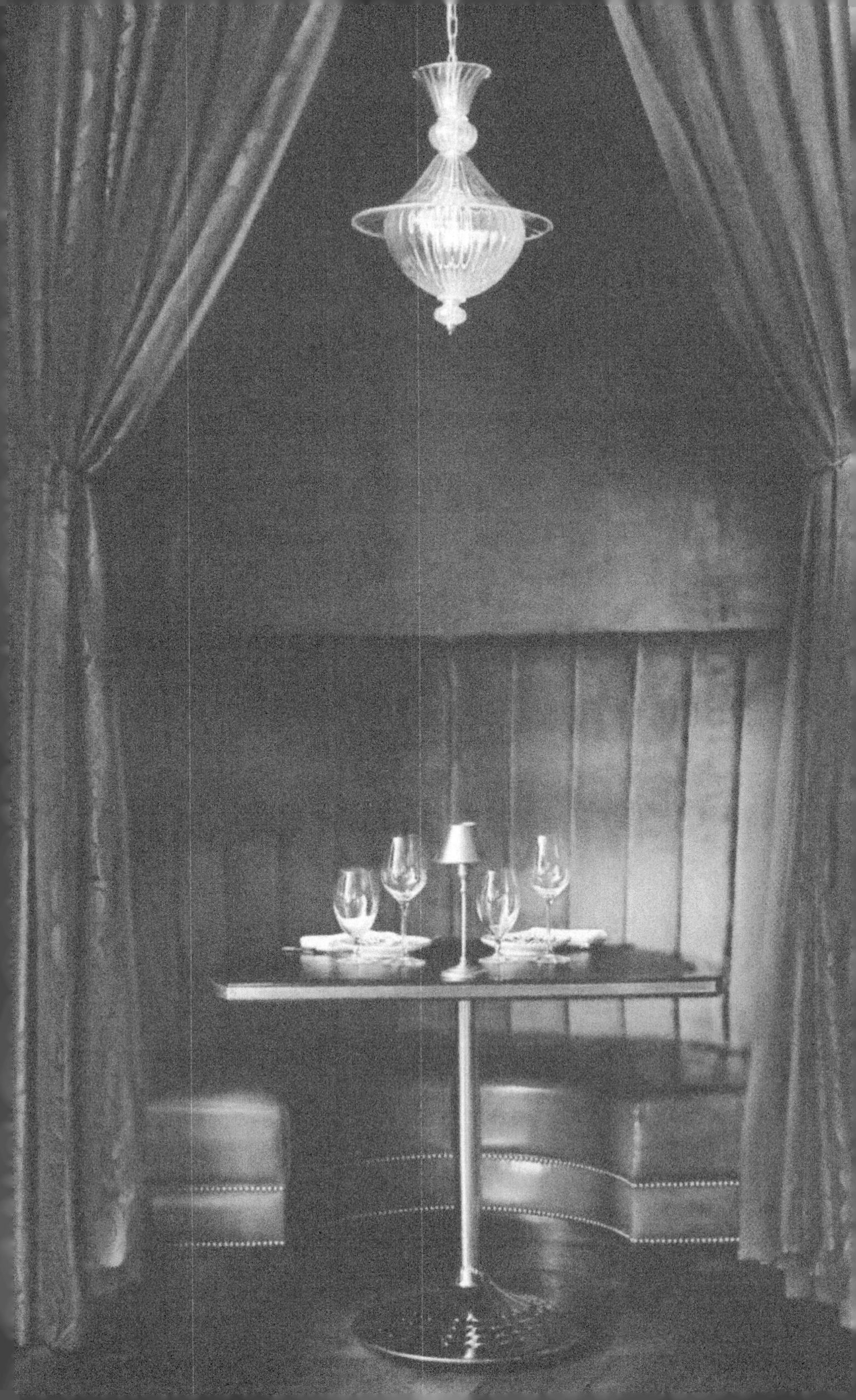

Four

Parker

F*uck me.*

Why did she have to wear something like that to a fundraiser? The sleek satin dress hangs perfectly off her slender frame, dipping just low enough that I get an impeccable tease of her chest. Her sky-high heels remind me of the pain they caused when they were digging into my back.

FUCK, stop thinking about her like that.

Ava's boisterous laugh filters from the circle of people she's been chatting with, and my hand tightens around my glass. She must be a real comedian since her surrounding group is all cracking up at whatever she has said. It's a side of her I'm not well acquainted with and, for some reason, that pisses me off even more.

I remember that first night I met her here at Kings Hideaway, and how drawn I was to her. I also recall how quickly I dismissed her when I heard her last name. Just another entitled socialite, too spoiled to know the meaning of hard work, and too rich to care. I've dealt with my fair share of her kind before, and I had no intention of adding any more to my rich prick list. But the more I'm around her, I'm beginning to wonder if my assumptions were unfounded.

I need a distraction.

My gaze settles on a woman who's been standing across the bar from me for most of the night. I nod and raise my glass in her direction. She responds with a shy smile and heads my way, tucking a piece of her auburn hair behind her ear. *Shy, my ass*, she's been begging for my attention for the last two hours. I noticed her staring for a while now. At the time, I couldn't focus on anyone else besides the brat, but now, after several rocks glasses full of amber, I welcome the distraction.

She sidles up next to me, and I'm immediately assaulted by her overbearing perfume. It's too sweet and sugary. "Hey there, I'm Molly," she says, then bites her lip.

She's beautiful, just not what I want at all, but the feel of familiar hazel eyes boring into the side of my face convinces me to play along.

"Parker Cole. Nice to meet you." I hold out my hand like the gentleman I was raised to be.

Placing her petite hand in mine, she shakes it softly. Her eyes travel to where we are joined, and she stares at my tattooed hand and forearm on display, thanks to my cuffed sleeve.

"Why don't we find a place to sit," she suggests with fluttering fake lashes.

I glance up and lock eyes with Ava for the first time tonight. Though her expression is neutral, the gleam in her eyes tells a different story.

"Sounds good." I follow her to one of the booths across the floor of Kings Hideaway, and we situate ourselves in one of the more intimate seating areas.

"So what's your connection to the charity?" Molly asks.

"I'm friends with Wesley, who Greg used to manage a few years back."

"Damn, you and Wesley King… Could your circle of friends get any hotter?" she blurts unabashedly. Do I dare tell her my best friend is the heartthrob, star closing pitcher for the Carolina Bulls? *Nah.*

I smile politely, unsure of how to respond, before adding, "I'm here for moral support and to help out however I can," trying to redirect the conversation away from my good-looking friends.

"That's so thoughtful of you," she purrs, her hand now resting on my arm. "I'm childhood friends with Greg's wife, Claire."

"Well, I hope nothing but good news for them over the next few months," I say, then take a large gulp from my glass. I let my gaze roam over Molly as she inches closer. She's an attractive woman, but she's trying too hard. I can smell the desperation leaching from her mixing with the horrendous perfume she bathed herself in.

"Thank you… That is so sweet."

We continue with the bullshit small talk for a while longer, but I'm bored. There's no pull, no spark…nothing. She breaks the lull when she reaches for her purse and excuses herself to use the restroom.

I wave my hand in a *go right ahead* gesture and take another sip from my glass.

"Now, don't you go anywhere." She winks before walking away. Guess she's thinking things are going better than I am.

Leaning back in my chair, I observe all the patrons here in support of Greg and his family. There's a great turnout tonight, and I truly hope things take a turn for the better. I'd never tell Molly, or anyone else, this…but I'm also here because I'd do anything to support a family going through that hell. I certainly wish people cared enough about my family when we were going through it; any assistance would have been welcomed. For fuck's sake, our own family wasn't there to support us…

My eyes search through the crowd. Seeing Wes and Sloan deep in conversation with several guests across the way. He nods in my direction, and I return the gesture, knowing we will catch up later once the fundraiser winds down. We spoke briefly before, but they've been bombarded with people since the door's opened.

I'm scanning for the leggy blonde with an attitude but trying my hardest to deny the reasons why. Finally spotting her back at the bar with her head in her phone, I can't help but wonder what is so deserving of all her attention.

Molly returns a few minutes later, breaking my stare. She bites her freshly reapplied lip and I know what's coming next. "So, I'm thinking of heading out. I'm staying at a hotel not too far away… I'm not normally this forward, but would you want to join me?"

My response is instantaneous. "I'm flattered by the offer, but I still have some people to catch up with tonight," I say, gently letting her down. I may be a dick, but Molly has been a nice way to pass the time. She doesn't deserve me being an asshole.

Disappointment creeps into her expression, but she brushes it off quickly. "Guess I misjudged. I'm sorry for coming across so bold."

"No need to be sorry. It was a pleasure meeting you." I stand to hug her goodbye.

Leaning in, she gives me a lingering kiss on the cheek. "Maybe we can meet up some other time. I'm in the city often," Molly whispers as she places a business card in my hand. I accept it, but only nod once.

"I'll catch you later, Mr. Cole," is the last thing she says before walking away.

My name leaving her lips sounds all wrong. Not at all like the temptress who taunts me daily with the sweet sound. The fact that she's the first person who pops into my head has my jaw tensing.

And yet again, I seek Ava out. Her back is still facing me, and before I know it, I'm striding over to her.

Ava

"What's so interesting on your phone?" Parker asks, pulling the bar chair back and sliding his big frame in next to me.

With a firm side-eye in place, I respond. "He does know how to speak… I was beginning to wonder." I'm being a smartass. I'm more annoyed with myself that I let his dismissal tonight get under my skin.

"I've been busy networking."

"Yeah, she looked like someone who has a lot to offer you professionally," I retort, and before he can accuse me of being jealous, I flash him my phone, which has the ESPN app pulled up. "Quinn was texting that Eli's in the bullpen."

Parker glances around the bar. "Damn… I get TVs aren't a true speakeasy vibe, but I may have to talk to Wes about adding some."

That makes me snort. "Now, Mr. Real Estate Developer, you know that is not going to fly. He loves the authenticity of this place."

Nodding, a smirk lifts his lips. Silence falls upon us as we both take another sip of our drinks.

"There's a sports bar two or three blocks over… You want to go catch the end of the game?" he asks in a tone I've never heard from him.

My mouth falls open. "Wait, did you just nicely extend an offer to me?"

He rolls his eyes. "Oh fuck off, it's not that big of a deal."

A shit-eating grin takes over my face because yes. It. Is.

"Put it this way, Legs, I'm heading to the sports bar down the street to watch my best friend pitch." Standing, he finishes off the rest of his whiskey, and I can't help but quiver at the way his throat moves when he swallows. "If you are coming…let's go." He starts heading in Sloan and Wes's direction, and even though I love defying him, for once, I don't. Maybe since we aren't at work, he will let his guard down. I'm curious to see what hanging out with him one-on-one would be like.

The only other time we were ever alone…there wasn't much hanging out involved.

And with that thought, maybe this isn't the best idea.

"Since you don't have any TVs in this place, we're going to head out and catch Eli closing out against the Orioles," Parker says in a teasing tone to Wes as they do that bro hand-shake/hug thing.

Sloan pulls me into an embrace. "So now you guys are hanging out?" she questions in my ear.

"It's not like that," I hiss and pinch her butt.

"Hey, hands off my woman's ass, Av." Wes pulls Sloan into his side, laughing.

"She likes it," I taunt, leaning in to hug him bye as well. "Tonight was great... I hope Claire does well with her treatments."

"Thank you both for coming... I'm glad we were able to do this for them."

Parker turns his attention to Lo. "Oh, and speaking of Eli, I was going to text you all tomorrow, but I arranged a private box big enough for the whole crew when the Bulls are in town next month. Once we can narrow down the game he's likely pitching, they'll get it all set for us."

So, he can be nice.

"Thank you for doing that. I knew you'd have connections. It would be so much easier if my brother was a catcher or fielder, so then we could pretty much guarantee seeing him play. But thank you for arranging that on standby."

My phone chimes with another text from Quinn. She knows watching baseball is my guilty pleasure.

"He's going in now... Let's go, boss," I say to Parker, then blow Sloan one last kiss before heading toward the door.

"Bar or cocktail table?" Parker asks.

"Let's get a table... Don't tell Wes, but those hors d'oeuvres weren't enough to fill me up. I need some food."

He chuckles, and it slides over me like a new song I've never heard but want to keep playing on repeat.

"Table for two, please," Parker says to the hostess. "And can you put us near a TV playing the Bulls and Orioles game?"

"Sure thing, follow me."

Once we're seated, it's the bottom of the seventh inning and the Bulls are batting, so we both check out the menu while Eli isn't on the field.

"I'm in the mood for a beer so I can pretend I'm at the game in person, but what's that saying?" I ponder, thinking out loud. "Is it liquor before beer... No, it's beer before liquor, never sicker...so I'm set." I do a little dance in my seat, excited for a cold pint.

"I never thought of you as a beer girl."

"That's the problem... You don't know me even though you think you do."

The waitress stops by, and before I can speak, Parker orders. "Bring us two of your Brooklyn Summer Ales, please." Then he looks at me with a smirk. "Do you know what you want to eat?"

I narrow my eyes at him with a playful smile. There's always an intense energy between us, has been since the first night I met him, but this is something different, something light-hearted.

"Yes, I'll take eight of your honey habanero wings. With ranch, please."

"You bet," our server says at the same time Parker speaks up again. "Make it two eight pieces and a basket of fries. Thank you."

The waitress leaves to place our order, and I turn to Parker. "Wow, I didn't think you ever drink anything other than whiskey."

"Sometimes I like to be reminded of where I came from, and there was a time in my life, I could barely afford a beer, much less Blue Label or Pappy."

That's the first time he's ever told me something personal... and I want to know so much more.

"What's your excuse?" he asks.

"Well, you may think I'm a private suite and champagne kinda girl, and while I do enjoy those things from time to time, I'm much more of a *mid-level in the stands, with the real fans, drinking a cold pint of beer* kinda girl."

Parker cocks an eyebrow. "You sure fooled me, brat."

I give him a heavy eye roll as our beers are placed in front of us.

"Eli's going in."

We tune in, watching our friend carry his team to another victory, not allowing any hits.

Drinking beer after beer, he's still an asshole, but for once, I'm not walking on eggshells around him. In fact, we're laughing, sharing smiles here and there, and getting messy over some wings.

It's, dare I say...fun. I especially enjoy the way he watches me lick the buffalo sauce from my fingertips. Not sure if he's turned on or shocked by the lack of etiquette this Upper East Side princess actually has.

By the time I check my phone, it's almost one in the morning.

"I better get going... I need to get back to Binx."

"Who the hell is Binx?" Parker asks incredulously.

I chuckle at his tone. "He's my kitty."

His nose scrunches in disgust. "You have a cat?"

"Yep, and he is perfect. I will hear no shade about my baby."

"What kind of name is Binx?"

I scoff. "Are you serious? You never saw *Hocus Pocus*, the all-time best Halloween movie ever? I don't think we can be friends, after all."

"Oh, the one with the three witches? One has the crazy red hair?" he asks, and I nod with another laugh. But then something flickers in his eyes as they latch onto mine, his face transforming with a mischievous smirk. "Also, I never said we were friends."

I wave him off, ignoring his last statement. "So you have seen it?"

"I don't remember watching it, but I do remember that my mom liked it." His voice softens on the last part, and I don't miss the way he used past tense when speaking of his mom.

"Well, it's settled, then…*friend*, we need a movie night so you can brush up on the Sanderson Sisters."

He shakes his head with a small smile on his lips. "Me and you?" Parker points from himself to me. "A movie night? That sounds like trouble."

My pussy clenches at the memory of said trouble. And with the way he's looking at me, we're definitely sharing the same memory.

The waitress brings us our check, and Parker pays while I use the bathroom before we head outside. It's the perfect time to shake off whatever moment we just shared.

"I think I'm going to call an Uber," I say, holding my finger up. "And before you tease me about being a brat, I typically walk almost everywhere, but I'm in this nice dress and I've had a few too many beers. I'm not walking."

"Well, smartass, I already called us an Uber. Luke and his Tesla will be here any minute. I put in the West Village, but we can update the drop-off address once we get in there."

Did I tell him where I live? I don't think so, but he's never told me either, yet I know all about his penthouse in Tribeca.

"Oh, okay, thank you… I'm so used to you throwing my last name in my face," I say, and my breath hitches, realizing how close we are standing.

His thumb reaches out for my lower lip like he did that first day in the hotel. "What's the deal with that? Why don't you take advantage of your family's pull in this city?"

A big part of me wants to explain…wants him to understand me and not think of me as the snotty rich girl from the Upper East Side.

Swallowing, his thumb slips from my lip, but he doesn't stop touching me. My body tingles as he moves his hand around the back of my neck, cupping it as he tilts my face up to look at him. This isn't friend territory; he was right about that.

I have to clear my throat before I can speak.

"Long story short…I love my parents, but I decided a long time ago I would never fit the mold they created for me. Growing up, the only time I felt like myself was when I was out at my grandparents' place in the Hamptons. They let me get dirty, explore, put my elbows on the table, eat dessert." I laugh because I know that sounds childish, but back then, I was a kid, and I needed that freedom more than I realized. "And then in college, when I met Sloan and Quinn, not being placed in the perfect little bubble my parents created for me was the most freeing thing I had ever experienced."

His stormy grey eyes bore into mine like he's soaking in every word until they drop to my lips. I find myself leaning into him, begging his mouth to take mine.

Just when I think he's going to kiss me, a horn behind us honks, causing us to both whip our heads toward the interruption.

A man calls out from the window of his Tesla, "Parker?"

Again, to my surprise, he takes my hand in his, leading me to the car. "That's me." Parker opens the door, guiding me into the backseat. He gets in as I scoot across, but stops me in the middle, not letting me move over to the other side.

His leg resting against mine reminds me of how strong and powerful he was as he pounded into me that night. I'm salivating for a repeat, even when I know I shouldn't be.

My phone chimes in my crossbody. I pull it out quickly, worried because of the time that it could be important.

> **LOGAN**
>
> Hi gorgeous, just wanted you to know I was thinking about you. I had fun with you the other night.

"Why is he texting you so late?" Parker growls from beside me, and I practically feel his hackles go up.

"I'm not really sure." I keep my tone casual. Logan and I have been texting often and I'm enjoying getting to know him better, but a text this late is unusual.

"Don't play dumb, Ava. Did you let him come in the night he walked you home?"

"Not that it's any of your fucking business, Parker...but no, he did not. He's referring to our dinner on Wednesday."

"Oh, so you did go on a date with him?" he sneers, and that has me narrowing my eyes.

"I can date whoever I want."

"Not when it's going to cause issues on one of my biggest projects. A project I took a chance on by hiring you in the first place."

"Wow…" I say, scooting as far away from him as possible. Praying this ride will be over soon. "You know what…fuck you."

His jaw tics, but he doesn't say anything else.

We were having such a good time, and he's just ruined it in a matter of seconds. I was ready to kiss him, dammit. *Ugh.*

"For your information, we went as just friends. Olivia tagged along too…but you know what, I'll probably text him back right now and take him up on his offer for a date, just to prove to you I can handle myself professionally and personally just fine." I practically spit the last part.

He grabs the wrist, holding my phone. "You better fucking not."

"I do what I want, Parker… Get used to it." I flick my wrist out of his grip, sitting back with a huff. I couldn't be any more relieved seeing we're close to my apartment.

I open the door before the Uber even comes to a stop. "Thanks for the ride."

Barely glancing over my shoulder, I grunt, "And thanks for ruining a great night, boss."

"Ava…" Parker reaches out, but I swat him away, not in the mood for his up-and-down shit.

"Yo, Ava…" I hear from down the sidewalk, where I see my neighbor and a few of his buddies walking up to our entrance from a night out. The distraction allows Parker to grab my wrist again from where he has moved over toward the open door I am halfway out of.

"Hey, Ben," I say, looking up from where Parker's touch is lighting a fire under my skin.

"You should come up… We are going to have a few more drinks at my place." As soon as the words leave Ben's mouth, Parker drops my hand like it's on fire. I feel his asshole exterior rebuild in record time.

I don't even want him touching me when he's being such a jerk, so why does him letting go bother me so much?

When I try to meet his gaze, he won't look at me, and I can practically hear his teeth grinding. He speaks, but his eyes stay straight ahead.

"Seems to me like you have plenty of *friends* to choose from. Have a good night, Ava."

BABES GROUP CHAT

SLOAN

Guess who Ava left Kings Hideaway with after the charity event?

QUINN

Shut up... who?

SLOAN

Her boss 😏😏

QUINN

Oh shit... details now Av!!!

QUINN

Also, highly recommend banging your boss. 10 out 10.

ME

Calm your tits, both of you! It wasn't like that.

ME

We literally watched Eli pitch and then Parker's assholeness started showing per usual.

SLOAN

So you guys didn't bang last night?

ME

Hell no. I ended up hanging out with my neighbor till like 4 am.

QUINN

Big Ben?

ME

😂😂

ME

Yes he's going to make some girl very happy one day. But honestly, I wasn't feeling it last night. We just hung out and I went home to Binxy Boy

QUINN

Aw I miss Thackery

SLOAN

Good news is... Wes owes me a massage because he bet me you guys were finally going to have sex.

ME

Tell his ass he owes me one too for putting up with his friend.

SLOAN

PS: If you decide you are up for a little fun with a stranger, don't forget about the speed dating event next Sunday night at Masqued.

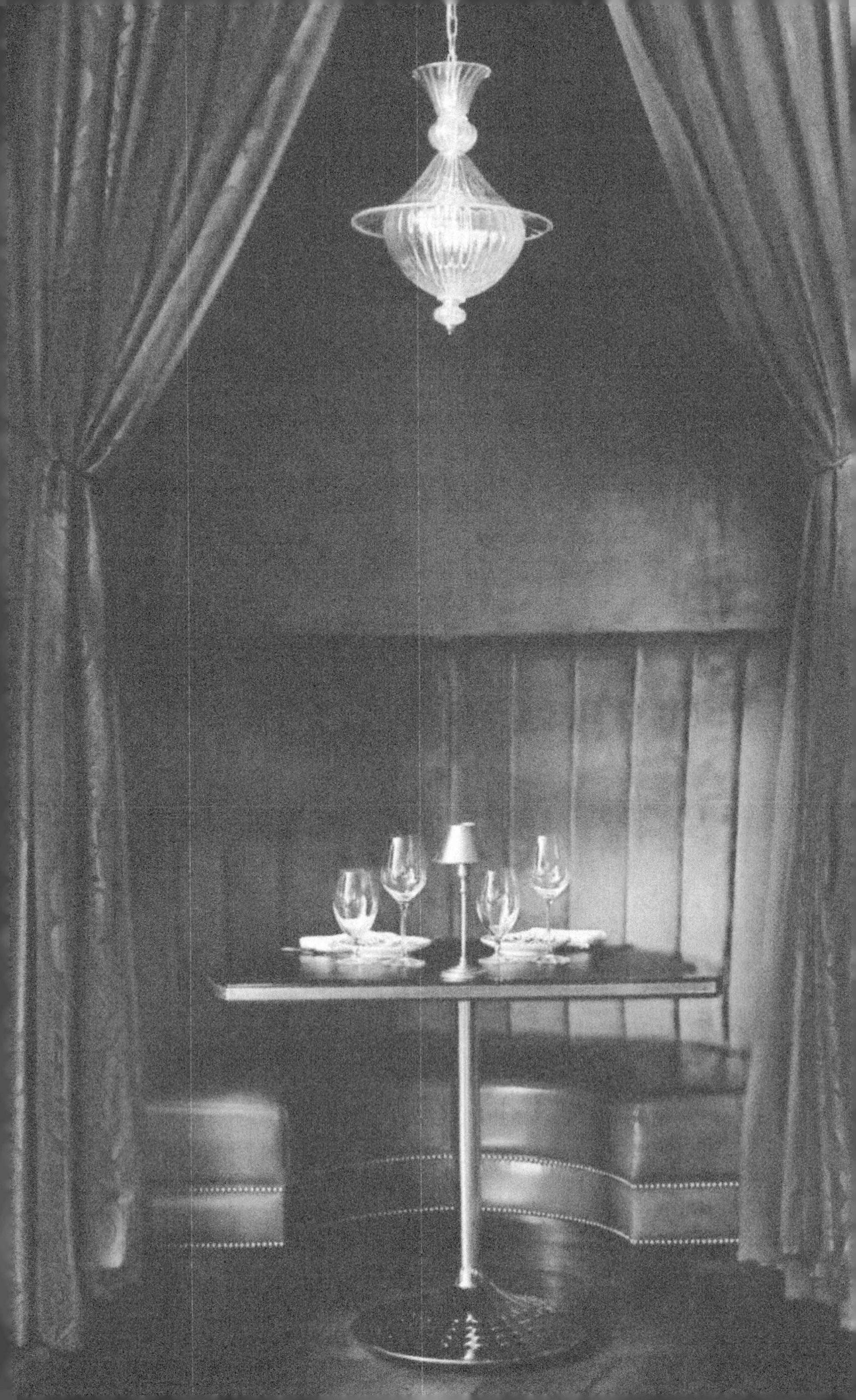

Five

Ava

"It's such a pretty day," Olivia chimes from beside me as we make our way through SoHo from Luxure to Bryant & CO's office a few blocks away. Taking advantage of the beautiful May weather.

"It truly is. I just hope it stays like this for a while before it turns into an inferno," I say, knowing how hot it gets on these city streets in the summer.

"Me fucking too." She laughs.

"Do you think he hates the counter tops we picked out?" I blurt out, my thoughts running rampant with why Parker only wanted to see Olivia and I today.

"I mean, how could he? They're perfect." She smiles over at me, and she's right, they truly are.

"No, I think there is something more to it. It seemed less about us and more about Logan," she states, and my brow furrows in confusion.

"Really? Why do you think that?"

"I can't put my finger on it, but he's different with you... almost territorial."

I scoff, trying to brush off the thought. Part of me knows she's right, but when it comes to Parker, I have no clue what that means. "No way... He's just an asshole to me."

"An asshole who pays you a whole hell of a lot of attention," she says matter-of-factly.

"What do you mean?"

"Well, for starters... Do you remember that night he showed up at the bar when we first hired you?"

Thinking back to that night, I recall her and Logan's strange reactions to him being there. "Yeah." I nod, unsure how to feel about where this is going.

"He never, and I mean *never*, cares what we do after work or even during work, as long as we get our shit done. The minute he heard you were coming, he had so many questions."

"Then the fact he showed up..." She slows her pace, moving both of her hands above her head and throwing out her fingers like the universal sign for mind blown. I laugh at her dramatics, and she continues. "The only time he has ever hung out with us outside of work has been at special events we all had to attend. And the occasional time he and Braxton get together. But never ever after work for drinks."

I take in her words, pondering what they could mean. If he wanted to make a move, it's not like I haven't been willing. I certainly wasn't pushing him away when he was inches from my face the other night. Either she's overthinking this, or maybe he's the type that doesn't do repeats so he's fighting our tension. Regardless, I'm not going to wait around until he figures it out. No matter how good it was.

We stop at a crosswalk, and Olivia pulls me from my thoughts. "Can I ask you something? Don't feel like you have to answer."

"Of course." I nod.

"Do you guys have history? I mean, it's obvious you know each other somehow."

I don't want to lie completely, but even though I trust Olivia, my two best friends in the whole world don't even know that secret.

We start walking again as I answer, "His college best friend, Eli Barton, dates my best friend, Quinn. And Eli's sister, Sloan, is our other best friend. But he decided the minute he heard my last name, exactly what he thought about me, which is why you guys had to convince him to even give me the job."

"I wouldn't say we had to convince him… In all honesty, I think Logan feels the tension between the two of you and says things like that about Parker as a defense mechanism."

Interesting.

"So today when he insisted it be me who brought you over and not Logan, it just solidified even more that I think he wants you… He may not even truly realize it himself, but he hates the thought of you and Logan alone together."

Could that be true? If it was true, he could have easily had me on Saturday. Instead, he let his male ego get in the way of what could have been an amazing ending to a good night.

"I don't know… I think he is more worried that Logan or I will fuck things up within our team if we get involved. Plus, there is the no fraternizing rule."

She stops right as we approach the building. "The what?"

"Parker told me about the rule against fraternizing within the company."

Olivia laughs, shaking her head. "That shiesty fucker is smart."

"Huh?" I ask, not following her accusation.

"Girlfriend, there is no rule against that. Mr. Bryant himself has been banging every secretary he's had since the 90s."

My mouth falls open.

That son of a bitch.

Maybe I will take Logan up on that date after all. He's hot, extremely interested, and not a complete asshole.

PARKER'S ASSISTANT Tasha greets us, lacking the enthusiasm she normally shows when Logan is around.

"Mr. Cole will meet you in here," she says as she sashays out of the meeting room she showed us to. I can't help but wonder if he fucks his secretary the way Mr. Bryant apparently does.

"Do you think we should also tell him we want to change the color scheme he and Logan decided on for the cigar lounge?" Olivia asks, interrupting my wayward thoughts.

I giggle because we totally agreed to let the boys have complete say over that room, but we had an idea today when we were picking out countertops, and now we can't unsee it.

"Let's feel him out first and make sure he isn't giving off over-the-top asshole vibes."

We both laugh until a deep voice interrupts, "What in the world could be so funny?"

"Oh, nothing, Ava's just hilarious," Olivia says, brushing him off.

"Could have fooled me. I figured it must have been the asshole Ava was referring to. But then again, I know she has many talents…" The pause in his sentence makes my skin prickle. "I just didn't realize comedian was one of them."

Many talents, huh? Those talents didn't mean much to you the other night when you couldn't get me out of your Uber quick enough.

But I guess we're pretending that never happened, which seems to be our MO.

"She really could be, but anyways…what did you need to see us about?" Olivia tries to change the subject. And I have to give her credit, because she's dodging this awkwardness like a pro.

"I wanted to commend you guys on the vanity countertop choices." Pride swarms my insides at his praise. I guess that's one good thing about someone who never gives positive feedback. When they do, it's like a drug.

Again, red flag central. And I can't stop myself from wanting to play capture the fucking flag.

I pull my head out of my ass when I hear Olivia thanking him and follow suit.

"And because of that, I have decided to hand the task for the actual bar tops off to you two as well. I know I said I wanted that decision, along with the cigar lounge, to be left up to me with the help of Logan, but you two proved yourselves today."

"Wow, thank you." I'm so surprised by this, and by the look on Olivia's face, she is as well. "So you are saying that we will now have full control over those areas as well?" I clarify.

"Yes, I trust you both as manager and designer, but any bigger changes or decisions, I still expect you to run by me."

Who knew he could be so reasonable?

"I'm going to be pulling Logan to help on a smaller project at times, so this will free him up and take some of his responsibilities off of him."

We both nod, barely containing our excitement about the opportunity to have more creative freedom. Parker and Olivia discuss a few things that Mr. Bryant wanted her to focus on, and my mind wanders back to our conversation on the walk over here.

Would Parker purposefully pull Logan away from this project just to keep our interactions at work to a minimum? I shake my head at the thought. I can't wrap my head around why he would go to that extent.

I stare at his side profile, taking in every detail. He's so handsome it's sickening.

What are you and that perfect fucking jawline up to, Parker Cole?

We spend the next hour going over the final floorplan for the rooftop, including the décor. Olivia's phone chimes right as we're wrapping up.

"Perfect timing. That was my reminder for our class at Dance Hub in thirty minutes." We both stand to leave, and I grab my oversized bag with my gym clothes.

Parker raises his eyebrows in Olivia's direction. "So you took up a new hobby, after all?"

"Yeah, I was hooked after the first class. I get the hype. See ya tomorrow, Parker." She calls out the last part as she heads out the door.

I wave goodbye, catching his eyes trailing down my legs, and I swear I hear him whisper, "Yeah, I see the hype too," as I walk away.

Babes Group Chat

ME

Ok what the hell am I wearing to this speed dating thing?

SLOAN

OMG, are you finally breaking your streak and coming to something at the club?

ME

Yes, I need something exciting in my life. I'm so close to giving in to a date with Logan.

QUINN

Speed dating will be fun... but why not just go on a date with Logan if you are into him.

ME

I just don't feel like I know him yet and I'd hate for it to be awkward at work if things got weird on the date.

QUINN

That makes sense but maybe try hanging out with him again as friends... ya never know.

SLOAN

True! But so excited you are going to Masqued. I'm actually letting Cass run the event but that's probably better for you. If I was there you'd just try to hide out in my office all night.

ME

You know me too well.

QUINN

I can't wait to hear all the details. I'm so intrigued.

QUINN

Definitely wear those black knee-high boots you have. Hello sexy!

SLOAN

Oooo yes with your black leather mini.

ME

Okay I'll send a pic for approval later =]

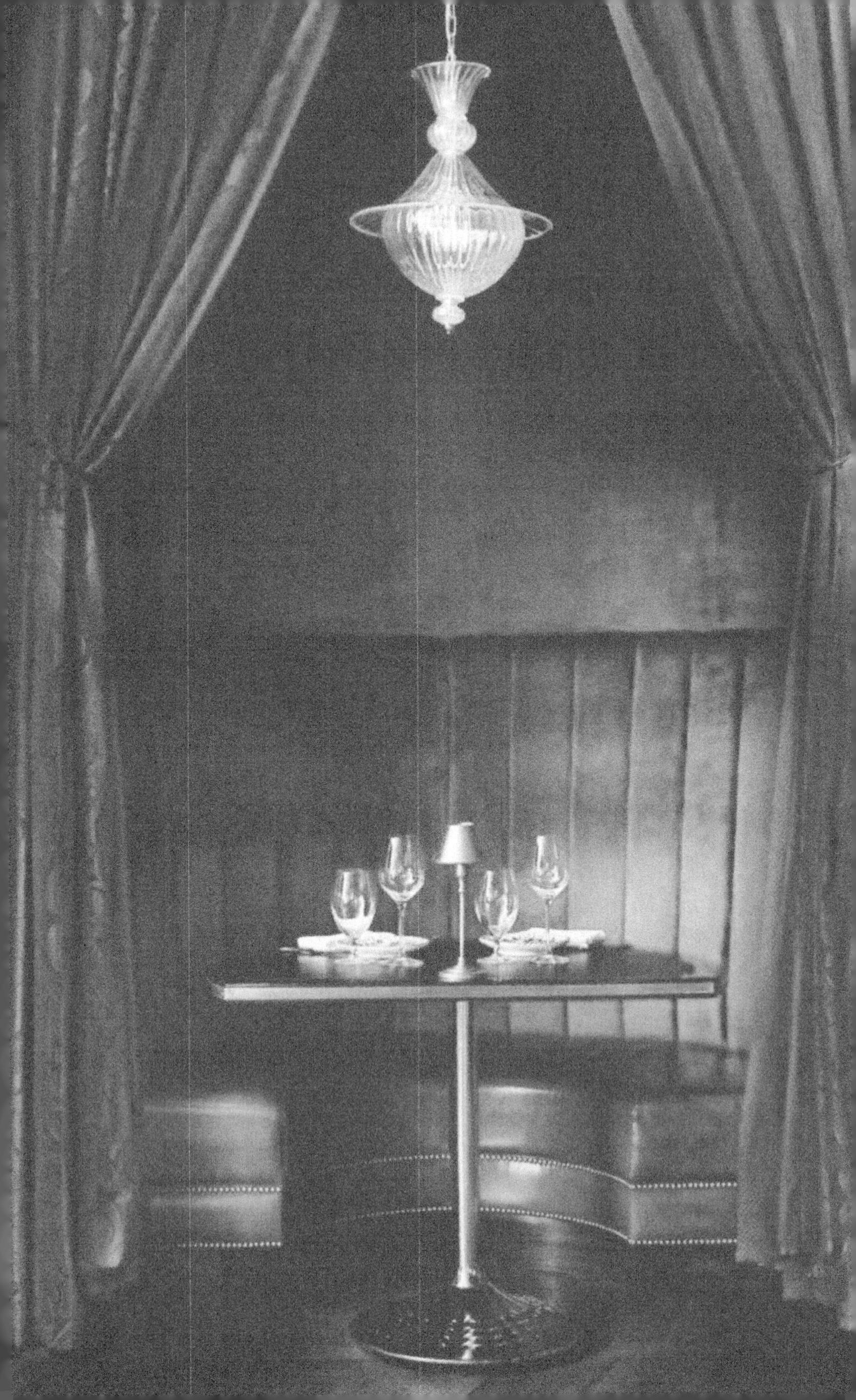

Six

Ava

"What are you doing here?" I practically growl at a smirking Parker, who is currently leaning against the bar right beside me.

"I'm enjoying the luxuries of a club I pay good money to be a part of, Miss Pierce," he answers smoothly, trailing his eyes from my mini skirt to my knee-high boots before ordering a Johnny Walker Blue Label. The blush that spreads up to my cheeks has me suddenly wishing this wasn't a maskless event.

I shake my head at him, so annoyed that he's here. "I just figured an event like this was beneath you. It's not like you have a whole lot of personality to offer a woman in general, much less during a five-minute speed date."

He chuckles at that. "I can be very charming."

"Well, I've certainly never seen it." I roll my eyes and take a sip of my pinot noir.

"Yet you've let me eat your cunt. I must have done something right."

I almost sputter my wine all over the bar at his statement, but I recover quickly.

Refusing to let him have the upper hand, I snark back, "Don't flatter yourself so much. I was horny… Any stranger would have done." I love the way his eyes get stormier with every word, so I keep going. "Which is exactly why I'm here tonight…for a *stranger*."

When I turn to move away, he reaches out, grabbing my arm, pulling me to him until his lips touch my ear. "We will see about that, little brat."

My whole body shivers and my pussy pulses just thinking about the first time he called me that.

Stick your tongue out and open wide, little brat. I can't wait to fuck that smart mouth.

I twist free of his grasp as Cass, Sloan's bar manager, greets the crowd.

I wasn't horny when I arrived, but I sure am now.

So this speed dating thing is actually pretty fun. I haven't met anyone I've had undeniable chemistry with, but they have all been handsome and fun to talk to. Cass set up tonight's event with cards on the table that have preloaded questions. It's perfect because it takes the anxiety out of knowing what to say.

"Okay, next question…" my current date, Daniel, says as he flips over the card. "If you could take a red eye tonight, where would you take it?"

"That's easy! Either Paris to visit with my aunt or North Carolina to visit my best friend."

"I love that your response is about seeing loved ones. Most people would say something extravagant, like the Maldives."

"Well, I mean, Paris isn't too shabby, but thank you. I love my people."

He chuckles. "I agree I love Paris. My company partners with a business based there, so I go several times a year."

Honestly, he would *so* be Aunt Samantha's type, but that may be weird to tell him in the middle of our date.

Before I gush about my favorite places to eat in Paris, the timer goes off. Daniel picks my hand up, placing a soft kiss to the back of it, and I will my body to feel something.

And I do…but it's a set of grey eyes watching me as he moves to his next date. Little Miss Yellow Dress devours him when he sits down in front of her. Parker's eyes are still on me, and he raises his eyebrows suggestively from his table to mine. That's when I realize this is my last round of a reprieve.

"Hi, I'm George," my next date greets, sliding into the chair across from me. He's an attractive man, definitely a bit older, with a little salt and pepper in his well-trimmed beard. But there is something very familiar about him.

"Hi, I'm Ava." I give him a smile, and he studies me the same way I am him, trying to determine where we know each other from.

"Wait, Ava Pierce?" he asks, eyebrows pinched.

When he says my last name, it hits me. "Oh my gosh, Mr. Thomas."

He chuckles. "Yup, but please call me George here… Even though I feel quite strange sitting across from you at one of these events, but I know you are an adult now."

George is a business associate of my family. My father took him under his wing when he first got into investing, and now he's created his own empire.

Thank God for the NDA that is non-negotiable with the membership. My parents heard about Sloan opening this exclusive club, and I got to hear all about their thoughts on the matter. I definitely don't care for them to know I come here occasionally to get laid by a stranger.

"Please don't be worried about me seeing you here, Ava. I promise. How have you been?"

That's the weird thing, I'm not that concerned; I just don't want to be lectured about it. I gave up on worrying about being the perfect little socialite my parents wanted me to be many years ago and they know it. Even though they still try to tell me their thoughts about any and all things not Pierce approved.

"Thank you. I'm doing good. Staying busy with my own business now."

"That's great. What is it you do?" It still stings, but it's no surprise my parents haven't told their friends about my entrepreneurship.

"I have my own interior design company," I tell him, and since my parents won't brag for me, I decide to do it myself. "I designed this entire club with the owner's wishes in mind."

"Seriously? That's amazing, Ava. You did an incredible job. Why haven't I heard this news before?" he asks genuinely.

I give him a pointed look that says he knows exactly why, and he nods in understanding. I have to remind myself I did make it clear I didn't want my parents' help in this industry. Who knows if they were even truly willing to, but I refused to take anything from them to just have it held over my head.

I wanted to make my own way.

"Well, I typically wouldn't do this here, but since this is a different situation," he says, pulling out his wallet and sliding a card across the table, "call me this week. Let's set up a meeting. I want to discuss some investment properties I have in the works."

The conversation turns to two of my favorite people in the whole world, my grandparents. And before I know it, the timer is going off again.

Giving George a hug, we promise to stay in touch. I feel Parker's hovering presence before I see him.

"George," Parker practically growls.

"Calm down, Mr. Cole, your time hasn't started yet," George says before kissing my cheek and moving on to his next date. It makes sense they would know each other. New York City may be a big place, but it can be small when it comes to business circles.

I sit back down, glaring at a brooding Parker, my defense mechanisms going up like armor.

"Why did he give you his card?" Parker asks as he sits across from me, arms crossed as he leans back in his seat.

"He may have some opportunities for me." I shrug. I don't owe any more of an explanation.

"Well, you're busy right now."

"Parker, seriously…it's none of your business, as usual. Now just draw a card and let's get these five minutes over with." I wave him along, over his confusing reactions.

He stares at me for a few seconds before slowly pulling a card. His tattooed hand has me wiggling in my seat. He may annoy the fuck out of me, but he's still the sexiest man I've ever seen in real life.

Parker reads the card, and a smirk takes over his face. "What is your number one fantasy?"

I gulp as visions of that night run through my head. Of course, my first sexual question of the event would be with Parker, of all people.

"Want me to answer for you?" Parker asks, still sporting that sly grin on his pretty face.

For some unknown reason, I want to hear what he thinks.

"Since you think you know me so well, please do." My tone is taunting as I lean forward on my elbow, resting my chin on my hand.

"I do know you, little brat," he whispers, and my pussy clenches. Parker continues in a hushed tone, leaning forward across the table. "I know you want me to call you that again with my cock so far in your throat you feel your airway cutting off. I know you want me to take you down that back hallway to a room and spank your ass until it's red, making your tight pussy so wet I could slide right in and fuck you like the bratty slut you are."

My breath hitches and my nipples tingle under my lace bra. Fuck, that sounds good.

Parker drops the question card onto the table and reaches into his pocket. I glance down, noticing the question had nothing to do with my fantasy and everything to do with my favorite street food in the city. My stomach dips, knowing he intentionally went off script for me.

I look up at him as he slides the gold card across the table, and his eyes sear into mine. "Now spare me another boring five-minute session and let's go."

My body and mind fight with each other as he gets up and heads down the hall.

Don't give in to him.

But it will feel so fucking good.

No, he's an arrogant asshole.

Yeah, but you've never experienced pleasure like you had with him.

Body humming, heart racing, without any more hesitation, I push my seat out to stand.

Fuck it.

I WALK into the dimly lit room, letting the door close behind me. Parker sits in the lounge chair across the way. His suit jacket is gone, and the top two buttons of his black shirt are undone, showcasing his rose tattoo. He sits back so casually, whiskey in one hand with his other resting on the ankle he has crossed over his knee.

Sexual dominance practically drips off him.

Parker holds up his Rolex-covered wrist, flicking his hand in the air for me to stop. And just like the first night, I listen to his command.

"If you want to play, leave your defiance at the door."

I nod, having no issue doing that in this room. Not with him. As soon as I said *fuck it*, I understood what I was agreeing to and, for some odd reason, I trust him.

"Ava, I need your words. Tell me you understand."

I swallow roughly. Not from nerves, but from anticipation.

"I understand."

"Good girl... Now show me what you wore under that mini skirt for your stranger tonight."

Excitement thrums along every inch of my body as I slowly push my skirt down past my hips and let it drop to my feet, stepping out of it.

His eyes darken. "Turn around," he says, and I do, showing him my dark purple strappy thong.

"As sexy as those are, I want to see your sweet cunt. Lean forward and peel them off."

When I do, the groan he lets out has goosebumps littering my body. When he speaks again, his voice is even huskier this time. "Leave the boots on and look at me." When I spin around, I whimper at the sight of his cock in his hand.

"Fuck..." he growls. "Those long legs leading up to that tight pussy, I could come right now," he says, pulling on his perfectly thick cock. "You are so ready for me, I can see you glistening from here."

I flush as his eyes move up to my barely covered breasts. "Did you really think I was going to let anyone else here see you like this? Fuck that. Fuck them for even thinking about it." Parker's possessiveness turns me on way more than it should.

Slowly, he motions with his pointer finger for me to come closer. I walk until I am standing between his widespread legs, my eyes unable to look away from where he lazily strokes himself. "Take it off," he grunts, and I unfasten my bra, letting it fall from my body.

"There they are. As perfect as I remember." His gaze is darkened and full of a lust that drives me crazy with desire to feel his hands on me.

Parker reaches up, running two of his fingers over my lips. "Open," he commands, and his fingers enter my mouth. I swirl my tongue around them and suck, pretending it's his big dick instead. His eyes roll back and his cock twitches between us, just slightly brushing my inner thigh. My clit pulses, so needy for attention I can hardly stand it.

Removing his fingers from my mouth, he trails them leisurely down my neck, giving a gentle squeeze, and I moan.

"Don't worry, I'll give you something to choke on soon."

I bite my lip, trying to hide the smirk fighting its way onto my face from his words.

He continues his journey, trailing his fingers between the mounds of my breasts, gently over my belly button ring, and finally grazing right where I'm desperate for it. "Yesss…" I moan, jolting into his touch.

"Fuck, you are dripping," Parker says, running his fingers through my wetness and rubbing it into my clit.

"Please," I beg, and he withdraws his finger. He doesn't speak, pulling me to the side of his chair as I gasp. Wrapping his hand around the back of my neck, he shoves my face down on his cock. My breasts lay across his thigh and my ass is in the air as my body folds over the armrest.

"Now suck me like the good little brat you are," he growls.

My jaw stretches to take him all the way in. Flattening my tongue along the underside, I groan at the feel of the veins in his hard cock. Inch by inch, I take him a little more and more as I begin to suck.

He shoves the back of my head down farther, and I gag around him.

"Breathe through your nose."

I do as he commands, and he lets up only for a second before he does it again. Just like the first night, I feed off his desires and the unknown of how far he will take things.

I feel Parker's strong hand brush over my ass cheek before moving between my legs. He pushes two fingers into my pussy, and I hum loudly around his cock. "You want to be filled so bad, don't you, Ava?"

I nod eagerly, still sucking up and down. My mouth falls open around his long length when he starts to stroke that sweet spot deep inside over and over, the friction from my nipples rubbing against his slacks creating more sensitivity.

He continues in and out, using his thumb to rub the perfect pressure on my clit. Spit trails down my chin as I suck and swirl his length like it's my favorite treat. I am completely feral for his touch and the way he thrusts into my mouth at the same pace as his fingers in my pussy.

I'm so close to coming already. Threading his hand through my hair, he grabs a fistful and pushes me to the hilt again. "I want to feel your throat spasming around my cock and your pussy squeezing my fingers. You're gonna come for me, just like this."

I moan loudly, but it's muffled, moving my hips against his hand as I chase my orgasm.

"Yes, that's it, come for me."

Seconds later, I come so hard that I lose all my functional ability, screaming around him. His fingers fuck me through it, rubbing and thrusting just right, as his cock twitches against my tongue. I'm still sucking him as I come down from the high, panting as his touch slows.

Parker's grip on my hair, taking my mouth off his cock, brings my focus back. "Fuck, Av...it's taking everything I have in me not to come down your throat," he says, pulling his fingers out of me.

I stare up at him in a haze, wanting more, more, more. As he drags his fingers, wet from my pussy, across his lips, the sight has my core pulsing. The aftershock of what those fingers just made me feel makes me shiver.

He closes his eyes, savoring the taste. "You may be a sour little brat, but you taste so fucking sweet."

His words thrill me. I thought I enjoyed pissing this man off, but there is nothing like being on the other end of his praises.

"Thank you, Sir," I say submissively, and by the way his nostrils flare, he's eating it up just as I knew he would.

"Take my shoes off," he demands, and I kneel in front of him, removing both of his Prada Oxfords. Parker stands to his full height as I stay on the ground. As he slowly unbuttons the rest of his shirt, I revel in every tattooed inch he exposes. Last time, he barely took his pants off before we fucked.

Wrapping his hand around my neck, he pulls me up to stand in front of him. "Get on all fours." He motions with his head to the bed beside us. I do as he says and peer over my shoulder, admiring every thick muscle in his body as he rolls the condom on his thick cock.

"Like what you see, Angel?" he teases, and the sweet name makes my heart stutter. His praise is fucking with my head more than he already does on a daily basis.

I bite my lip, nodding. I have spent way too many nights chasing the high I felt with him the last time we were here.

He slaps my ass with his cock. One. Two. Three times. I moan at the weight of it against me. Just when I think there is no way he could be any sexier, he holds his dick steady in his hand and a trail of spit falls from his mouth, getting himself wet. I whimper at the sight, and he enters me slowly. Making sure I feel every centimeter, he stretches me to fit him perfectly.

"So tight," he groans and pulls out, just leaving the tip for me to clench around before slamming into me. Again, and again. No one has ever fucked me as hard and as thoroughly as this man. His hands roam all over my body, worshiping me in a way I'd never tire of. Tweaking my nipples, up and down my spine, slapping my ass. I can feel him everywhere.

"It's so good… Too good," I groan, needing him to know.

His fingers dig into the top of my ass, pulling me back onto him with every stroke. "I'm going to come so fast, fuck."

Parker pulls out, and I'm pleading instantly. "Parker, don't stop, please."

"Flip over, I want to see your face when you come," he says, practically turning me over himself.

I push up on my elbows, wanting to see his cock as it disappears inside of me. I expect him to fuck me relentlessly, but instead, he shocks me. His hand finds the back of my head, pulling me up toward him, and his lips touch mine for the very first time.

I have thought so much about that night and how he seemed to intentionally not kiss me. I tried to act like it didn't bother me, but there is no doubt it did, especially when he pretended it never happened whenever I would see him.

But right now, as his lips devour mine, I honestly wish he'd maintained that rule. I already knew no one else would compare to him sexually, but this is something different. He is ingraining himself into me with every brush of his treasuring yet hungry lips. I have never felt this connected to someone as I do in this moment.

And when he breaks away, his cock still inside of me, I know he felt it too by the way he admires me, almost like he just saw something for the first time.

Thankfully, he breaks the spell, pounding into me. "I need you to come for me again. Fuck, I can't hold off much longer. You feel too good."

Making a dominant man like Parker so desperate has me feeling powerful and even more aroused. His moans, how he grips my hips tightly, the strength in his arms and chest as his muscles flex with each thrust, send me over the edge, and I claw at his chest as we both come.

I swear I hang in the clouds for a few minutes, somewhere between life and death, until my eyes open to his cock sliding out of me. Parker tosses the condom in the small trash can and flops down on the bed next to me, letting out a satisfied sigh.

"Thank you, Sir." I can't help but giggle from the smirk I see out of my peripheral.

"You'll never be able to call me that again without gaining my cock's attention."

"That's the point...Sir," I smart back, raising my eyebrows suggestively to him.

Our eyes meet for a few moments, and he gives me the most genuine smile I've ever seen grace his face. My stomach stirs with what feels like a million pigeons fighting over scraps in Central Park.

"Fuck, that was phenomenal." He breaks the silence.

"I don't think phenomenal even begins to describe it."

"I've been waiting on that for over a year and a half." Again, his slight admission sends my emotions in a tailspin, trying to navigate what he's saying without saying.

"Well, you know you didn't have to wait for me to show back up here." I've thought so many times about seeking him out at Masqued since that first night, but any time we were briefly around each other, I always got the notion he had no intentions of reliving our rendezvous.

Until recently.

"That reminds me of something I've been wondering. Why haven't you been here much, if at all, since then?" He raises his eyebrows as mine dip. "I mean, you obviously like sex, and it seems like you are still looking for something you haven't found, so why not?"

I ponder on that for a few beats, but I'm not sure I even really know the answer. "How do you know I haven't been here, Mr. Cole?"

He smirks. "I have my ways…or maybe it's just an assumption."

I turn onto my side, trailing my fingertips up his arm. Parker watches the touch, and this time when his eyes meet mine, I see something new within his stare. An emotion I can't quite grasp.

"You know we could keep doing this… It doesn't have to be here, and it doesn't have to be anything serious."

I feel him stiffen under my fingertips. My words have him sitting up abruptly.

"We would keep it outside of work too, of course. I know how touchy you are about me taking my job seriously. Just a casual agreement, whenever we are both free," I rush out.

He runs his hands through his dark hair, still not saying anything, and I feel like such a stupid girl as I continue to try to keep his walls from completely going back up.

"Even if we just meet here... That way, neither of us is going to the other's home."

Parker holds up his hand. "Ava, stop, please."

"Seriously, what's the big deal?" I say, sitting up, just as he starts getting dressed.

My question has him whipping around. "The big deal is, we fuck two times...one of which was a year a half ago, and you are already asking me for more."

Any lingering euphoria is wiped away as he levels me with his stormy grey eyes. "And I don't do more, Ava." The grimace on his face tells me there is so much more going on here, but I'm fucking over his wishy-washy behavior. "I'm a one-and-done type of guy... Occasionally, when it's good, I come back for seconds."

Parker pauses, staring at me for a few seconds, and then he's walking over and cupping my face, searing his lips to mine. For just a blink, I relish it, but then my brain course corrects, and I push him back with a shove, wiping my lips. My heart feels like it's in my throat.

He doesn't attempt to pull me closer, instead he practically growls his next words. "You tempt me every fucking day, so yeah, I needed seconds...but that's it."

Now I'm officially nauseous from this conversation. And pissed.

"Well, fuck you and your seconds, *boss*man," I say through gritted teeth, and then I do something I'll probably regret tomorrow.

I pick my clothes off the ground, clutch them to my chest, and waltz right out the door.

"Ava, put your fucking clothes on right now," he barks, and I flip him off. My feet carry me to the end of the hall without turning back. His heavy footsteps come shortly after, as he spits more demands at me, but I'm done following his rules tonight. I don't even hear a word he's saying as I focus on getting the hell out of here.

I punch in the code to the staff-only area, slamming the door before he gets there and finding my reprieve in Sloan's office. No one saw me doing the most embarrassing walk of shame I've ever committed, but you know what, it was worth it just to fuck with Parker *Asshole* Cole.

Babes Group Chat

QUINN

Two dates in one week... damn girl.

SLOAN

Leave her alone. At least she met this one at work and not on tinder.

ME

There is nothing wrong with meeting a stranger from the internet. Some people meet their soulmates online.

QUINN

Please read that back to yourself... I feel like meeting a stranger on the internet goes against everything we were ever taught growing up. haha

SLOAN

She does have a point.

ME

Ugh with the two of you.

QUINN

Who you kidding you love us.

SLOAN

We're the best.

ME

Mmhmm.

QUINN

I gotta go Addy just took off her diaper and is running around ass naked. I can't make this shit up.

SLOAN

You might need to wrap her waist in duct tape. It's tamper proof.

QUINN

Are you speaking from personal experience?!

SLOAN

😅😅

ME

Hahah love yous. I'll let you know how it goes.

QUINN

xox

SLOAN

Send us pics 📷

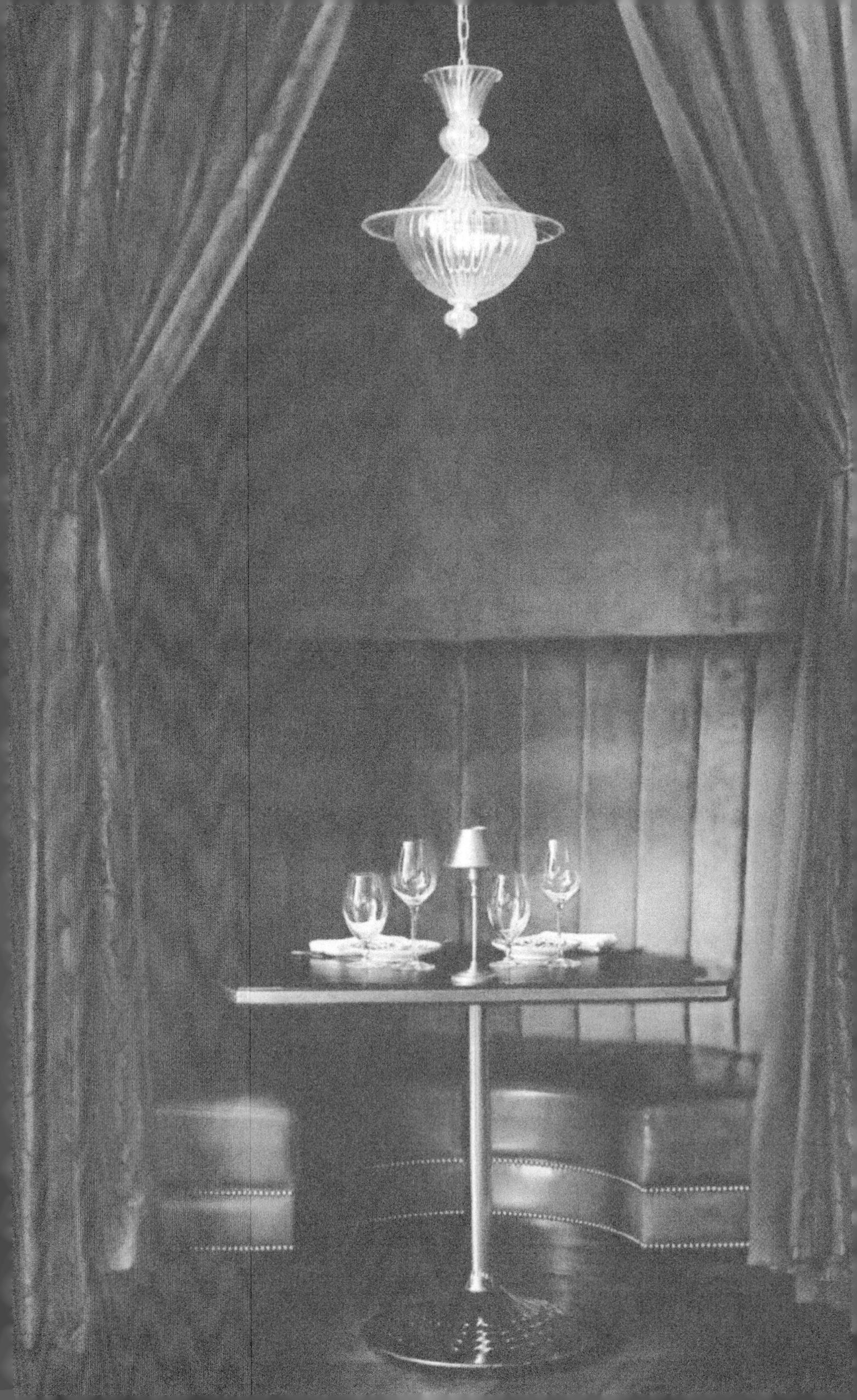

Seven

Ava

M*eowwww.*

"Aww, is that my Binxy boy," my grandma croons from the other end of the phone.

I chuckle. That woman is obsessed with my cat. "Yes, it's him, trying to be all cute. Acting like I didn't just give him treats five minutes ago."

"Ha! That's my boy. Grandma will come and visit you soon, little man... Speaking of which, are you still planning on spending your birthday with us?"

Trying not to trip over said cat, I walk over to my fridge to grab a drink.

"You bet I am. I'm looking forward to a nice weekend out there."

My grandma scoffs. "Out there... You make it sound like we live so far away."

"Okay, sorry, out east."

"Well, that's too long not to see you. How about I come into the city, and we go to lunch or something?"

That makes me laugh. Only she would consider not seeing me for a few weeks too long. Unlike my parents, who can go months. I'm not mad at that, though.

Lunch with my grandma is the soul cleanser I need. Best of all, she'll never judge you. Another trait opposite of my mother, who cares far too much about the naysayers.

"Oh, I'd love that. You'll just have to give me a heads up on what day so I can plan accordingly."

Meaning, I have to tell Mr. Dickhead that I will be taking an extended lunch that day and try my best not to throat-punch him when he gives me a wise-ass comment in return.

"Perfect… I'm thinking within the next week or so," she says, along with the sound of rustling papers.

"Sounds good to me," I say with a smile.

"I'll let you go get ready for your date… Give my boy some extra treats for me."

"You know it's nothing serious." By the way she let the word "date" roll off her tongue, I know she's already planning my wedding at her Hamptons estate. I just needed to clarify.

"Mmhmm, dinner the other night and now this. Sounds like it could be something," she sing-songs.

Rolling my eyes, I sigh with resignation. "I'm still not sure how I feel about it."

"Trust me, honey, when it's the right one, you'll know," she says with a lightness in her tone. No doubt she is thinking about how she and my grandfather met all those years ago. It was my favorite story growing up. She was on a date with a gentleman her parents had arranged for her, and by the end of the night, my grandpa was the one who wound up walking her home. She said she just knew he was who she was supposed to be with, and they have been together ever since.

"I'll let you know when Cupid's arrow sticks," I joke, pushing away the one person who slips into my mind.

"I love you, Aves."

"Love you too."

Looking at the clock, I realize I have less than an hour before Logan will be here. I'm eager to see how the night goes. Leaving Parker at Masqued that night was my push to move forward.

So when Logan asked me earlier this week if I would like to be his date to a company function celebrating one of Mr. Bryant's latest achievements, I finally agreed. I'm not sure if it was solely because I'm interested in the man, or if it's to mend my bruised ego.

Dating Logan should be easy enough. He's handsome, intelligent, charming, funny—all the things one should want in a partner.

I rustle through my closet to find the perfect dress, settling on a plum-colored sleek satin low-back dress. The front offers enough coverage that it's appropriate to wear around work colleagues, but I still feel sexy in it. I apply a fun smoky eye shadow and throw my hair up in a messy but cute chignon, using a tutorial I found online.

Strapping on my favorite pair of Jimmy Choo heels, I'm ready with less than two minutes to spare. *The girls would be so proud of me.*

"Have I told you how stunning you look tonight?" Logan whispers into my ear, causing a smile to break across my face.

"Maybe once or twice," I reply shyly, observing the crowd from the cocktail table we've been occupying. It's not a lie; he's been very generous with his compliments tonight. Not in an unsettling way, but subtle enough that he makes me feel wanted and beautiful.

"Well, it's true. Come on, let's get a refill and go mingle," he says, then places his palm on my lower back as we make our way through the crowd. This move is something he's been doing all night. Maybe it's because of the cut of the dress, or his need to touch me, or a combination of both, but I'm not mad at the way he's asserting a little possessiveness over me.

After numerous introductions and bouts of small talk, we're finally seated for dinner. I'm feeling good about the night so far. Logan has been nothing but attentive and has been praising my work to anyone who would listen. Of course, there was a bit of awkward conversation when people recognized my last name and then proceeded to inquire about where my parents were. Trying to use me as a steppingstone to them, like usual.

Honestly, that's why I wanted to branch off and do my own thing without the Pierce name, much to my parents' disappointment. For my talent and my accomplishments to be mine, and not because of who my family is or what strings they have pulled.

My gaze roams around the room as conversations continue around our table. But I'm frozen as soon as I collide with a pair of stormy greys. His jaw is clenched, and by the way he's gripping the tumbler of his favorite amber liquid, I can tell he's in a mood. I've felt his eyes on me for a better part of the night, especially when Logan is nestled in close, or has his hands on me. It's funny, for someone who says they are a one-and-done, and in our case two-and-done, he certainly looks pissed.

As a matter of fact, he's been in a mood this entire week, especially once he overheard Logan talking about our Tuesday night dinner plans. *"You sure do move on quickly. Jumping from my cock to his?"* My anger resurfaces at the memory of his hateful words.

He had his chance. Besides, I've been enjoying spending time with Logan. He's not the fuckboy Parker made him out to be. He's been a nice reprieve from the usual assholes I've dated in the past. Having similar upbringings has helped us connect on a certain level, the main difference being he's leaned into the perks of his last name, whereas I've strayed.

"So, I asked the driver if he wouldn't mind idling for ten minutes because I knew I'd be thrown out as soon as I showed my face inside. And as a matter of fact, it was within six minutes, my ass was back in that car." Logan's boisterous laugh fills the air, followed by several others joining along.

I bring my focus back to him, disregarding Parker's incessant glares. After several moments, I realize we're sharing embarrassing stories from growing up. Logan's was his first time meeting a girl's family. Not realizing that he had dated the girl's older sister a year prior. The father basically slammed the door in his face.

"I can't believe you didn't realize they were related," I tease as I sip my glass of champagne.

"Yup, it wasn't until the morning of when she gave me her home address that I put all the pieces together. In all fairness, I only went on a few dates with the girl, but she was adamant I met her family before we took things further." He lets out another laugh when I swat his arm.

Another guy chimes in with a shitshow of a story about trying to sneak into a club and being tossed out after attempting to dance on the bar. We all laugh in unison when he mentions his date stayed at the club without him.

"I remember sneaking in there when I was in high school. They had the best DJs on Friday nights. We would dance our asses off," I add.

"Ah, to be young and stupid again." Logan sighs and finishes off his drink.

"Here, here!" Several people at our table cheer and down their drinks as well.

Logan leans over to whisper in my ear. "I'm patiently waiting for the day you show me those dance moves of yours. Maybe I can get a private showing?" He waggles his eyebrows playfully, and my body heats.

"Maybe if you're a good boy I'll reward you," I tease as a smirk curls my lips.

"Oh, Ava, you have no idea how good I can be." With a wink, he situates himself back in his seat, but not before adjusting the bulge in his suit pants. I try to conceal my flushed cheeks. Logan certainly knows all the right things to say.

Conversation and liquor are flowing freely around our table, and I can admit I'm having way more fun than I thought I was going to. During a lull, I excuse myself to the bathroom with a big smile on my face.

A tall, dark, and broody asshole is leaning against the wall opposite the women's room when I exit. Rolling my eyes, I attempt to walk right past him. Within a few steps, he matches my stride.

"You seem to be enjoying yourself tonight," Parker says, but I ignore him and keep walking. "I bet he's charming as fuck. Entertaining the whole table, I'm guessing."

I stop in my tracks and turn to him. "We're on speaking terms again, huh?"

His jaw tics, and I continue. "Actually, I am having a great night, no thanks to the constant feel of your death stares."

"He certainly likes to have his hands on you. Possessive much?" he sneers like the dickhead he is.

"Oh, I'm sorry, is that a hint of jealousy I hear? Remember, *asshole*, you had your chance. You told me you didn't want anything else from me. Therefore, I agreed to go out with someone who genuinely wants to spend his time with me and not just for a one-and-done fuck." I poke at his chest to emphasize every word.

He scoffs. "You're delusional if you think he has good intentions… You probably assume you were his first choice as a date for tonight too."

"Yeah, yeah. I've heard your whole spiel already. Save it for someone who gives a shit." My frustration is getting the best of me, and I know better than to continue arguing with him.

"If we're done here, I'd like to return to my date," I say as I look him right in the eye. I'm hoping to see a glimmer of something, but I don't know why I care.

"We're done here. I'll see you at the office on Monday. Enjoy your *date*," he says, practically growling out the final words.

We part ways, and I head back to where Logan is standing at the bar. Chancing a glance in the direction Parker stormed off, I see him heading toward the venue's exit. For some reason, my stomach drops slightly, knowing he's gone for the night.

Plastering on a smile that no longer feels natural, I continue toward Logan. A grin breaks out on his face as I approach. Tucking away his phone, he grabs my new glass of champagne and raises it to me.

You assume you were his first choice.

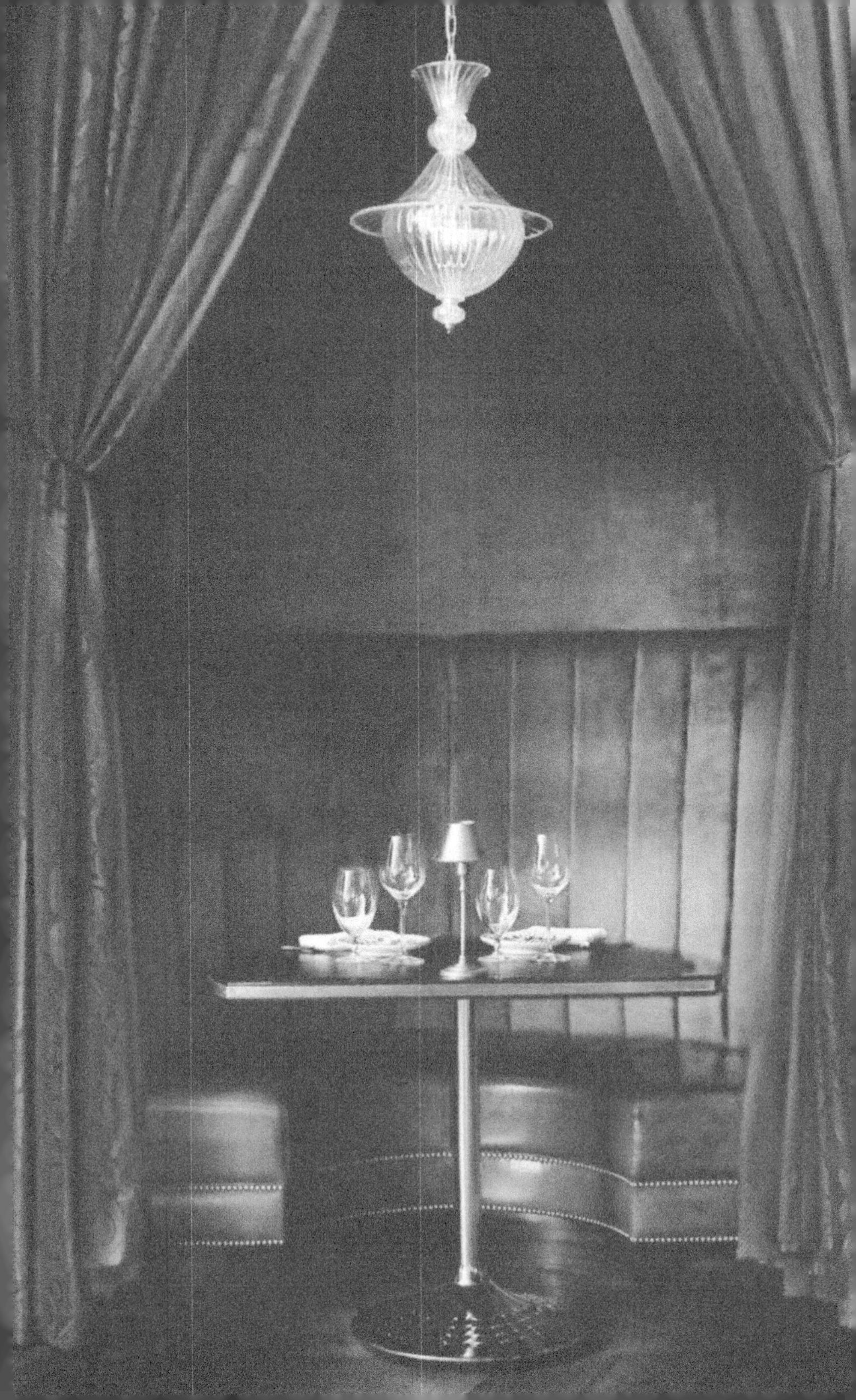

Eight

Parker

"I'm so glad you could make it this weekend," Quinn says, embracing me in a big hug.

"I wouldn't miss these little munchkins' first birthday for anything." No sooner are the words out of my mouth does Eli come to greet me with the twins in each of his arms.

"Glad you returned him in one piece," Quinn teases.

"Who you are kidding, we talked about the girls for most of the night."

Eli met me at my hotel in downtown Charlotte last night to catch up before the madness of the party.

The girls are trying to wiggle free from his arms, desperate to go wreak havoc on the rodeo-themed party decorations.

I take a good look around and smile at the over-the-top décor. But in all honesty, I wouldn't expect anything else from Quinn, especially when it comes to Sophie and Addy.

"What time is everyone coming?"

Eli peeks at the clock. "I'd say within the next hour or so."

"What can I do to help…"

Addy lunges out of Eli's arms toward Quinn, and I think my heart almost stops for a minute. Little gremlins always seeking out ways to scare the ever-living shit out of the adults.

Eli wrangles her in quickly, then turns to me. "Actually there're a few more outdoor decorations that need to be hung up. Would you mind helping with that?"

"Sure, no problem," I say as I make my way to the back doors.

"Perfect, Ava knows what needs to be done!" Eli yells after my retreating form.

Of course. For some fucked-up reason, the universe loves throwing her in my face as often as it can.

It's bad enough I had to see Logan's arm around her all night at the Bryant & Co. dinner last Friday. Right after the best sex of my life at Masqued just the week before. I wanted to break his fucking arm every time it slid down her exposed back. It's my damn fault, though. I turned her down, *again*. And from the devastated look on her face, that was officially the last shot I had with her. There's only so much disappointment someone can take before they give up on you.

As much as I hate to admit it, it's better this way. I'm not here for anything serious. I learned a long time ago I wasn't meant for that. And from what I can tell, Ava is on the hunt for something deeper than just sex. It just kills me to know that she's the only person to hold my attention these past few years, but I can't bring myself to offer her more.

I find the current thorn in my side wrestling a string of balloons near the front gate. She's so distracted by the escaping balloons that she doesn't notice my presence.

Her body freezes at the sound of me clearing my throat.

"Looks like you could use some saving," I tease, not able to stop my smirk.

"You're the last person I'd ask to save me," Ava quips. Her tone causes my dick to twitch.

"Why's that? I always thought I'd make a great knight in shining armor."

Her scoff is followed by a glare. So I continue. "Unfortunately for you, Eli has tasked me with helping you. What are we doing?"

Ava rolls her eyes and thrusts a handful of balloons into my hands. "We need to string these along the fence and tie off some bundles by the gate."

"Okay, simple enough."

"I've begun tying them individually—"

"That's silly. Why don't we string them in one long line first and then attach them," I suggest.

"The wind could knock some loose, and then if they're all tied together, we will lose the entire set. I figured individually we will have less of a chance of losing the whole lot of them," Ava retorts, grabbing back the bunch.

I reach for the bundle. "Yeah, no. Then we will have to worry—"

"If you're not here to help me, then you can go inside. Sometimes you need to let other people take control."

"Sometimes you need to not be such a smart-mouthed brat and take direction. Especially when your way will take us double the time."

"I thought you liked me being your little brat, Sir," she bites out with another eye roll. "You know, I've never met someone so unable to compromise. It's ridiculous."

"Feeling's mutual... Maybe that works on your little boyfriend, but I'm not him."

"Yeah, you're certainly not." My jaw tics with her jab, stomach twisting with unwarranted jealousy. I had wondered what was going on between the two of them, and now I have my answer. I just hope she realizes the type of guy she's getting herself involved with. I warned her once already.

After a minute of stewing in the tension-filled air, Ava finally speaks. "Fine, you can do your half of the fence your way, and I'll do mine how I want. Just remember to keep a bunch for the gate itself."

"Whatever you say, Miss Pierce." I bow slightly, grabbing my allotted bundle and stalking away.

The wind has picked up slightly, and it's making it extremely difficult to hold on to the balloons and tie them off at the same time. I'd hate to admit this, but this would be a hell of a lot easier if Ava and I worked together. Moments later, I hear a frustrated growl and a slew of curses, and a smile spreads across my face.

"Everything alright over there?" I call out, teasing.

"Everything is fan-fucking-tastic," she yells back.

"Okay, just making sure." I can't help it; I love getting her riled up.

"Just do me a favor and stop talking. You're distracting me."

"I was just trying to help out."

"I don't need you to *help out*. I'm fine on my own," she seethes as she wrestles with her balloons as a gust blows by. Eventually, a small batch breaks free and flies in my direction, and I'm able to catch onto them before they're gone forever.

She huffs and marches toward me. Holding out her hand, she reluctantly says, "I'll take those, thank you."

"Look, this is ridiculous. Why don't we just work together? These balloons seem to have it out for us…"

Ava contemplates my suggestion, and I take the time to ogle her. She's sexy even when she's pissed off. Her cowgirl boots and fringe-covered shorts showcase her amazing legs and ass. By the time my eyes make it up to her face, she looks smug as fuck.

"Are you done?" she taunts, eyebrows raised.

"For now." I lick my lips in memory.

"I think you're right. We need to work together," she says begrudgingly.

"I'm sorry, what did you say? I couldn't hear you."

"Just hold the damn balloons and I'll tie them." She shoves another bunch into my hands.

"I have a few tied in a string already. Want to start with those?" I suggest, knowing she didn't like my idea the first time, but it's already done.

She stares at the offending string like it pains her to use it, but she eventually takes it. As a team, we make progress down the longest part of the fence line.

I'm doing my best not to gloat about how well my method is working, when another big gust whips past us and takes out the entire row we just completed. Ava and I try to grab onto the runaway string of balloons, but it's a lost cause. They're already up and over Eli and Quinn's roofline.

Ava turns to me with a scowl. "I told you that wouldn't work, but noooo, you didn't want to hear it. Now we barely have any left."

"Maybe you aren't great at tying things. As you can see, my string didn't unknot, but yours did."

"I can't with you… You are impossible to deal with!" she bellows, and although she's mad, my eyes watch her cheeks pinken and chest rise in fall with frustrated breaths.

"Let's just tie the remaining to the gate and call it a day."

"By all means, go ahead, master knot tyer," she says, waving her hand in that direction.

"Watch a pro. You might want to take notes." I wink, and she flips me off in response.

Always a brat. I've never been one to find that type of attitude attractive, but partner it with a long pair of legs and pouty lips and… Nope, stop that train of thought right fucking there.

Besides, she seems to be enjoying Logan's company.

Ava

"Sooo tell us more about this *boyfriend* of yours?" Quinn says, turning her head and narrowing her eyes on me. "And don't even think I've forgotten about the other bomb you dropped on us earlier, but first, I want to hear about Logan." She leans back in her Adirondack chair beside Sloan, waiting for my response.

The three of us sit around their firepit, looking out over the lake. Eli and Quinn's moms insisted on putting the girls down and cleaning up so that they were able to enjoy some adult time with friends since all of us are in town. Their moms are two of the funniest people I know, and I'm so thankful they accepted me into their big family circle all those years ago. I almost begged them to let me help inside, just to avoid my best friends' third degree, but I knew they would have no part in it.

"Okay, so first off, he's not really my boyfriend. We've only gone on a few dates and the first one didn't count because I told him it was just as friends."

"You're the one that called him that," Quinn retorts, and she's right. I'm not sure why I did. Maybe it was the reminder I needed, knowing I was going to see Parker here today.

"I know, that was a slip-up."

I do like Logan. He's hot, fun, and sweet, but there just isn't that explosive chemistry I've been looking for over the last eighteen months. Recently, I've been wondering if that chemistry is overrated and not worth it anyways.

"Well, you must like him a lot if you're accidentally calling him that already." Quinn's assumption makes sense, but even if I hate to admit it, that's not the reason.

"Orrrr she's trying to sell it so hard to someone else, she's even convincing herself."

Damn you, Sloan.

I slouch back into my seat and let out a huff. "Maybe," I whisper. Being around him today has been as confusing as it has been frustrating. The lingering glances and the energy that always thrums between us causes me to forget about the way he has treated me.

"Okay, so now explain to us what's going on there," Sloan says, referring to Parker. After our balloon incident, I was annoyed, and my friends thought the best way to work out that annoyance with Parker was to fuck him, so I nonchalantly let it slip I may have already been there and done that.

"It was him at the opening night of Masqued, wasn't it?" Quinn asks, narrowing her eyes.

Both these bitches know me too well.

I bury my face in my hands, trying to hold back a smirk. I may hate his guts, but both experiences I've had with him are the types you run and squeal to your girlfriends about. The fact I have been holding this in and not telling them has me ready to burst.

"Oh shit…it was," Sloan says, and I see the light bulb go off in her head. "It was him you hooked up with on the speed dating night too, wasn't it?"

When she asked how that night went, I brushed it off and said I had hooked up with one of my dates, but left it at that, bringing attention back to the fact I had an awkward experience with one of my dad's associates to distract her.

So I proceed to tell them everything. All the nitty-gritty details. *Well, most of them.*

"I knew he would be amazing in bed… All that attitude has to be good for something," Quinn responds. "But fuck him for treating you like that afterward."

"I am not sure if his actions have to do with him losing his parents or if something else happened to him. Either way, it seems like he has been through more than most at his age." Sloan always was the most rational out of us. Though I've wondered the same thing at times, especially after the girls filled me in on what little they knew about his parents. He may be the biggest asshole I know, but I still have a heart, and it aches for his loss.

Guilt suddenly consumes me at my avoidance of my own parents, who are still perfectly alive and well.

"Wait...that reminds me," Quinn says, holding her stomach as she grimaces.

"You okay?" I ask, concerned.

"I'm fine, just some gas pains. Probably from all that birthday cake the girls kept insisting on feeding me."

"Do you need some meds?" Sloan asks.

Quinn waves us off. "Back to the other thing. Now that you say that, I kinda remember Eli mentioning something back in college about Parker's girl doing him really dirty. At the time, I didn't know him well, so I don't recall details."

It's hard for me to imagine a younger, more vulnerable Parker going through all these painful events that caused him to be the closed-off man he is today.

"There they are." Sloan nods toward the wakesetter pulling back in, Eli at the steering wheel with his twin Maddie at his side. Wes, Parker, and Quinn's brother, Brayden, are all sitting around the back, beers in hand as they guide the boat in from their sunset cruise.

"One last question before they walk up here," Sloan says, observing me. "What made you keep it from us? You're normally the first to run to the girl chat and tell it."

I contemplate that for a second and give them the raw answer I don't even like admitting to myself.

"The way he makes me feel...it scares me."

"Like, you have feelings for him?"

I shake my head. "No, or at least I don't think so. But I have never had such a primal need for another person in my life, and it's unsettling."

The knowing look Quinn and Sloan give each other does nothing to settle those feelings seeping in as I watch him walk up the hill from the boat dock.

THIRTY MINUTES LATER, Parker and I are the last two sitting around the bonfire, and I have no doubt in my mind that my friends made sure it happened this way. I almost get up, unable to handle the tension flowing across the flames between us, but I can't bring myself to walk away from him.

Thankfully, a comfortable silence settles around us. One we've never been in before. It's peaceful almost. When I gaze in Parker's direction, I notice him staring off at the massive rose bushes lining the edge of the yard. The setting sun enhances the varying colors and shades of the flowers. It's actually quite beautiful.

"Gorgeous, aren't they?" I ask.

"Huh…oh yeah. They are," he responds absentmindedly. His thoughts are clearly elsewhere. "I didn't realize Eli and Quinn were rose connoisseurs."

"I wouldn't go that far. I sort of insisted Eli put the garden in when he hired me to decorate the house," I admit.

His gaze stays focused on the roses for a few minutes more before he shifts in his seat. Then with his chin resting in his hand, he sets his stormy greys on me.

"Why the roses?" he asks.

"There's something so fascinating about a rose. How it flourishes amongst its thorns, colors shining proudly. Their scent draws you in, but those thorns keep you away from their beauty."

A small smile spreads across his lips. "My mom loved them too."

I try my best to hide my surprise at his candidness. This Parker sitting before me is in complete contrast to the one I wrestled balloons with earlier today.

"Did she have a garden too?" I ask, hoping like hell he continues sharing and doesn't shut me out.

"She did." His smile softens, as if picturing her. "She would always be tending to them. The peach ones were her favorite. She had a bench in the middle of the garden, like her own little sanctuary. I'd find her reading out there all the time."

That explains the rose tattoo on his neck.

I study his face for a few moments plastered with an expression of complete serenity. It's definitely a drastic change from the grumpy asshole I'm so used to. However short this fleeting moment is…I relish the fact he's opening up about something that he clearly holds dear to his heart.

"What was her name?"

He searches my eyes for a second. "Miranda."

I offer him a warm smile. My 'thank you for sharing this with me.' And to my surprise, he offers me one back. Fuck, he's gorgeous…even more so when he's not being a dick.

Knowing I need to keep my eyes off the Adonis, I shoot off a text to Logan. We haven't talked much since I left for North Carolina.

> **ME**
> Hi! Just letting you know you were on my mind. Hope your weekend is going good.

> **LOGAN**
> Hey beautiful... boring without you. I miss you more than I should say.

His words are sweet, but don't stir that longing deep in my belly. I've had fun with Logan this past week and my attraction to him only grew each time we were together, but then I get around Parker and lose all normal thoughts.

My phone chimes again.

> **LOGAN**
> It was good to see you earlier. You looked gorgeous as always. I'm free tonight... You down to keep me company?

I read and reread, thinking I'm missing something, until I let out a sardonic laugh.

Fuck boy, bye.

I see the bubbles pop back up. He must be thinking of a way out of this. I hope for our working relationship, he just owns it.

"What's so funny? You sound scary." Parker's deep voice draws my attention.

"Nothing," I say, my lips twisting to hold in the truth because part of me wants to tell him, but I hate giving him a reason to say he told me so.

"I don't believe you. Tell me, Av."

When I make up my mind to share with Parker, I convince myself it's because this is too comical not to. And absolutely nothing to do with the fact that somewhere deep, deep down, in some fucked-up way, I want him to know for other reasons.

"Logan just sent me a text he meant for someone else."

"What kind of text?" he asks slowly, likely trying to gauge my reaction a little closer.

I read him the message, and as I do, Logan tries calling me.

"Now he's trying to call, but I really don't want to hear a weak excuse or lie."

Parker stands, walking over to me. "Give me the phone."

I contemplate it. "No. It's annoying, but I wasn't invested like I should have been either."

He listens for once and takes the seat beside mine.

"Yeah, but he was also the one pursuing you from the very first day," he says, looking into the firepit, jaw tight and eyes narrowed.

His concern is almost laughable when the way he treated me was the ultimate push I needed to say yes to Logan. But Parker has a point Logan made his intentions clear from our first meeting, so why go to all that trouble, and then blow it before you even give me time to feel something for you?

"That's true. I knew exactly what he wanted from day one. He was very convincing, and I did think someone wanted more than just sex from me for once." Thankfully, I wasn't ready for that step last week after how things went down with Parker. Something just didn't feel right, and I knew it wouldn't be the same. I thought if I waited, maybe I would forget how good it was with Parker and me.

Parker's hard gaze turns on me. "So, he got what he wanted and immediately jumped ship?"

I level him back with a stare to match. "If you want to go fishing, you should head down to the dock. If you want to ask me something, just ask. It's never been an issue for you before."

"Did you fuck him?"

I shake my head. For someone who doesn't normally do repeats, he certainly seems invested in my sex life. I take a second to get my thoughts together, hoping my words hit him where I want them to. "No...I thought maybe if I made him wait a little bit, it would work out better since primal instinct fucking doesn't seem to end well for me."

He flinches, but then I see him visibly relax at the truth about Logan and me. His initial reaction makes me question if he is remorseful over his complete disregard for me after our last encounter at Masqued. I'm getting really sick of the head games he's playing... *What is going on inside that mind of yours, Parker Cole?*

I notice Quinn and Eli's dads heading our way from the back patio, so I stand from my seat, ready for some alone time. Stopping right beside his chair, I trail my fingers lightly down his tattooed arm and speak in a low tone.

"I don't get you, Parker. It's like you don't want me, but you don't want anyone else to have me. You act like I ask you for so much, when in reality, I just asked for sex. That's all I want from you anyways, because I know that's all you are capable of."

Before I can walk away, he grabs my wrist and whispers back, "Maybe that's the problem, Ava. Maybe I'm not only capable of that."

BABES GROUP CHAT

ME

Boarding now. Somehow I was upgraded to first class. How's Quinn?

QUINN

I have my phone now. The procedure went well, just resting on the couch now. Have a safe flight.

ME

I'm so glad to hear that. You scared the crap out of us last night. But I know you're in good hands... otherwise, I would have never left.

QUINN

Mmm, Eli's hands are good...

SLOAN

I love you, but eww.

QUINN

Haha... Sorry, I'm still a little doped up. PS: Lo just filled me in on Logan. He wasn't the one for you anyways. Bye fucker!

SLOAN:

💯 !!! Don't worry Av, we will take care of her. We love you have a safe flight.

ME

For sure! It was for the best, but now he won't stop blowing me up.

ME

I'll check in on you when I land. And if I need to come back to help you do anything at all, I'm sure my boss would allow it since it's you.

QUINN

Thanks Av. I'll be ok. Talk soon. I love you!

SLOAN

I would put money on the fact that bossman upgraded you to first class.

ME

You would have won that bet. I just got to my seat and non-other than Parker fucking Cole is sitting next to me.

QUINN

Mile High Club here you come.

ME

Yeah, you must be high.

SLOAN

He upgraded you, that's sweet. Don't be a brat.

ME

If you only knew.

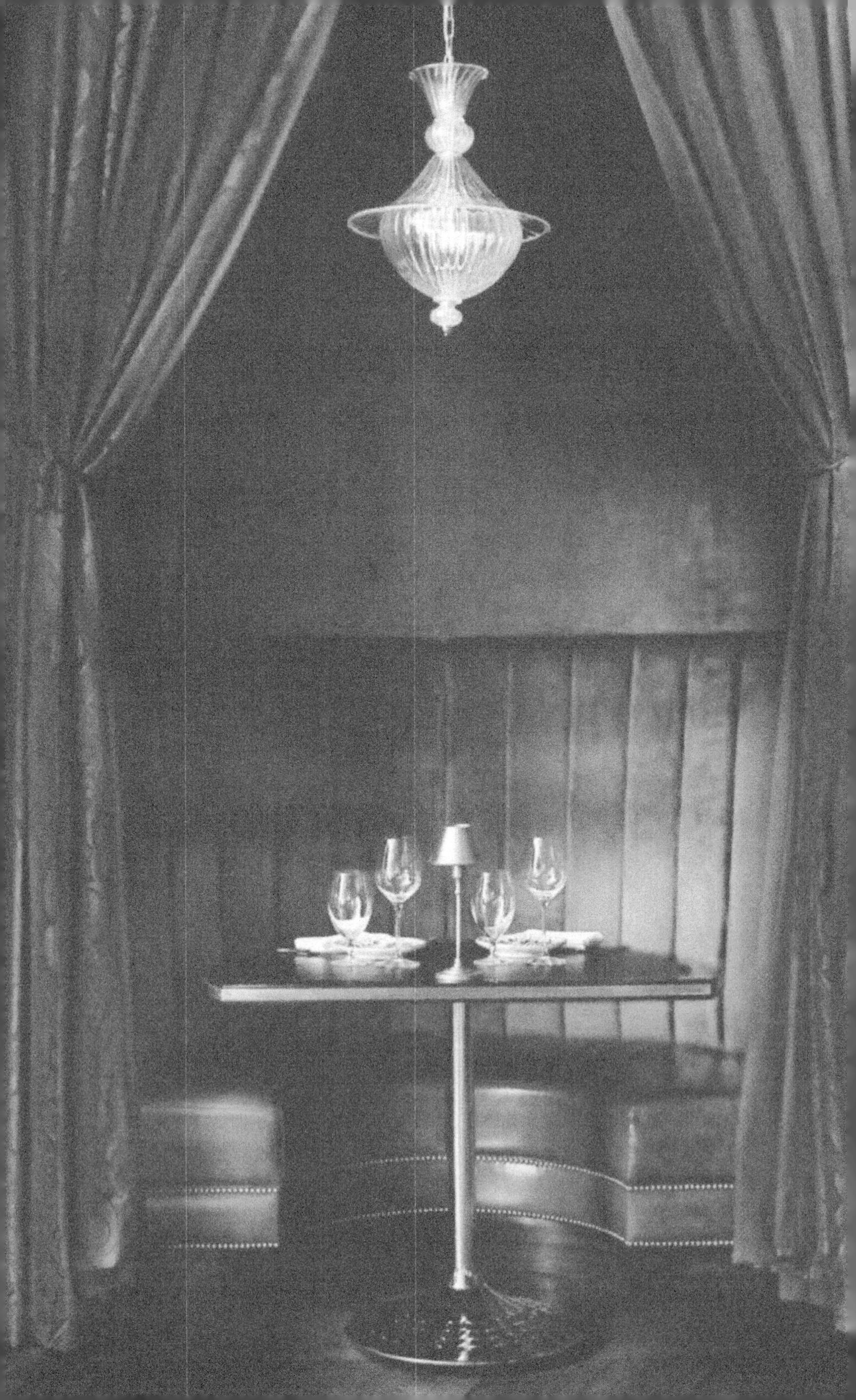

Nine

Ava

"Thanks for the upgrade, boss," I say as I slide into my seat beside Parker. In first class.

He smirks at my greeting. "Well, I couldn't let a Pierce sit amongst the peasants in good conscience."

Asshole.

Today, he is dressed in casual black jeans, and to my surprise, a white t-shirt. The material clings to his every muscle. The lighter fabric against dark ink covering his tan skin is sexy as sin.

"You, Mr. Cole, are the one I could never imagine sitting anywhere but first class," I retort as I adjust my neck pillow.

He doesn't look at me when he speaks next, and the tone of his voice tells me his words are nothing but the truth. "Not that long ago, I couldn't even afford to fly coach, much less first class."

It is a known fact that Parker is a self-made billionaire who has worked his ass off to get to the top. A college baseball legend who was hurt his senior year, losing his chance at the MLB.

But the connections he made in baseball allowed him to get himself on the real estate map in New York City when he helped Eli along with other former teammates and friends of friends buy their homes. After that, his business took off, but still, you don't go from broke to real estate sales to one of the top investors in the city without hard work and dedication.

And yeah, so, I may have done my research after the first night I officially met him. He was an asshole from the start, but I was immediately and unfortunately intrigued. If I'm being honest, it started long before that night.

Busying myself with my seatbelt, I don't look at him when I respond. "Look at you now, you could have your own private jet if you wanted one."

"Spoken like a true princess," he grunts.

I roll my eyes and dig into my carry-on. Parker mimics me, also pulling out his headphones.

We settle into a comfortable silence as the plane prepares for take-off. I can't help but wonder what type of boring podcast or Audible he's probably listening to while I blast my EDM playlist I have downloaded on Spotify just for airplane mode.

But apparently, the jokes on me because my AirPods stop working mid-song. Fuuuckk. I forgot to charge them before my flight.

Parker looks over at me curiously. I wave him off and continue searching for my charger. The flight from Charlotte to JFK is only a little over an hour, so I decide to give up and try to take a nap. Until the stewardess stops by, offering a drink menu. Parker has his eyes closed so he doesn't see her. I scan the menu and know exactly what he would order without asking.

"Yes, I'll take Titos and Sprite and he'll have The Macallan 12."

She comes back a few minutes later. "Here you go," she says, setting mine down first, which draws Parker's attention as she serves him his drink. Surprise flashes in his eyes as he removes one of his ear buds.

"What is this?" he asks, his question direct but his tone soft.

"The Macallan 12, sir. Is that okay?"

"Yes, it's perfect, thank you," Parker says, and I watch his throat swallow the first sip.

The stewardess shifts her attention back to me. "Good choice. Let me know if either of you need anything else."

"Ordering for me now, Legs." He smirks at me.

"Your drink order is no surprise to anyone who has spent more than one evening with you. Plus, I didn't want to interrupt whatever murder case file you are taking pointers from right now."

He chuckles, and fuck, if it doesn't stir a million flutters in my stomach. "Speaking of, what happened to your AirPods?"

I make a gun with my fingers and point toward my carry on under the seat in front of me. "Dead. I forgot to charge the stupid things."

"Why are they stupid? You are the one who forgot?"

"Oh, fuck off," I playfully growl, trying to stop myself from smiling.

His hand reaches out to me. "Want to listen? This one is interesting and…informative."

Unable to resist, I put his AirPod in my left ear. Of course I keep the thank you to myself. Gotta maintain my brat persona he loves so much.

He presses play, and to my utter surprise, he is certainly not listening to a podcast. I bust out laughing, causing the row beside us to nearly break their necks.

"Really?" I laugh harder, reminiscing on the twin's birthday party. This is the last thing I thought he'd be listening to. "'Save a Horse, Ride a Cowboy'?" I say as the song pours through the small earpiece.

"It's my favorite right now," he says with a teasing smile. I love this side of him.

I turn to look at him, holding his stare. This just so happens to be what was blasting through the speakers as I was riding the mechanical bull at Eli and Quinn's yesterday. The bull Eli insisted on having at his one-year-old's first birthday party. Obviously, a party favor for the adults.

"Is the image of me busting my ass when it threw me off, playing on repeat in that sick head of yours?"

"Nah, I'm recalling something much less decent than that, brat." His dark and stormy eyes penetrate me with every word. Suddenly, my mouth feels like it needs more than this drink.

His words from last night flit through my mind.

Maybe that's the problem, Ava, maybe I'm not only capable of that.

I hate letting him know the way he continuously affects me. Giving him that satisfaction feels like defeat at this point.

Gently smacking his chest, I retort with humor instead. "Perv…you were at a children's birthday party."

His eyes pin me with a suggestive stare that traces from my face to my yoga-pant-clad legs.

"You were the one riding the bull in those little jean shorts, showing off those legs. I was jealous of a piece of fucking machinery."

"Aw, poor bossman," I say, keeping it light as my heart thuds harder at his confession. This is exactly why I fell asleep to thoughts of him instead of overanalyzing the text I accidentally received from Logan. While annoying, that text was likely an easy out for me in the end.

The tune winds down, and Parker passes me his phone. "What's your favorite song right now?"

That's easy. I'm doing a routine to this one so it's always on repeat. Within seconds, Selena and Rema bleed through the speakers, the beat making me want to move my hips in the seat.

"I knew you'd pick this." His knowing tone has me trying to remember if I have ever had it on blast in the office. "How?"

"Just a good guess," Parker says, not meeting my eyes.

I narrow my stare, but let it go as the words to "Calm Down" play. I can visualize my routine from start to finish. It's one of my favorites because it is a mixture of hip hop and pole.

A question pops into my head. Part of me worries that it's a sore subject, but I still decide to ask it.

"What was your favorite walk-out song in college?"

For a split second, he stares at me, and I worry I really did take it too far until a rare smile brightens his face. It almost stops my heart right then and there.

"My favorite was probably the 'Wipe Me Down' remix. How can that not hype you up?"

I smile back as he plays it, and I follow along, pretending to "wipe myself down," the song taking me back to high school dance party days.

To my shock, he pretends to wipe off his black leather Christian Louboutin low-tops. Who the fuck is this man? I wish I had really known him when he was younger and more carefree.

"I figured it was 'Gasolina'?"

His eyebrows furrow again, gaze searching mine.

"How did you know that was even an option?"

I laugh. "I came to a game my sophomore year with the girls. You would have been a junior."

"Really?" he asks, still astonished.

"I remember you walked out to Daddy Yankee and then jacked one over the fence. I think I immediately had a little crush," I admit, but seriously, he was hot as hell back then too.

"Why didn't I meet you? I remember meeting Sloan and Quinn on multiple occasions."

"Maybe you met me too," I tease, wanting to make him question it, but his response twists up my insides.

"No, I would never forget you. I still remember what you had on the first night I met you at Kings Hideaway."

I bite my lip and ask my next question so I can analyze it for days to come. "What was I wearing?"

"A hot pink blazer with matching heels and skintight black pants. Your hair was down and curled. And you had in these tiny gold hoops and a small flower stud in your second piercing. And I knew right then and there you were going to be a pain in my ass."

Wow. I retrace every word until he speaks again. "I can't believe you were at my game." Parker chuckles, and as the song ends, he passes the phone back to me.

"Okay, let's switch it up. Now a song that always makes you feel a little melancholy or sad. As long as you aren't going to start crying on me."

I wrack my brain and one I randomly heard again recently comes to mind.

"'100 years' by Five for Fighting. You ever listened to it?" I ask and select it on his screen.

He nods. "Yeah, I actually remember the first time I heard it as an adult and really understood the meaning."

"The older I get, the more I understand how that one hundred years can fly by."

Parker glances out the window. "Some people would be thankful for half of that."

The pain in his voice hurts my soul. He's thinking of his parents, I'm sure.

We sit there listening, and I don't ask for his sad song because I worry that would be too much for him right now. He scrolls through one of his playlist, and when the song he selects starts playing, I know just by the melody that he's gifting me with something painful to him.

I dabble in country here and there, and this song has been on the top charts for a while now, so I immediately recognize it. "I Remember Everything" by Zach Bryan and Kasey Musgraves.

Looking over at Parker and seeing his eyes closed but his face so full of anguish, brings tears to my eyes. I reach my hand over and rub my thumb along his. I expect him to push me away, but instead, he intertwines our fingers. We remain quiet during the whole song, and when it ends, he peers up at me, emotion flaring in both our gazes.

"Parker," I whisper. "Who does that song make you think of?"

"My parents, they met in 1988," he whispers back. Taking a sip of his drink, he speaks again. "My mom was a rich girl from the city and my dad was an aspiring musician who took a bus ride there on his last dollar. The song isn't necessarily their story, but the emotion in it, and some of the parts that resemble them, always overwhelm me with thoughts of the past." He pauses again, but I stay silent, my chest thundering with the fact he is trusting me.

"He also had a bottle of cheap whiskey in his hand every day after my mother died of ovarian cancer until he drank himself to death."

Rotgut Whiskey.

Tipping his drink in my direction, "That's why I only drink the high dollar stuff, plus I know how to control myself."

I turn my head slightly to the side, twisting my lips, trying to control my agonizing emotions. It's not about me, and I know Parker doesn't want my pity. But what do I say to that? No one should have to go through that. I know Quinn mentioned this, but I guess hearing it from him and how it went down makes it a million times worse. No wonder he is so closed off; I would be too.

Parker tugs on my shoulder. "Hey, now that you've got me baring my soul thirty thousand feet in the air, can you pick a happy song, please?"

I attempt to smile through the tears I'm trying desperately to hold in. This time, when he passes me his phone, I think of my aunt. She played me this song as a pick-me-up after one of the many nights my parents treated me like crap. And then I turned it into my first solo dance routine.

Missy Elliot's raspy voice blasts through the speakers as I wipe the loan tear that escaped from the corner of my eye.

Another chuckle passes through Parker's lips. *Thank God.* My broken heart needed to hear that.

"This takes me back to some sweaty college dance floor, lots of grinding and girls thinking they could rap like Missy." Parker smiles lightly.

"I was totally one of those girls."

"No doubt in my mind. And I've seen you dance, so I know every dude in there was trying to get a minute of your time."

I giggle at his compliment. "Luckily, if I wasn't in the mood, I had two guard dogs on standby. Quinn was my girlfriend multiple times, and Sloan would just give them a speech about respect."

"I can see that. I'm not sure which of them is scarier."

The girls would appreciate that.

"Now what makes *The* Parker Cole happy? I promise not to tell your secrets at work."

Humming, he smiles to himself as he thinks. "Top secret… but 'Pocket Full of Sunshine' is my go-to when I'm by myself."

I stare at him for a second before I bust out laughing again, pissing everyone in first class off. "Oh my gosh, that's the best thing I've heard all year. Are you serious? I can picture it now."

He laughs with me before confessing, "Fuck no, Av. That's actually my in-the-shower song."

I've never seen him like this, and all these different sides of Parker are just making it harder not to like him. He's showing me what's behind that asshole exterior, and I'm greedy for more.

"You want the truth?" he asks, pinching my arm.

I nod eagerly, and he scrolls through some pictures on his phone before he pulls up his Spotify yearly report from last year.

"Unforgettable" was his number one played song. I swallow thickly at the realization of what he's showing me.

That's the song I was dancing to that night at Masqued when he watched me from across the room. The desire in his eyes had me wanting him more than I had ever wanted anything else. I didn't care who he was or how much of an asshole he had been to me...I wanted him. Plain and simple.

Too bad it's not so plain and simple now.

"What made you accept my invite that night?" I ask the question I've been wondering for quite some time. *What made him change his mind?* I was fully prepared for him not to show considering how easily he dismissed me the first time we met, but I was too turned on by him watching me all night not to try.

Parker finishes off the liquor in his glass. "The same reason you did."

Undeniable, indescribable chemistry.

When we land at JFK, of course Parker insists on having his driver drop me off. I don't even fight him at the demand. He is still a bossy asshole, but after that plane ride, he suddenly feels more friend than foe.

Once we are settled into the blacked-out SUV, I turn off my airplane mode, wanting to check in on Quinn.

"Checking to see if Logan is begging for forgiveness?" Parker asks, hard-set jaw back in place.

There he is.

"For your information, I asked him to please stop calling me and to meet me for lunch on Monday to save our working relationship."

My phone vibrates over and over in my hand, and concern takes over my senses as I block out whatever smart comment Parker retorts with.

To my surprise, it's not Sloan or Quinn's names filling up my screen, but my neighbor Ben and my grandmother. Oh shit, is Binx okay?

I immediately listen to the voicemail Ben left me an hour ago.

"Ava, uh, hi sorry. Uh—Yeah, I have some bad news… I'm so sorry, if I hadn't of stayed out all night, maybe it wouldn't have been so bad…. They are saying a pipe busted, and not only did it flood my place, but yours too. It's uh—it's pretty bad. I'm so sorry, beautiful. Binx is okay. He is on the top of his cat house and wouldn't come out for me. I think you are coming back today, but if not, I'll try again. Just didn't want to traumatize him more. I did put his food and water bowl up top."

"Oh my… Fuck," I say on a breath, my mind racing with how bad this actually is.

As the homeowner, I am sure they called my grandparents, so I return her call immediately.

"What's going on, Av?" Parker asks.

"My apartment flooded," I rush out as my grandmother answers the phone.

"Hi, dear, did you talk to Ben?" my grandma asks, steady reassurance in her voice as she continues without letting me answer. "Don't stress. Grandpa and I will make sure this is fixed properly and safely." I don't even have the fight in me to refuse their help.

"He left me a message, but I called you back first. Is it truly that bad?"

"Honey, it sounds like there is two to three feet of standing water, and your grandfather said mold will start forming quickly with that much water."

Poor Binx. My stomach plummets with the need to get to him.

"But don't stress. I know you hate the thought of being near your parents, but you can stay at our condo until we can get this sorted out." The thought of staying anywhere in the Upper East Side makes me cringe, much less in the same exact high rise as my parents. After I graduated college, it took a lot of convincing to get me to live in the apartment my grandparents bought for my aunt many years ago, before she moved to Paris. When they finally settled on allowing Quinn and I to pay part of the homeowner fees, I agreed. The other perk was that it was far away from the Upper East Side. I love my grandparents, but not even they could convince me to live there again.

"Grandma, I don't think that will be necessary. I can at least stay at Sloan and Wes's tonight. I'll call once I see how everything looks in person."

"Okay, if you insist, and Grandpa has already put a call out to someone who can come first thing in the morning to assess the damages before insurance sends someone out."

"Thank you both. I love you and I'll call soon," I say, trying to sound less stressed than I am.

"So, what the hell is going on?" Parker asks, seriousness and concern coating his words.

I fill him in on what I know as we make our way toward my flooded apartment.

"So, if your grandmother offered you their other place to stay, why did I hear you tell her you are going to stay at Sloan and Wes's tonight?" he asks.

"Because I refuse to stay anywhere near my parents," I say bluntly, and I see his mind working as I continue. "Plus, I didn't want to worry her more, but I'm hoping Ben is just being dramatic and I can stay at my place tonight." I'm trying to put positive thoughts out there. Whether it's a reach or not, who knows.

"That sounds like the worst idea… They said there is standing water, Ava." He practically growls that last part.

The car approaches my building, and I wave my hand. "Welp, I guess we are about to find out."

"Ava, fuck no… This is unsafe."

Parker's voice booms through my apartment as I look around in shock. The amount of my things that appear ruined is hard to wrap my head around.

"This is definitely worse than I was picturing."

I advance farther into the space, only truly caring about one thing.

"Binxy Boy… it's okay. Mama is here," I coo, knowing he is likely petrified from the tsunami that hit my apartment.

"Ahh fuck, I forgot about the cat. Is the thing okay?" Parker comes up behind me.

Binx pokes his head out of the cathouse, which is thankfully outside of the area that got the brunt of the leak. But I can tell by his matted hair, he was most likely curled up on my bed when it all started. My poor boy probably had no idea what was happening.

I pick him up, and he purrs into me. I can almost feel the relief in his little feline body as he melts into my embrace. "It's okay, buddy. I'm so sorry," I whisper and continue to walk around on what feels like a pool deck. Peering into my room, it is obvious this side of the house got the majority of the damage. I see the standing water throughout my bedroom and closet.

Of course, Quinn's side was only touched by a bit of overflow water on the floor. With her half being empty right now, that would have made things so much easier if it had of happened on that side of the apartment.

"Looks like I need a thrift store and a cat-friendly hotel pronto."

Parker takes hold of my shoulders, his tone oddly soothing and one I've never heard from him before as he eyes Binx with caution.

"Your luggage is still in the SUV outside. I'm sure you have some things in there that can get you through the night. Why don't you just come home with me, and then figure it out tomorrow?"

I'm already shaking my head, but he cuts off my reply.

"And before you say no just to spite me…you know it's the simplest way to handle this tonight. I have extra rooms, so you'll have plenty of privacy," Parker says, and he's wrong because I have no willpower to spite him in this moment.

"What about Binx?" I shrug him toward Parker to grab his attention back from darting around the sodden apartment.

His gaze finds Binx again. He tries to stop it, but his nose scrunches up like his next words pain him. "The damn cat can come too."

I relent with a nod and offer him a soft smile, but the way my heart hammers from his protectiveness is a tell-tale sign that this is probably a bad idea.

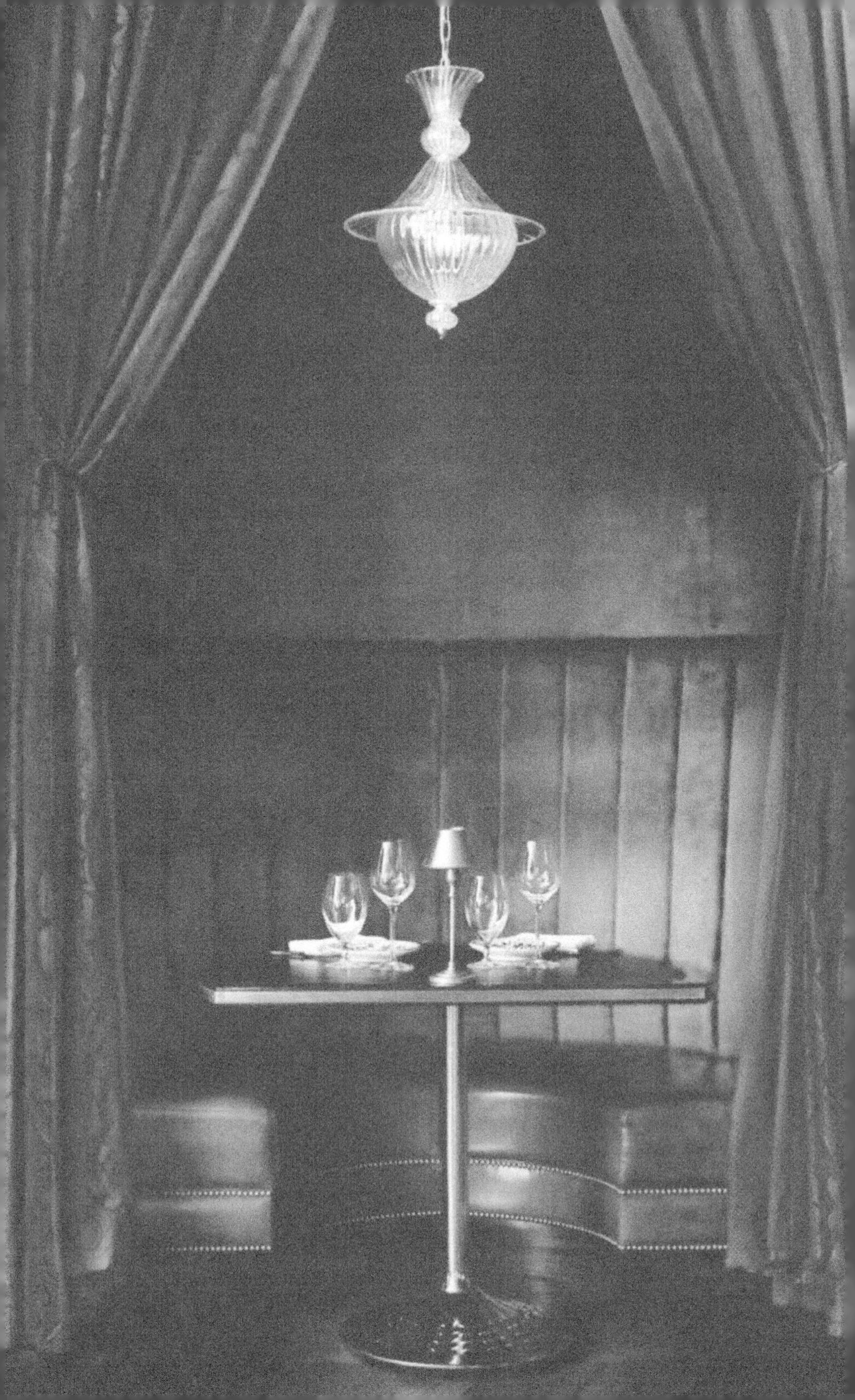

Ten

Parker

U*gh, my throat is scratchy.* That's my first thought when the heat of the morning sun beaming through the curtains wakes me out of a deep and restful sleep.

My chest feels strange. It's vibrating like it's a battery-operated toy... It feels sort of heavy too.

Fuck, I hope I'm not getting sick.

I open my eyes, dreading the aches I fear will be coursing through my body.

"What the fuck," I curse at the sight of the black fur ball curled up on my chest. I'm practically inhaling its fur.

It appears that said fur ball has no desire to leave its current resting place, seemingly unbothered by my loud voice. I slowly glide my hand under the cover to shift the thing off me, but the subtle movement has him moving into attack mode. He slinks down into a stealthy position, ready to pounce on my hand, so I pause, thinking he will lose interest.

I've never owned a cat, nor have I ever cohabitated with one either, so when he pounces on me with ninja-like quickness, I practically jump out of bed in both surprise and maybe a little fear. Not that I'd admit the latter.

"Really, dude," I groan as the fucking fur ball claims a spot in the middle of my bed. I point at his curled-up body as he eyes me with intent. "This is not your room."

The thing just ignores me and rolls onto his side like he doesn't have a care in the world.

I march into the kitchen to where Ava is fighting with my espresso maker. As if she can already feel my presence in the room, she spins to face me.

"How in the world do you use this thing? I've been trying for fifteen minutes."

I quirk an eyebrow as I peruse Ava in her pajamas. "That's quite the adorable set you have on. I would have never taken you as a bunny pattern type of girl, considering the unhinged black demon you have as a pet."

She chuckles. "Is that where he was? I've been looking for him. The pajamas were all I had in my suitcase from North Carolina. And besides, they are very comfortable."

"I can see that," I tease, as my eyes rake over her body once more. Fuck, she's gorgeous, even in the morning.

Ava's arms shoot out to cover her braless chest. I grin at the motion. "Come on, Legs, it's not like I haven't had them in my mouth before. No need to hide from me."

Her eyes flare and she shoots me an incredulous look. But I notice the way her chest heaves. My cock twitches at the thought of seeing what's underneath those flimsy pajamas.

She scoffs, and then drops her arms to her sides as I walk around her to get the caffeine flowing. Effectively breaking the moment.

"Espresso or cappuccino?" I ask over my shoulder.

"Mmm, a cappuccino, please. What can I do to help?"

"Grab the milk from the fridge, then I'll teach you how to use the machine," I say as I grind the beans.

"It's so quiet here. If it wasn't for the view, I would've forgotten we were still in Manhattan," Ava says as she takes a sip of her second cappuccino.

"I forget sometimes too, until I walk outside."

"You mean, until you almost get run over by a taxi, or a bike messenger. Oh, or yelled at by someone just passing by."

"Yeah, something like that." I chuckle.

"Ah, I frickin' love it here. The chaos and the beauty all wrapped into one crazy island," she says with a loving sigh.

"Do you ever get sick of it…the constant noise and people?" I ask, knowing she was born and raised here.

"Absolutely. That's when I escape out east to my grandparent's house. Or take a trip to visit friends. I used to visit Sloan in California before she moved back to the city. Where's your escape…beside here?" she asks as her hand motions to my apartment in emphasis.

"Upstate, Hudson Valley area," I answer honestly.

"I love it up there. Especially in the fall… The colors of the trees are so pretty that time of year," she says with a sincere smile. It's so beautiful, it makes my chest ache.

She's a lot easier to talk to than I had first presumed, based on the fact she grew up with a silver spoon in her mouth. But that's my own vendetta, and it's slowly dissipating when it comes to Ava the more I give myself a chance to get to know her. I find myself sharing stories and personal moments… Something I haven't felt comfortable enough to do with anyone in a very long time. It's a hard lesson to learn growing up, who you can trust, who will have your back and unfortunately for me, that lesson was learned the hard way.

"It really is…" I say, more to myself than her.

A peaceful silence falls between us as we finish our drinks and look out at my view.

With the little time left that we have before we need to leave for the office, Ava takes it upon herself to browse the floor-to-ceiling bookshelves that line the entire wall in my living room.

Her delicate fingers roam over the spines, inspecting each and every one. I swear my cock twitches with every twist of her hand.

"I would have never thought you were this much of a reader," she says, continuing her perusal.

"There's a lot you don't know about me."

"Hmm, that is true," she ponders, then switches her focus to the endless shelves. Her head tilts to read the worn spines of some of my favorite series. I swear I think I've read those at least a dozen times.

Ava turns her head in my direction and eyes me with interest. "This is quite the variety you have here."

"I'm a mood reader," I reply bluntly.

"Figures." She sighs, then steps back, and her eyes return to the shelves. Probably observing the fact that they lack pictures.

This back-and-forth between us feels too much like the closeness I dread when it comes to relationships. And that's exactly what she's looking for, although she'll try to deny it. But I remember that elated expression on her face when she caught the bouquet at Sloan and Wes's wedding last fall. All the women fawning over her, telling her she'll be the next one down the aisle. She looked absolutely stunning standing amongst the other bridesmaids beside Sloan. I found it hard to focus on anything else. The vision of standing at an altar flashes in my mind, but I quickly shake away those thoughts...

Needing some space, I place my cup in the sink, and then walk down the hall to my room without a word.

I shut the door behind me, taking a calming breath, hating that I love the fact that she's been here for less than twenty-four hours, and her smell is already infiltrating my space. But that doesn't stop me from inhaling deeply again.

Ignoring the black fur ball who has now claimed my bed as his own, I step into my ensuite and pull myself together for the long day ahead.

Ava is slinging her work bag onto her shoulder when I exit my bedroom. I clear my throat and her head whips in my direction.

"Do you want to walk together to the office?" I ask.

She stands there in silence as she contemplates my offer.

"Okay," she finally relents.

A gust of warm air hits us as soon as we step out of my building. "It's less than a ten-minute walk," I say, trying to break the awkwardness that has surrounded us since the elevator ride down.

"Great," she says with that fake, practiced smile. Knowing the difference between the two, I hate the fact she's using this one with me.

After a block or so, she speaks up. "I have several Airbnbs I've been looking into. I should hear back from them by the end of the day. So, I will be out of your hair soon."

My steps falter. *Wait, what?*

I know I'm a grumpy fuck, but have I made her feel unwelcomed?

We fuck two times…one of which was a year and a half ago and you are already asking me for more. My words from that night send a chill up my spine. Sometimes I don't even recognize the man I've turned into.

She needs my help right now. It's the least I can do to make up for my behavior. "Av, there is no rush to find something. I have plenty of room."

She side-eyes me as we continue our walk. "Are you sure? I don't want you to feel like I'm invading your place."

"I'm sure… That little black demon you call a cat is welcome too," I tease, hoping to bring back the lightness between us.

"I think he has daddy issues… Maybe that's why he was all up on you this morning."

We both break into laughter at that.

"Thank you, Parker. Honestly, it means a lot to me."

"I'm glad I can help," I say with a genuine smile. Even though the thought of sharing my personal space scares the shit out of me, it also fills me with a strange thrill. I've come to realize

I need to stop letting the past control my life. There's just something about her being around that makes me want to push forward...be better. I relish the fact that I get to actually be there for her in the ways I want to be.

We're about a block away from the office, and I can tell by the gnawing on her lip that she's deep in thought. But before I can ask her, she speaks.

"What's your favorite type of take out?"

I chuckle at the random question. "Hmm, If I'd have to choose, I'd say sushi or Thai."

"Mmm, I love Thai food," she practically moans.

Fuck, that sound is addicting.

"Can I ask why the random question?"

She turns to me as we wait for the light at the crosswalk. "Because I'm treating you to dinner tonight. As a thank you," she beams.

"You don't have to do that. I'm usually home quite late," I try to argue.

"I know, I know...you're a workaholic. Good thing Thai is easy to reheat." She winks, then begins crossing when the light turns green.

"I'll try to make it home at a decent time." No sooner are the words out of my mouth am I questioning their meaning.

"No worries, I have to hit up Target at some point today, then I have dance class. So I'd say I'll be home around seven-thirty."

"Sounds like a plan," I agree as we approach the main doors.

Something about all this has my stomach tightening. Her staying the night, seeing her in her natural state, making her coffee, observing her move about my space, walking to work with her, arranging to be home to have dinner together... I'm...enjoying it, and that makes me feel like I'm about to freefall into something I can't handle.

Ava turns to me with a sly smile on her face. "I'm going to head in first... You know, wouldn't want us walking in together to raise questions."

"I don't give a fuck what people think," I retort.

"Oh, I know you don't, bossman. But you know with that no fraternization policy, I wouldn't want any trouble." She quirks an eyebrow.

Trying my best to school my face, I gesture for her to go ahead. She nods and strolls past me. I don't miss the extra sway of her hips as she strides through the doors.

Well played, little brat... Well played.

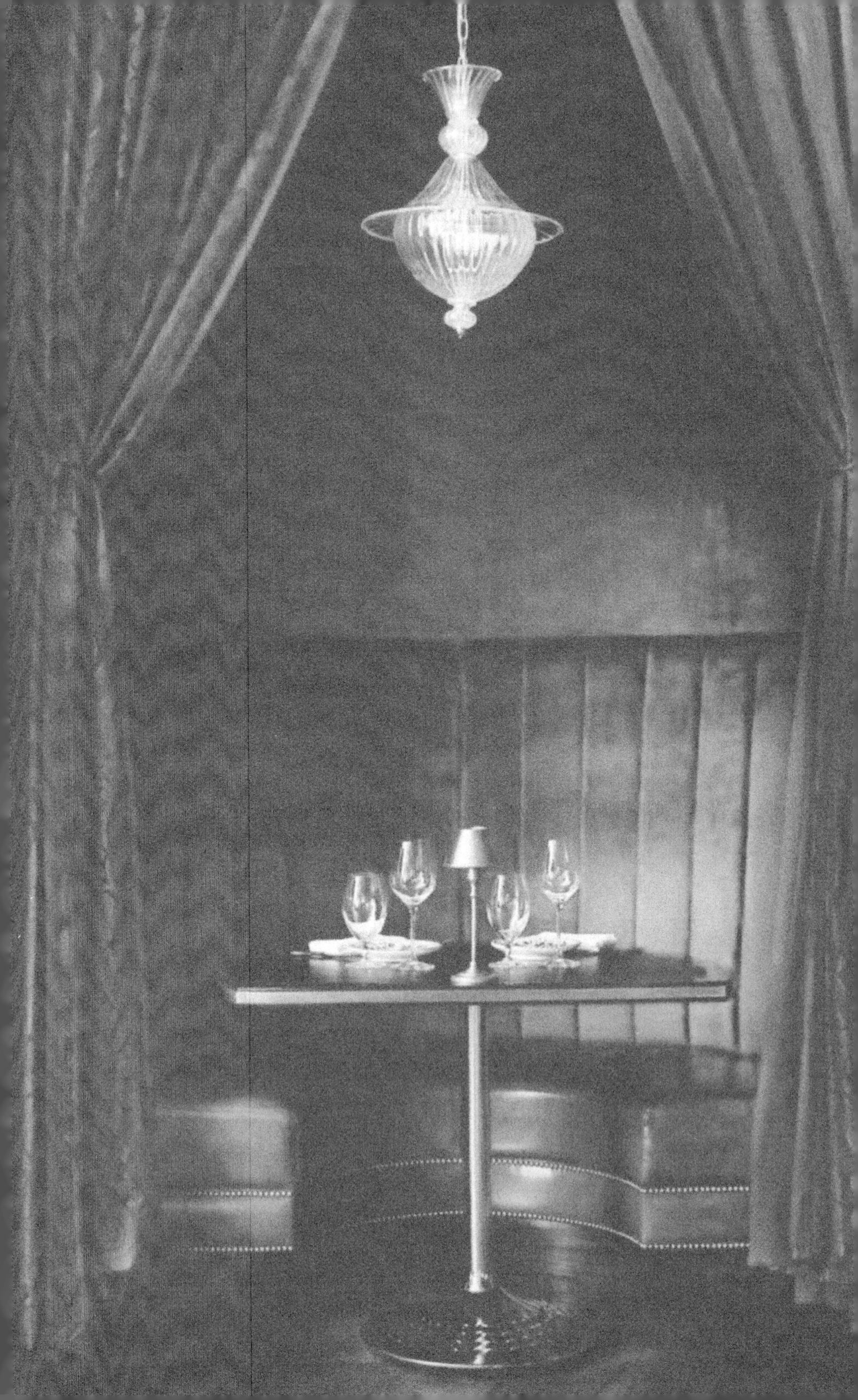

Eleven

Ava

I approach the temporary sitting area in the hotel lobby, and Logan immediately stands to greet me. Intentionally slowing my steps, I stop at the chair across from his. Our eyes meet, and thankfully, he reads the room and doesn't attempt to hug me. "Hi, Ava. Thanks for hearing me out."

After deciding that Logan really didn't deserve my time, especially with everything I have going on right now, I canceled lunch and asked him if we could talk for a few at the hotel.

"Logan, I'm not here to hear you out. My only intention is to clear the air so we can move forward for work."

His expression is full of regret as he responds, "I understand, but truly, that text wasn't as bad as it probably seemed. She's an old…" I hold my hand up, stopping him from making more excuses that are just going to piss me off.

"Look, I'd rather not hear your excuses. It is what it is. We never talked about exclusivity, so you didn't owe me anything, but I'd appreciate you not lying to me. From the very beginning of all of this, you have made your intentions clear with me. And you seemed to be pretty adamant about wanting a chance with me and only me, so how can I believe anything else you say when that was certainly not the case?"

He lets out a long sigh, and I continue. "I'm honestly not mad at you. I just have a lot going on and this is probably for the best. I would appreciate it if you would respect me as a colleague and not pursue me as anything more moving forward."

"Ava…" he whispers, and I cut him off again.

"No, Logan. I need you to respect my wishes. I look forward to continuing our working relationship, but that's all I'm willing to give."

And saving the day once again, Olivia waltzes into the lobby at that moment. "Logan…" She barely greets him, turning to me. "Ready to go, Av?"

"Yep!" I say, grabbing my purse from the chair and giving Logan one last glance. "You act professional, and I promise you, I will too. This project is important to me."

He gulps, looking at Olivia, who he is obviously not used to receiving the cold shoulder from. "It's important to me too. You have my word." Just before I turn to head out the door, he calls my name, and I give him one more glance.

"I'm sorry," he says sincerely.

I nod and give him a soft smile. At the end of the day, he wasn't right for me, and I know that. I was more pissed he seemed so invested and then really wasn't. I don't want to be played as a fool.

On the other hand, the man I can't get out of my head says he isn't invested, but lately his actions are speaking louder than his words. And I'm not sure he even realizes it.

"Glad to have that over with?" Olivia asks as we head toward the Target not far from the hotel.

"Yes, definitely…and you know you don't have to be mad at him, right? I don't expect that. It's not really that big of a deal."

"Yes, it is. You forget I was there from day one when he kept gushing about you to me. I even put in a good word for him, and for what? So he could go fuck it up over Tasha?"

I grab her arm, wanting to make sure I heard her correctly. "Wait, Tasha? As in, Parker's assistant?"

She nods, pursing her lips. "Mmhmm! When I confronted him this morning, I made him tell me who it was."

The sick side of my brain flits to Parker. I wonder if he thinks she's as worthy of his attention as Logan does. This is exactly why I can't hold a grudge against Logan. My thoughts always spiral to *him*.

"Wow, that's interesting."

"I know, right! No wonder she is always giving us the stink eye."

I giggle at that because she certainly does.

"I'll say this last thing, and then I want to drop the Logan topic. I appreciate you having my back, and I love you for that, but give him some grace. Deep down, I'm sure he could tell I wasn't all in, which is why I can't be so pissed at him. I hate liars, but he's young, dumb, and will hopefully learn from his mistake."

She laughs. "I swear I thought you were about to say he's young, dumb, and full of cum."

We both fall into a fit of giggles as we walk into the Target.

"Okay, so what do you need?" Olivia asks as I get a shopping cart.

"Basically, everything. If it wasn't in my suitcases from my trip, it's ruined."

"Fuck."

"Yeah, my grandpa called me a few hours ago after the contractor went to assess the damages and basically said my room, bathroom, laundry room, and half of the living room will require a complete gut because of the standing water and mold that's most likely growing in the walls." The news didn't come as a shock to me. After I saw it in person last night, I knew it was bad. Doesn't mean I'm any less upset about it.

"Shit, so what are you going to do in the meantime?"

I honestly don't know.

"I've been searching Airbnbs, thinking maybe I could do an extended stay."

I also thought about asking Eli and Quinn, but I feel like such a burden doing that. I know he is rarely at that condo, but they have a stretch of games here this month, so I hate the thought of inconveniencing them and the girls.

"If they aren't a fortune, that would be a good idea. I would offer mine and Braxton's couch, but that wouldn't be very comfortable for you."

"No worries. I could crash at Wes and Sloan's, but I feel like they are still enjoying being newlyweds, and I really don't want to be subjected to their nightly fucks." I laugh and know I have to tell Quinn and Sloan what's going on before they hear it from someone else. I just really want a plan together first because they'll both try to save the day.

Parker's words keep running on repeat. *Av, there is no rush to find something.*

"So where did you stay last night? Is that your plan for tonight, until you figure it out?"

Shit, I knew this was coming.

"Well…you see, Parker insisted on sharing a ride from the airport, so he was with me when—"

"Shut up! You stayed with Parker?" she practically shouts.

"Damn, woman, tell all of SoHo while you're at it," I whisper-shout back at her.

"Details, now…" She points her finger in my direction like it's a threat.

"Nothing to tell. He's still an asshole, just not a total one. Maybe like 50/50, or I guess I'll give him 60/40 because he did wake up to my cat on his face."

"Excuse me?" Olivia's eyes are bulging out, her eyelashes blinking fast.

Oh… ohhh. I laugh. "Get your mind out of the gutter, Liv. I'm talking about my actual cat, Binx. The cutest little feline you'll ever meet."

She bends at the waist laughing, tears coming to her eyes. "I swear I thought…" She laughs harder. "Not going to lie, I was def picturing you sitting on the boss's face."

Yet you've let me eat your cunt. I must have done something right.

Now I'm thinking about it. Abort. Abort.

"Just go ahead and erase that image from your head. I'm on the complete opposite side of his penthouse and the only man in my bed will be my Binx."

I just have to keep reminding myself of that.

"Uh huh," she says, eyeing me suspiciously. "So you're staying there tonight too?"

I search the shampoo aisle as I respond, "Yeah, he has been gracious enough to let me stay until I get something figured out."

"Gracious, my ass. More like ulterior motives," she mumbles under her breath, and I don't even try to argue that, because then that would require me to fill her in on our last Masqued encounter and the speech he afforded me with at the end of the night.

"Honestly, I think because he was with me last night, he probably feels sorry for me, and it turns out, he is a halfway decent human being with a massive place. He will barely know I'm there."

"Yeah, okay…let me know how that goes for you," she teases with an eye roll to sell it.

"Speaking of the boss. I need to kick it into high gear so we can get back to the office."

MONDAYS ARE NORMALLY my night that I reserve one of the studios for myself and I am extra thankful for the reprieve tonight. Group dance is always full of laughs and comradery, but after the last twenty-four hours, I've been in desperate need of some me-time.

"Calm Down" by Rema and Selena filters through the speakers. I try my best not to think about all things cluttering my brain… *My apartment, my living situation, Parker, Logan, Quinn, my parents, my apartment (on repeat), my grandparents…Parker.*

Slowly, they dissipate... Except one who isn't so easily forgotten, no matter how hard I try.

The room has wall-to-wall reflection. Near the glass door entrance, there is a section for viewing that is a one-way mirror, so that the dancers don't get distracted. As I move from the pole to the floor, my heart stutters. My mind must be playing tricks on me. *Parker.*

I stop dancing and walk over to peek out the door, only to see the hallway empty, everyone else in the dance class across the hall. I swore I saw Parker's reflection through the door. The man is constantly invading my thoughts, but the fact I'm conjuring him up while I'm dancing is concerning. I'm sure it was just someone running in late to class.

Shaking off thoughts of *him*, I go back to my routine, running it through a few more times before losing myself in my freestyle playlist. I dance until the alarm on my phone blares through the speaker, letting me know my allotted time is up.

By the time I walk out of The Dance Hub, the sun is starting to go down. The weather is ideal tonight, not too hot, not too humid. I suppress the giddiness I feel as I walk toward Tribeca on my way to Parker's penthouse.

With the hecticness of yesterday, I didn't even have time to feel nervous about staying at Parker's. I don't think it really hit me until I laid my head down on the pillow in his guest room and the thoughts crept in. But this excited anticipation is a dangerous thing when it comes to the broody bastard.

This morning, he almost looked—dare I say, disappointed, when I mentioned I was searching for Airbnbs. *But why?* Shouldn't this be, like, the ultimate step too far into the fortress he has built to keep me at arm's length?

I convince myself not to overanalyze his reaction, because it seems like any time I get a flicker of hope about Parker, he snuffs it out just as quickly.

My stomach grumbles a few blocks into my walk, and I really hope Parker made it home by now with the food. When we spoke on the phone this afternoon, he said it wouldn't be a late night for him, and since I had dance, he offered to pick up the takeout for us, promising I could treat him soon. Of course, he also inquired about how things went with Logan, and I could tell he was happy to hear that I didn't end up giving him much of my time.

His building comes into view, and the doorman must see me coming because he greets me with an open door and a smile as I walk up.

"Hi, Stuart, thank you!"

"Hello, Miss Pierce. It's a pleasure to see you again." According to Parker, he is the second shift doorman and his personal favorite. I can only imagine the disarray I must have looked like last night when we arrived.

"Same to you, and thank you again for your help with our things last night."

"No problem at all. Parker got in not too long ago with dinner. Even brought me a treat since he knows it's my favorite."

"Yum, I'm starving. Are you a Thai food fanatic too?" I ask as he walks us over, scanning me into the private elevator.

"Yes, and SoHo Thai has my favorite sweet chili tossed calamari."

Interesting. I expected him to grab it from one of the Thai places in Tribeca, but instead he walked the opposite way from the office to the one near my dance studio. Maybe my mind wasn't playing tricks on me. But why wouldn't he have said hello?

"Sounds delicious. Enjoy and have a great night!" I wave as the elevator doors to the penthouse close.

The shaft opens, and I inhale the flavorful scent of herbs and spices, causing my stomach to clench in hunger.

"Smells amazing and looks like you got one of everything," I say, dropping my purse on the entryway table and picking up a purring Binx.

"Well, I didn't think to get your order, and I didn't want to bother you during dance. I figured whatever we don't eat, we can take into the office tomorrow," Parker says from where he is setting everything up on the huge kitchen island.

I nod, and his mention of dance has the curiosity from what Stuart mentioned flittering back in. "That's perfect. I would love to try some dishes I haven't before. Where did you end up getting it from?"

"Thai place, not far from the office. It's one of my favorites," he rushes out, offering me a glass of wine.

Uh huh. Not a liar, but an avoider. Now I'm almost certain I saw him.

I smirk, eyeing him, and I swear I see a slight blush creep up his jawline. It has my stomach fluttering, and I want to push him a little more.

"Does it happen to be near my dance studio, Sir?" I say it in a teasing manner, but the way his eyes darken, I realize my mistake immediately.

He stops pouring the wine and turns fully to where I am standing against the counter. Two steps, and he is caging me in with one hand on either side of the granite behind me. My breath catches at how close he is, his cologne surrounding me.

"Careful, little brat," he whispers right above my mouth, and I could melt right here at his feet. Binx lets out a meow in between us, and a light chuckle escapes Parker's lips, but he doesn't move away. Instead, his eyes bore into mine as he asks, "You want the truth?"

I nod, not taking my eyes off his.

"About six months ago, I went there to get Thai food because Stuart told me it was the best around here, and I happened to see the sexiest pair of legs walking inside the dance studio next door. I knew them the minute I caught a glimpse, and like a kid in a candy store, I couldn't stop myself."

I blink rapidly, trying to process the timeline of what he is saying.

Everything falls into place. "On the plane… That's how you knew I was going to choose 'Calm Down' as my favorite song."

He nods and pushes my surprised jaw up with his tattooed hand. When he takes a step back, I set Binx on the ground, staring as he saunters off, still trying to make sense of all of this.

"And today?"

He nods again.

"I see your brain working, but I have no answers. I've been trying to understand it myself for six months—actually, longer than that—and I still can't." He pulls one of the chairs out at the kitchen island, motioning me to come sit down. "Don't overthink it, Av. Now, let's eat before it gets cold."

Yeah, that's easier said than done.

And by the way he avoids me after dinner, retreating to his cave to read a book, I know he's overthinking it too.

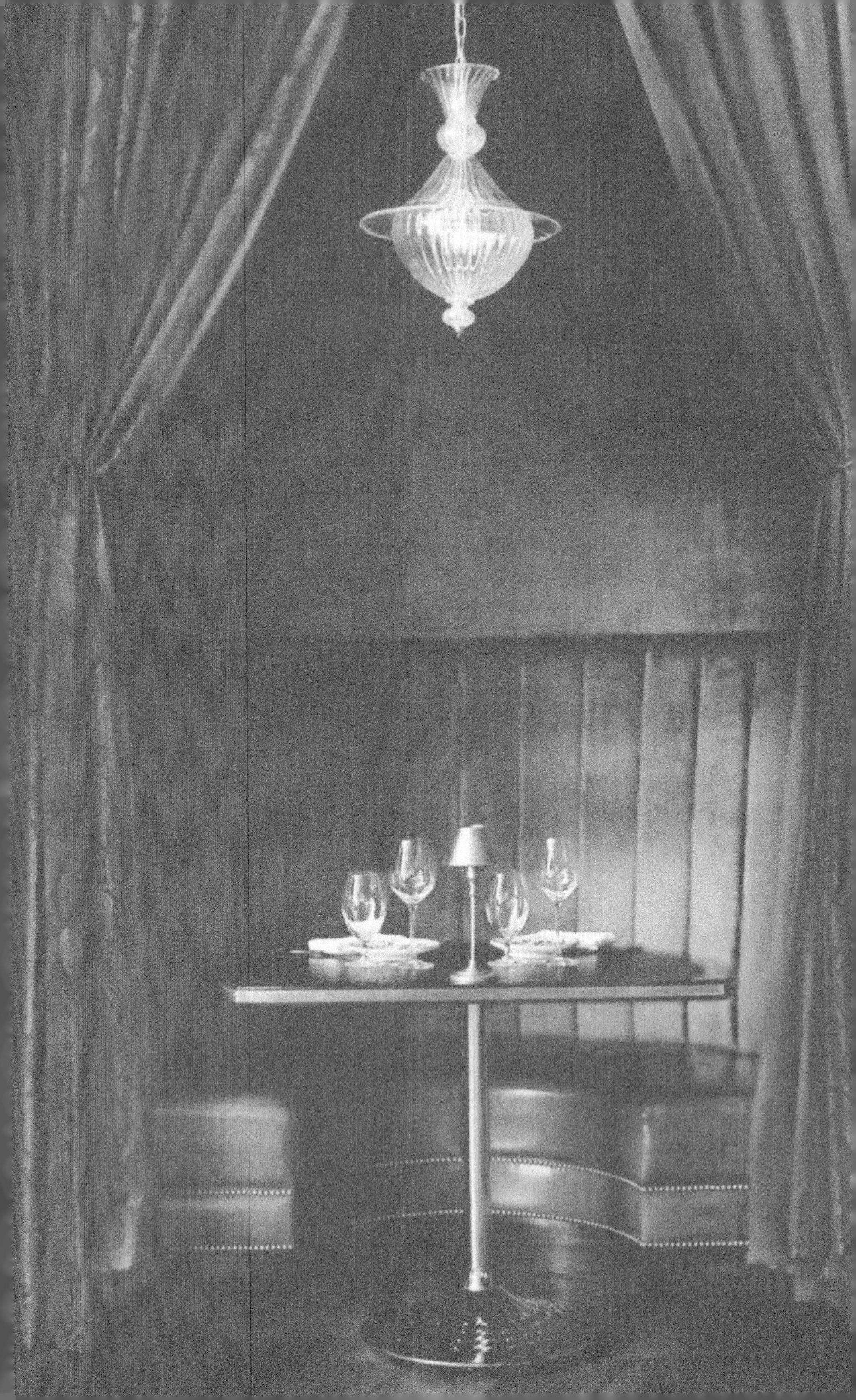

Twelve

Parker

No sooner am I through the door, I being nuzzled by the little black demon. "Meowww," Binx greets me as he weaves himself around my feet. I almost trip on him twice on my way to the kitchen, where he insists on hopping onto one of the stools at the island to watch me.

I place the beer and mango High Noons in the fridge, grabbing one of each for Ava and me.

On Thursday, we both realized neither of us had plans this weekend. Ava insisted she needed to treat me to dinner as a thank you, then afterwards we would have a *roomie* movie night. Her words, not mine. So I told her to choose the movie and I would pick us up some drinks.

Making my way into the living room, I stop and observe as Ava scurries about, making a nest for us on the floor with pillows and blankets. Binx darts into the room behind me, claiming a spot for himself. She has several cartons of delicious-smelling takeout on the coffee table.

"Smells great in here… What did you pick up?" I ask, interrupting her setup.

"Oh, you're home already? I didn't hear you come in," she says while throwing one last blanket onto the pile on the ground.

"Yeah, just a minute ago... You want?" I ask as I raise the hand holding the mango High Noon.

"Mmm, mango, my favorite." She smiles, then steps closer to take it from me.

"Took a guess." I wink. "What are we watching?"

"It's a surprise... Go get changed and meet me back in here in, like, ten minutes. I want to wash up too."

"Sounds like a plan."

Ten minutes later, I'm changed and sitting on the couch. Ava strolls in, fresh-faced and absolutely fucking gorgeous. Of course, this isn't the first time I've seen her like this. But it feels like the first time I'm able to sit back and truly take in how stunning she is. This week has been quite hectic between my late nights and her dance classes and checking in on her apartment, so we have spent little time with each other.

"Why are you sitting up there?" she asks, waving to the seating area she's constructed.

"We're eating, aren't we? I'm sitting at a table," I answer incredulously.

"Um, no, *roomie*, it's movie night. That means asses on the floor with takeout on our laps."

I can't help but chuckle at how adamant she is about our movie night plans. She's taking this very seriously, and by her expression, I don't think I'm going to win this one. So, I pick up one container and make myself comfortable amongst the sea of blankets and pillows.

"Better?" I ask when she sits down beside me with two dishes.

"Yes." She smiles, looking thoroughly pleased. "The girls and I used to do this once a week at school. We would have a movie night on the floor of our dorm room, using all the pillows and blankets available to make a nest. Stuffing our faces with whatever the wheel decided was our takeout that day."

"A wheel?" I question.

Ava laughs and a gorgeous smile lights up her face. "We could never decide what to eat, so we bought one of the mini-prize wheels to keep in our dorm. We filled it with our favorite restaurants and would let the wheel decide.

"That's a genius idea." I laugh, because who would have thought of that?

"It was! Saved us hours of debating."

"I bet with them being so close, it was a bit intimidating when you first met them," I say, knowing how close Quinn and Sloan were growing up. The stories that Eli has told paint them as always being together.

"Honestly, I was nervous at first. But we immediately hit it off. Like they were my long-lost sisters," she says with a smile, then opens the containers and serves the food.

"I ordered from Uncle Joe's. I heard they have the best chicken parmigiana," she says as she takes a big bite.

"Oh, yeah... No wheel necessary? Also, how did you know about Uncle Joe's chicken parm?" I ask, well aware I order from Uncle Joe's at least twice a month.

"Stuart told me...and he's not wrong. Damn, this is delicious," she moans while taking another bite.

The sound of her moan runs straight through me, and I will myself to look away from her mouth. I focus on eating my dinner and keeping my hands to myself. Because if one moan can put me on edge, I wonder what an entire movie night will do.

BY THE TIME the credits are rolling for *Hocus Pocus*, we're cuddling up close in the nest of blankets. Ava's body gradually made its way closer to mine throughout the night, slowly nuzzling herself into my side. I may or may not have inched over a few too.

The movie itself was alright, I guess, but Ava's enthusiasm made it more enjoyable. I could've watched her all night as she recited almost every line from the movie. She knew all the words to the songs too. It was quite entertaining.

Her head rests comfortably on my shoulder, with my arm wrapped around her, and I relish the feel of her body being this close to mine once again. It feels good being here with her like this. Easy almost, but I know this is a dangerous game to play. I'm not going to lie and say I didn't enjoy every minute of my night with her. Appreciating the efforts she went through to set it up.

"Thank you for tonight," I whisper, not sure if she's still awake.

Ava props herself onto her elbow, inches from my face, and studies me. Really studies me, and for a moment, I fear what she might see. But to my surprise, she doesn't pull away. Instead, her lips gently brush against mine. Tentatively at first, then surer the second time.

My cock aches and my hands roam over her body as she presses against me, pulling a groan from my chest. Her kiss is soft and sensual, but I need more. More of her, more of *this*. My heart races at the thought.

Grabbing the back of her neck, I crash my lips against hers. A moan escapes her, and I devour it. Savoring every minute of us tangled in each other. My other hand reaches to cup her ass, pulling her body so it's flush with mine. Letting her feel how hard I am beneath her.

Ava gasps when I kiss along her jaw and down her neck. But before I can travel any lower, she pushes herself up off my chest.

With a lustful daze, she stares back at me. "I had a good time too. Goodnight, Parker." She hesitates for a moment, but eventually, she climbs off me and heads down the hall to her bedroom.

Fuck was that?

My head falls back onto the pillow as I will my body to calm down. The motion causing her scent to permeate around me, and I inhale deeply. Cherishing the smell of her that seems to have infiltrated every corner of my home. Making it even more difficult to stop thinking about her.

When I come to my senses and decide not to storm after her like my cock is screaming at me to do, I head to my bedroom.

Once inside, I walk straight to the shower. A long stint under the water should help me relax, knowing damn well sleep isn't going to come easy tonight, that's for sure.

All this time, I have gotten by just fine living the way I've been, disconnected and cold. No need to give people more than they deserve. But is getting by ever enough? Being around Ava makes me feel like there has been something missing ... Nonetheless, those thoughts need to stay far the fuck away…for I know without a doubt I can't survive any more heartbreak.

"*Well, hello to you too, Ava.*" *My smirk stays fully in place as she stalks toward me.*

"*Are you sure you're ready for this?*" *I ask when she's just a mere few steps in front of me.*

"*Would I have invited you here if I wasn't?*" *she sasses, causing my dick to swell. Her and that bratty attitude.*

From the first night I met her, I've wanted to fuck that smart mouth of hers. Even though I shouldn't. The way her eyes found mine tonight, the way her body's every move enticed me, drawing me in like some sort of siren, I knew without a doubt my night was going to end this way.

I must have her.

Just this one time.

"*Get on your knees, Ava.*"

Her eyes widen, and she hesitates for a moment, and then slowly sinks to her knees without another word.

Good girl.

"*Take my cock out. I know you're desperate for it.*"

Ava's hands fly to my zipper, and I revel in the feel of her delicate fingers as they wrap around my shaft. With an eager smile, she strokes me confidently.

"*Stick your tongue out and open wide, little brat. I can't wait to fuck that smart mouth.*" *Her body visibly shudders at my words, right before she takes me down her throat.*

To say this image will forever be engrained in my memory is an understatement. She looks fucking stunning. Her hazel eyes stay focused on mine through the mask, making this whole thing even sexier.

"Fuck, your mouth feels good," I groan as her fingers play with my balls. My head falls back while I try my hardest to keep from coming down her throat.

I pull away from her, and the motion makes her luscious lips pop as the head of my cock leaves her mouth.

Ava eyes me in confusion for a minute, but stays in her kneeling position. I like her down there. Ready and willing to take my next command. I peer around the room, thinking of what I want to do to this beautiful woman at my feet. Then I see the chaise lounge across the way, and I know without a doubt I want to see what her pretty ass will look like with my handprint on it.

"Stand up, Ava. Walk over to that lounge and lean over the arm with your ass out."

She stands in front of me, pupils blown wide, the picture of pure seduction. Lifting the hem of her dress up and over her head, she's left in nothing but a lacy black thong. My jaw tics with the urge to consume every inch of her. Then, as if remembering my demand, she spins and sashays her way to the chaise.

I watch as she positions herself exactly as I asked, leaving her in place for a few minutes before I make my way over.

"Who would have thought you were so good at taking commands?" I ask as I trail my finger down her delicate spine. Her body arches like a cat before my words actually sink in.

"Who would've—"

Smack.

My hand flies to her right ass cheek before she can finish her retort.

"Ahhh!" she yelps in surprise.

"None of the sass, little brat. You asked me to be here. Enticing me all night, knowing exactly what you were doing," I say as I caress the reddened cheek. She pushes back into me, begging to be touched.

"Yes, Sir," she moans, and I don't think she realizes the words slipped from her lips.

"Say that again." My fingers trace over the soaked lace of her thong as my dick throbs. I need to hear those words again; they do something to me.

"Yes, Sir," she says with a smile on her face.

"Mmm, I like the sound of that coming from that sinful mouth of yours." Pulling the fabric to the side, I stare at her.

"Please stop teasing me. I need you to touch me," she begs, with an edge of frustration in her tone.

That earns her another palm to her ass.

Smack.

She rasps the most erotic sound, and I can't wait to hear more.

"What do you want, Ava, for me to touch you or fuck you?" It's taking all my restraint not to ravish her.

"Please fuck me."

In one swift motion, I rip the black lace from her body, leaving her perfectly exposed to me. Her body shakes as I run my finger through her slippery slit.

"Are you ready for me, Ava?" I ask as I roll on a condom.

She nods in response over her shoulder, her back heaving in anticipation.

With her body perfectly poised over the arm of the chaise, I line up behind her. More than desperate to feel her.

"Hold on," is all the warning she gets before I'm pushing inside her, sliding in easily with how wet she is for me.

"Ohhh, fuuuck," she groans before I'm even fully seated.

"You feel so good," I breathe out as she adjusts to my size, clenching around me.

"Please move, I need you," she begs and rolls her hips.

My left hand smacks her ass cheek almost instinctively. I rub my palm over the warmed flesh as I thrust my hips. The feel of her warm, wet pussy as it grips me is unreal.

Grabbing her ass with both my hands, I use it as leverage as I drive into her harder.

"Oh yes… please don't stop," she moans, gripping onto the chaise with whitening knuckles.

"Don't plan on it. You a screamer, Legs?" I ask when I feel her cunt pulsing, making me even harder than I thought possible.

"Not… usually… oh shit," she pants, releasing a whimper as she thrusts back to take me deeper.

My breath catches as hands release her ass, and I smooth my palms over her tender cheeks. The sensitivity of her skin combined with the steady roll of my hips, has unintelligible words slipping from Ava's lips.

Fuck, I love the sounds coming out of that bratty mouth of hers.

I lean over and grab her shoulder, pulling her body up toward mine. My hands explore as she begins to bounce back on my cock. Brushing up the front of her thighs, then over her core, up her waist to her perfect breasts.

"Fuck… I didn't think you would feel this good," she says when I tweak one of her nipples.

I did.

She is soaked, practically ruining my suit pants that I now realize never made it off my body. Using one hand to continue playing with her nipples, the other traces down her tight abs to between her thighs. Her rhythm is thrown off slightly when I apply a little pressure to the sensitive bud.

"I'm going to come," she moans as her nails dig into my thighs at her sides.

I pull my slick hand from between her legs and bring my fingers to her lips. Without hesitation, she sucks them into her mouth. Twirling her tongue eagerly, she moans in delight when my other hand sinks back between her thighs.

Ava's body is a live wire beneath me, basically vibrating with raw sexual energy. Writhing uncontrollably, her pussy works my length over and over, moving faster as her moans grow louder.

Fucking. Incredible.

She better come right the fuck now, because this is all too much for me.

"Parker… ah, shit. I'm coming!" she screams, body trembling, and my fingers slip from her mouth as her head falls back onto my shoulder. Hearing my name from her lips in pure ecstasy is my undoing.

And I fall.

I'm woken up by my aching cock, begging for attention. That night is something I think I'll dream about till the end of time. The way her body reacted to my touch. How she obeyed my every command…

Dragging my hands over my face, I release a deep sigh. Fuck, it's going to be a long and torturous day. I don't think I have the willpower to be in this apartment after how she left us last night.

Ava and I had talked about going over some of the floorplans for her apartment restoration. Apparently, the pipe that busted was leaking for quite some time and there's more mold and damage to the structure than originally assessed, resulting in her apartment needing a complete gut from top to bottom.

This means her place will be out of commission for longer than she had hoped. This also means she will be here testing my restraint for an unforeseeable amount of time... Unless she starts with that Airbnb shit again. The idea of her living anywhere but under my roof has me on edge, and that fact alone is part of the reason why I desperately need to keep my guard up.

Tread carefully, my friend.

Walking out of my room, the fresh scent of ground espresso beans leads me toward the kitchen. Where I find Ava successfully making a cappuccino for the first time this week.

"Finally got the hang of it?" I ask, stepping in close and reaching above her to grab my espresso cup.

"Fifth time's a charm," she says cheerfully, spinning around before I can back away. Putting us in close proximity yet again. She licks her lip, effectively teasing me, then raises the cup I didn't realize was between us to her mouth.

"Mmm," she hums, leaving me with a wink and walking to the kitchen island where Binx perches upon a stool, staring at the two of us.

Does she realize what she's doing?

A glance in her direction gives me the perfect view of her slender neck as she swallows. Reminding me of how good her lips feel wrapped around me and how I desperately want to feel them again. Fuck, I need to stop thinking about that.

I'm well aware this is a dangerous game to be playing... especially when I already know I'd be on the losing side. But that doesn't stop the words that fly out of my mouth next.

"You up for a drive today?"

She hesitates for a moment, and my stomach sinks. Damn, I guess I didn't realize how badly I wanted her to join me. The idea of sharing my special place with her should have warning bells sounding, but for the first time in what feels like forever, they're muted.

"I have dance at ten-thirty..." she says, gnawing on her lip as she contemplates. I wait with bated breath for her answer.

"How far we talking?"

"An hour...two tops, depending on traffic," I answer quickly.

"You know what, I can skip dance this week," she says with a smile that stirs something I thought was long dead inside of me.

"Yeah?" I reply, hoping the excitement in my voice is somewhat contained.

"Sounds good to me. What time do you want to leave?"

"How's eleven?"

"Perfect!" With a smile, she prances off to her room as I stare at her perky ass swaying in her little sleep shorts.

Now I just need to muster up the strength to keep my hands to myself for the rest of the day.

Babes Group Chat

SLOAN

Just a tidbit of information I'd like to share. I just called our sweet bestie Ava to see if she wanted to go to the farmer's market with me, but she had to turn me down because she is currently going on a day trip to Hudson Valley with her new roomie.

QUINN

Does this really surprise you??

ME

You are both so dramatic.

QUINN

No, you are delusional.

ME

I figured you guys would be happy that we are finally on friendly terms.

SLOAN

Oh, we are... That's not the problem.

ME

Well, what the hell is?

QUINN

Friends don't look at each other the way you two do.

SLOAN

What she said 👆👆

SLOAN

Also bring me back some fresh strawberries since you are unavailable to go with me to the market today.

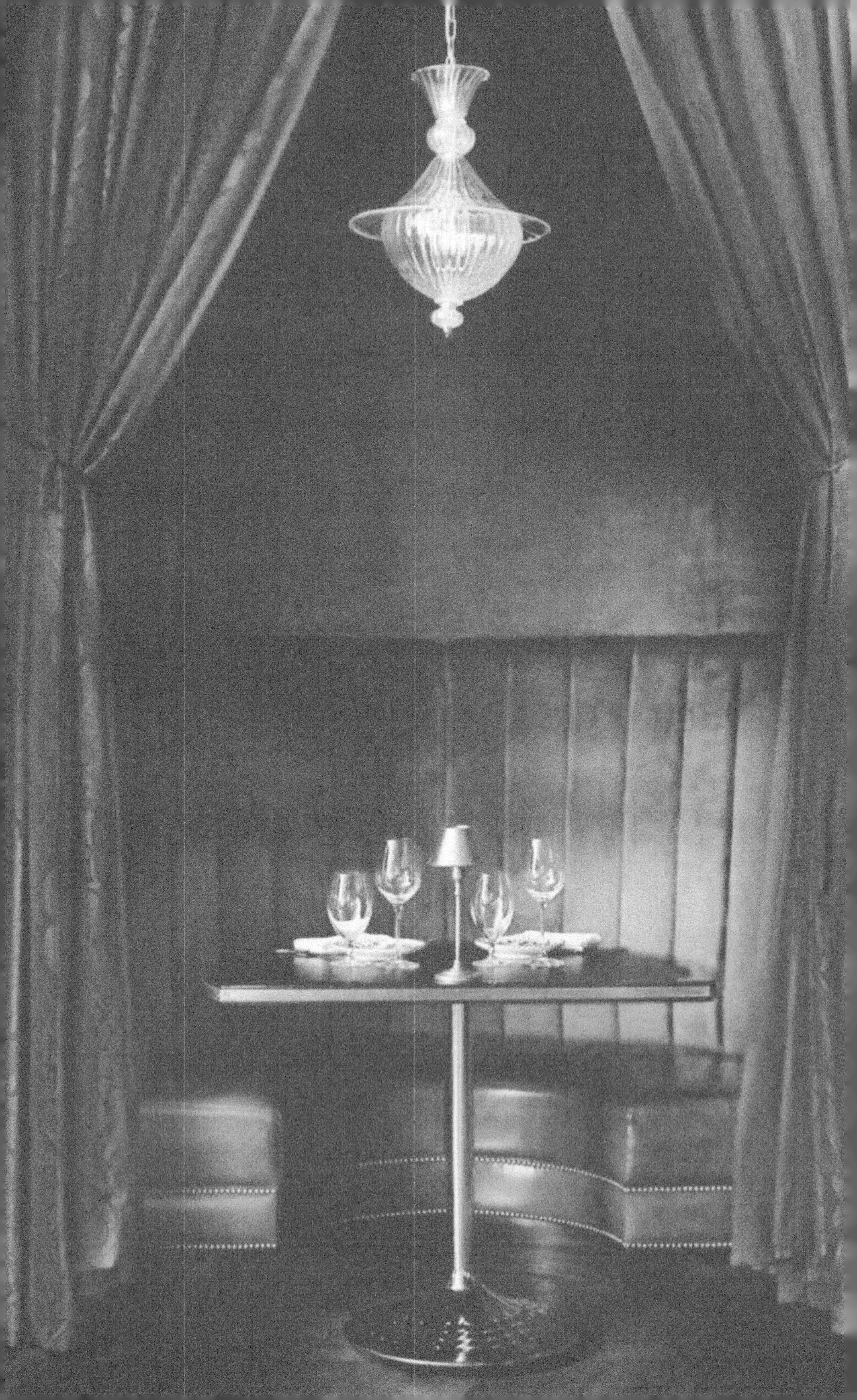

Thirteen

Ava

"It's been so long since I've taken the time to drive up to the Catskills," I say, admiring the beauty the farther away from the hustle and bustle of the city we get.

"Did your parents ever bring you up here?" Parker asks, and my eyes trace the way his hands wrap around the wheel of his black-on-black Rolls Royce Wraith.

I scoff. "Heck no. This wasn't up to their standards for a vacation." I didn't come up here until the fall of my freshmen year when Sloan, Quinn, and I took our first girls' weekend getaway. I fell in love with the quietness.

"Not even a day trip?"

"A day trip in their eyes is taking a helicopter out to the Hamptons." I remember one time we took a small plane up to Toronto for my dad's business meeting. I begged and pleaded to make a pit stop to see Niagara Falls and you would have thought I was asking to go dumpster diving by the way my mom turned her nose up. *"That's for silly tourists,"* she had said. If it didn't involve a good shopping spree or the bragging rights to talk about trips to Europe, then they didn't want to do it.

"Sounds luxurious," he says with an eye roll.

"Sounds boring," I retort. "I mean, don't get me wrong, some of my best memories were spent at my grandparents' house in the Hamptons, but you don't know how badly I wished as kid to do simple things like this."

"Why does it always seem that we want what we can't have?" he says, and I don't miss the way his eyes linger on my face before looking back at the road.

"As a kid, did you want the lavish things you have now?"

He thinks about it for a minute and shakes his head. "No. I've been around people with money my whole life, and none of them ever seemed as happy as my parents." Parker pauses for a minute, then adds, "Well, before my mother's diagnosis, at least."

"How old were you?"

"She was diagnosed my senior year of college, but they didn't tell me until I came home that summer, and she was gone six months later."

Fuck. I can't imagine. I don't share an overwhelming fondness for my mother, but I would never want her to go through something like that.

I picture a beautiful brunette with Parker's eyes. Retracing his apartment in my head, I don't think he has any pictures of actual people, now that I think about it. But then again, I haven't been in his room. I can't help but wonder if I'm right, or which parent he resembles most.

"Tell me something about them."

Emotion passes over his face before he answers.

"My mom gave up everything for my dad and my dad gave up everything for me. But somehow, it always felt like we still had it all."

A soft smile lifts his lips, like he's reminiscing, as my mind conjures up a younger, more carefree Parker.

"My mom's family cut her off financially when she chose to marry my father, and my father gave up his musical ambitions when she became pregnant with me. They bought a small house on Long Island and made it into the perfect home for me to grow up in. Our spare time was full of music festivals and baseball tournaments, camping trips, day drives up here. They didn't just love me, they believed in me. Believed I could do anything I set out to do."

That makes me smile, thinking of the support and love I always got from my grandparents. I'm happy Parker was able to experience that.

"Sounds like an amazing childhood. Did you ever see your mom's family?" I wonder if they are who he was referring to when he mentioned being around people with money.

He hesitates, and I notice the dark look that washes over his face. "Yeah, not because of my mom. My dad grew up in the system and refused to let my mom give up her family for him completely. We went to holidays on occasion. And in the summer, I would spend time with them." It makes me wonder if they were there for him when his parents died, but I'm scared to ask.

"Where are they all now?"

"Some are in the city, some live out east in the Hamptons." The sneer on his features doesn't go unnoticed, and I take that as my cue to stop prying.

The next sign I see offers me the perfect distraction and change in subject.

"Ooooh, fresh strawberry shortcakes. That sounds delish." I point, and Parker grunts in approval.

The strawberry patch sign reminds me of Sloan's text from earlier. I finally three-way called her and Quinn on Wednesday to fill them in on my disaster of an apartment—I may have thought they planned the whole catastrophe themselves if I hadn't of been with them in North Carolina that weekend.

They were *way* too excited about my current living arrangements. Quinn, especially, reminding me of what the close proximity turned into for her and Eli.

The difference is, those two were written in the stars from the very beginning. Parker and I may have an undeniable chemistry, but I'm no fool to think he would ever love me.

My gaze wanders from his big hands to his flexed forearms, every tattoo on his skin a true work of art. I can't help but want to test his restraint, because that kiss last night took every bit of mine to pull away from. But I refuse to be the one who initiates things again, I want him to want me as badly as I do him. My body is still completely agreeable to just sex with him, but my mental can't handle the rejection again. Especially not with the progress we have made with not constantly being at each other's throats.

"We're getting close," Parker says, and I don't ask questions. He said he'd explain once we got there.

I stare out the window, enjoying the peacefulness. Parker's phone rang on and off about work for the first hour on the way up here, until he finally said he was turning it to *Do Not Disturb*. Unfortunately for me, Parker handling his multiple business matters while I sat beside him quietly was not annoying at all. Instead, it was a turn-on, hearing him handle all the different things he has going on with ease and dominance.

Dominance. Something I never knew I liked so much.

WE TURN onto a gravel road lined with trees along each side, and my mind continues to run with possibilities about what he is bringing me here to see.

The trees start to fade, and suddenly the view opens up. Beautiful fields of green grass lead to the base of the mountain. I roll my window down, enjoying the summer breeze and fresh valley air floating through the window. So different from the smells of the city.

Mountains upon mountains surround the picture-perfect view. To the left, I see a river flowing through the valley and a small bridge you can cross over on foot. Parker stops the car, and I follow as he gets out, still not saying anything.

This place is a hidden gem. I'm wondering if it was special to his parents.

I walk behind, still taking in all the natural beauty, and I see a large home in the distance. It appears to have quite a bit of age to it, from what I can see from here. But I love it. Like an antique, it will be full of character.

We walk onto the bridge and Parker leans his forearms onto the railing, looking down at the water traveling under us. I take a second to admire him like this. I don't think I've ever seen him so at ease.

"What is this place, P?"

The little nickname slips out. I'm not even sure where it came from, but I think I like it, and by the smirk on his face, I would say he does too.

"P, huh?"

I shrug. "It's better than asshole, right?"

He chuckles. "Definitely."

"This is my next investment... Well, hopefully. I'm still in negotiations with the seller. My dream would be to make it a small resort. A mixture of luxury and outdoors." He points out into the distance. "I'd love to have some more lavish cabins away from the main property, but then make sure the main rooms are affordable for your average family."

"Parker, you have to do it," I say in awe, excitement thrumming through my body. A wide smile takes over my face, and I mentally start planning out décor themes and floorplans.

Looking back at me, he smiles. "I see that brain of yours working a mile a minute right now."

"You have no idea. This would be a dream job. I know I said that about the hotel, but this is on another level. You could create an oasis here, truly."

For the first time when my eyes find his, I notice light blue clouds mixing with the stormy grey ones. *He's happy.*

"Well, if the hotel is up to my expectations, you just may have yourself another job lined up." His brow furrows. "Unless you aren't willing to leave the city."

"Are you kidding me? For this, I would leave in a heartbeat." My smile only grows as I think back on my first sketchbook.

"One of the first designs I ever created before I was even in college was an elaborate bed-and-breakfast layout."

"Really?"

"Yeah, I went to visit my aunt in Paris, and she took me out to this quaint countryside town in France. We went to a retreat that was unreal. It was my high school graduation present from her. I literally created a whole plan with that as my inspiration, but with my own additions.

"That's quite impressive," Parker replies. Shifting ever so slightly closer to me.

"I had already decided to go to NYU, but my parents were still trying to push me to basically any degree other than what I wanted. They wanted me to be educated for the clout of it, and just never use it. But my aunt is nothing like her sister, and she told me I had to pursue this."

"All it takes is one person to believe in you," he says as he gently trails his fingertip over my hand resting beside his. The light touch and his genuine words make my belly dip. "I'm glad you have your aunt and your grandparents."

"Let me show you the farmhouse," he suggests, waving me to follow him toward the home off in the distance.

We start walking through the field, and I ask, "What made you want to get into real estate?"

"When my baseball career went up in flames, all I had was a bullshit degree in business. But I was determined to make a name for myself in the city. One people would know."

My lips to the side. I'm kind of surprised by that statement, but don't know if I have the right to say it.

"What?"

"Huh?"

"You are doing that twisty thing with your lips you do when you are trying to stop yourself from saying something."

I roll my eyes at his accurate assessment. "It's just the way you have always made comments about money to me. It seems unusual that it was so important to you back then."

He stops at the bottom of the old broken front steps, pondering my statement.

"I had something to prove back then. My mom had just passed, and I was pissed at her family for how they always treated us, needing an outlet to place all my blame and anger."

I nod. That makes sense.

"There were other driving forces too…" He stops himself, shaking his head and looking off toward the river. "I can't believe I'm actually going to tell you this shit."

My heart speeds up at the anguish in his voice, and Quinn's words about a girl hurting him come back to mind.

"I was engaged once."

Oookaaay. I did not expect *that*. I bite the inside of my cheek to make sure my mouth isn't hanging open in shock.

Parker must read the shock on my face. "Yeah, I know it's hard to imagine me engaged. But I was. She was my high school sweetheart. We dated all through college."

So many puzzle pieces fall into place about this broody man.

"What happened?" I whisper.

He lets out a sardonic laugh. "It wasn't your typical breakup once she realized I wasn't going pro. No, worse than that. She made me feel like she was with me, no matter what. Told me numerous times she didn't care about that."

I wait on bated breath for the *but* that's coming with this story. I've only ever had casual boyfriends, so it's hard to imagine this man in a situation so far beyond that.

"But what I didn't know was two summers before that, she had hooked up with a rich prick and it had continued going on from time to time."

She wanted to have her cake and eat it too. Well, I hope the cake is small and stale now. *Bitch.*

"How did you find out?"

"Typical shit. I'd been in a funk because it was my mom's birthday week, the first one since she passed. My fiancée was out in the Hamptons. I dragged my ass to a party she had originally invited me to because I was trying so hard to be who she needed me to be, when in reality, I was falling apart."

My chest literally aches from the pain I can feel wafting off him. What kind of person treats someone that way? Someone you are supposed to marry and cherish forever. *I hate her.*

"Sounds like she wasn't being who you needed at that time. You were the one struggling."

"I was more than struggling, and now I see that. She held my hand through the funeral, but she wasn't really there for me as I would have expected. And it took me walking in on her riding another guy's dick to see it."

I could vomit.

"Let me guess, she begged and pleaded, saying it was a mistake."

"On multiple occasions."

I wonder if she still does. My stomach coils again at the thought.

"I hope you told her to fly a kite."

He nods, releasing a heavy sigh. "Told her more than that."

"Good… Did the guy know?"

"Oh, he knew."

When he doesn't elaborate, I decide I've pressed my luck enough, and who cares anyway? Fuck them both for doing that to him, especially with everything he was already going through.

"That year changed me in a way no amount of therapy will ever fix."

Taking a deep breath, I nod in understanding, but look around at the property. "I truly think this project here may be one of the best things you'll ever do for your healing."

His eyes trail around, and a genuine smile takes over his face. "I think you're right, Av."

Fuck, when he calls me Av, it feels like a million butterflies are having a rave inside my belly.

"Let me show you inside." Parker steps ahead of me and reaches his hand back for mine. "It's an old home, so follow right behind me." Placing my hand into his, I let him lead the way. The feel of my small hand in his sends tingles through me, from the top of my head to the soles of my feet.

Parker ducks to get into the house. "Obviously, it needs a lot of work, but I would love to still utilize it somehow." His grip on my hand tightens. "Come. I want you to see this back patio view."

We walk through the kitchen area, and I immediately understand what he wanted me to see. If I thought the ride in had amazing views... *This.* The hills and fields roll and roll for what seems like miles. "Wow," I exhale. "How many acres is this property?"

He lets go of my hand to open the double doors that lead out on the back patio, and I instantly hate the loss. "200 acres."

"Endless possibilities."

He nods. "My thoughts exactly."

I move ahead to step out on the patio. "Ava, no!" Parker commands, grabbing my arm and halting my movement. The sharpness in his tone startles me, and I suck in a breath.

"It may not be safe. The wood looks rotten. I don't want you to get hurt." His tone softens as he nods toward the deck I was going to step onto naively.

When I exhale, he chuckles. "Sorry, I didn't mean to scare you." We're so close, his mouth hovers over mine.

Dominant and sweet. How the hell am I not supposed to throw myself at this man and beg him to fuck me right out there in that tall green grass?

"Why are you laughing then, bossman?" I tease, pinching his side.

"Because I don't think I've ever seen you listen so well without back-talking me..." A sly smirk takes over his face. "Well, that's not entirely true either."

My teeth slip over my bottom lip, lightly biting down at the thought of what gave him pause. Which leads me to another question I've often contemplated many times. "Are you a Dom?"

His expression is a mixture of shock and comedy.

"Did I just ask that out loud?"

"Yes, you absolutely did." His voice grows huskier than before. His hand still gently holding my arm feels like a flaming torch lighting my insides on fire.

"Well, are you going to answer the question?"

"It's a question I've asked myself frequently, especially over the last eighteen months."

Eighteen months... Since our first time.

"And?"

"I'm not in the sense that I don't actively practice as a Dom, but I think it's pretty obvious I have certain tastes and a naturally dominant personality."

I swallow, and Parker pushes a strand of hair behind my ear. "And you are naturally submissive in bed."

I try to disagree—for what reason, I have no clue. But he shushes me, placing his finger over my lips, and my tongue dies to reach out and taste him.

"Don't even try to deny it. You thrive as a submissive." I know he's right. Even right now, with all my clothes on, the sexual energy is so charged between us that I'm obeying his every word.

"An alpha in the streets and a submissive in the sheets," he says with a chuckle, and I can't help but laugh.

"Did you just make a joke, Parker Cole?"

"Told you, I can be charming." He grins, finally releasing his hold on me and taking a few steps away.

If he can control himself, so can I.

"Thank you for bringing me here," I say as we pull back onto the main road. We spent the last two hours exploring the property. We even found two Adirondack chairs that looked over the river, where we sat in silence, just enjoying the scenery. Both of us imagining a future for the beautiful land.

I hope with every fiber of my being that the seller agrees to let Parker buy it. He needs this passion project. There is something there meant for Parker, meant to help him heal the pain he has been through in this life. Maybe it's in the soil, maybe it's in the memories he has of this area, or maybe it's because this has everything to do with joy and nothing to do with making money. Either way, he needs this.

"Let's hope it won't be the last time."

I know he means that as his interior designer and, honestly, I'm okay with that. The fact he would trust me with something this meaningful to him would be an honor.

I squeeze his hand. "It won't be. I feel it, Parker. It's going to work out for you."

We drive a few miles before he flips his turn signal. I look around in confusion until I realize he is pulling into the strawberry patch I pointed out on our drive up.

"So you were listening to me earlier? Or maybe you just love strawberry shortcake too."

He turns into a spot, his Rolls Royce grabbing the attention of the parking lot bystanders.

Reaching over, Parker runs his knuckle along my jawline. "Don't you know a Dom always rewards his sub?"

RIP Ava Pierce. I'm not strong enough for this shit.

"Don't tease me with a good time... Sir," I say in a hushed tone before pressing the button to open the door.

I hear him growl "little brat" as I hop out of the car, leaving one mouthwatering temptation for another. *This one just won't be nearly as satisfying.*

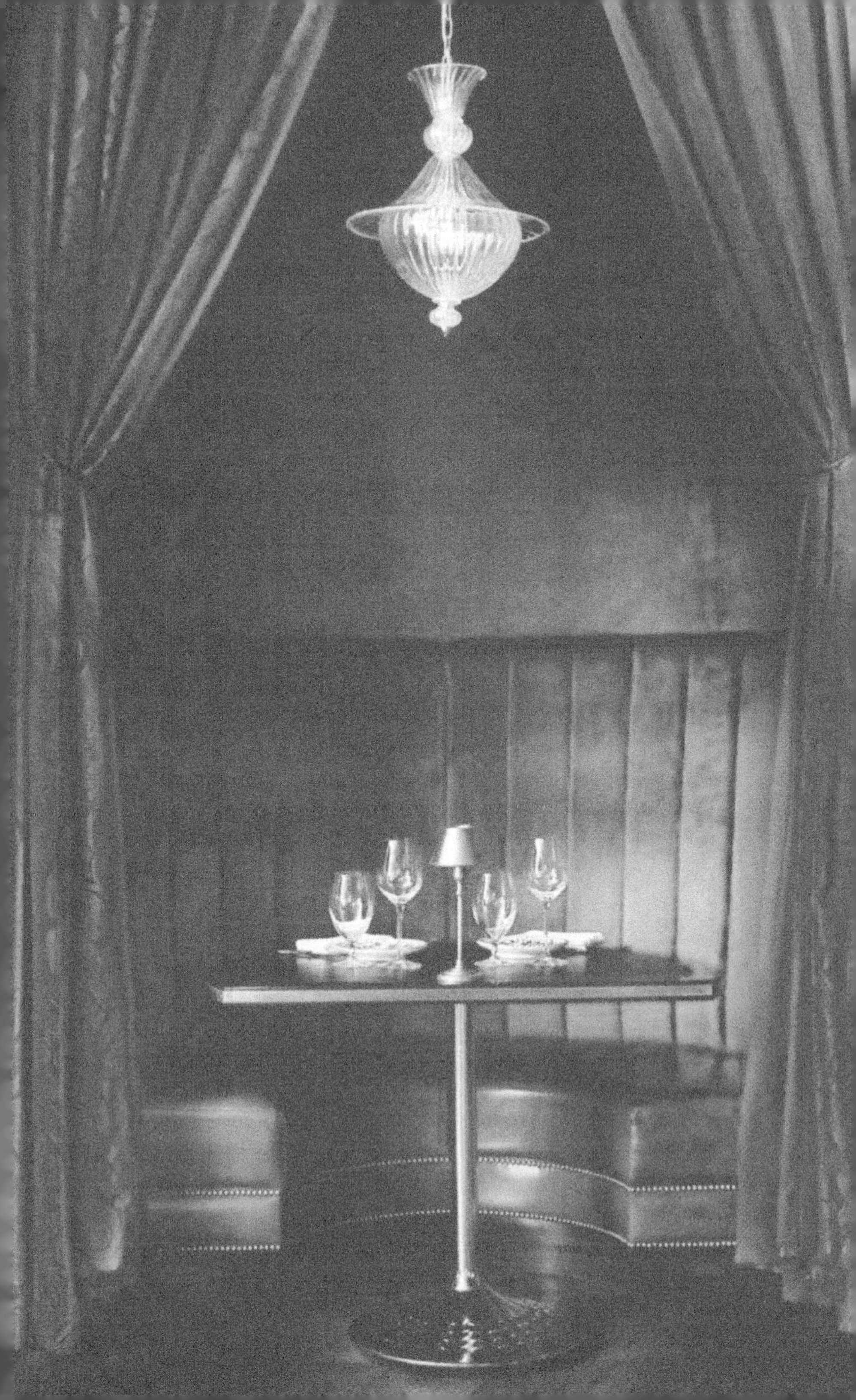

Fourteen

Ava

"Don't let us forget to order to-go food for Stuart," I say, pointing my chopsticks in his direction. This Pad Thai is hitting the spot after dance tonight. It was one of the harder classes I've done in a while.

Parker finishes his bit of Khao Soi. "I was just thinking the same thing."

When he called me today offering to meet me after dance, I couldn't help my excitement at spending more time with him.

"I think it's officially Thai Mondays at this point," I tease in an attempt to get out of my head.

"Thai Mondays for the foreseeable future," Parker declares. "Stuart will definitely be happy about this news."

Foreseeable… I wonder what that means, exactly. My place needs at least a month's worth of work, per the update this week, and I'm just choosing to ignore all the red flags as usual when it comes to Parker and shacking up in his guestroom. Our lives have so easily intertwined over the past week, between walking to work together most days, to numerous meals, I even have him drinking hot tea with me on his rooftop in the evenings. I love spending time with him, way more than I ever thought I would, but I can't lie and say I'm not disappointed he hasn't tried to kiss me again.

I get the reasons he wants to keep emotions to a minimum because now I understand who he is so much better. The thing is, I should walk away before my own feelings get involved and this becomes more than just sexual chemistry. Right now, it's like that new favorite candle you want to burn any chance you get, but I worry my heart won't know when to realize it is time to move on and that flame will turn into an inferno I can't blow out.

"So how was dance tonight?" Parker asks.

"The class was actually really challenging. I learned some new moves, but damn if my back and neck aren't going to be sore tomorrow." I wince at the reminder, rubbing my free hand up my neck, already feeling the muscle ache.

His eyebrows furrow in concern and the devious side of me says I should milk it just to get his hands on me, but I decide to brush it off.

"I'm good. It was fun to be challenged."

Parker's expression relaxes, and it brings warmth to my chest. "What got you into dance?"

"My parents put me into ballet at a young age, and that was fun, but I'll never forget the first time my teacher invited me to take a hip-hop class. I immediately knew it was my forte. I actually asked my Aunt Samantha to sign me up for the class, since at that time, she was still living in the apartment that I live in now. She was the one taking me to dance class anyways, because she found out no one ever went with me to watch.

Either my nannies or driver had always dropped me off before her."

"Did they ever find out?"

"They had no clue until they came to the recital, and I did my routine." I laugh, remembering the look on their faces that day.

"What did they do?" he asks gruffly.

"They were pissed. It didn't fit the prima ballerina persona that had created for me. That was the only time I have seen my aunt mad. She went head-to-head with my mom, and let's just say, I was able to sign up for hip-hop the next year as well."

Parker laughs at that. "This aunt of yours sounds like a good time."

"She's the best. Her and my grandparents are the people who have always loved and supported me, no matter what." I smile as I take a sip of my water.

"I'm sorry your parents are shitty, but I'm glad you have the rest of your family."

A thought pops in my head. My grandmother has been begging me to come to visit her, and she has so many questions about my new boss/roommate. Maybe Parker would like to come too. I'd love for him to meet them, but would that be too much for him?

He showed me a huge piece of himself this weekend in Hudson Valley, so why can't I show him something important to me?

My home away from home, that was much more about the people in it than the location or the size.

I untwist my lips, deciding to ask him. "Speaking of my grandparents... They want me to come visit soon, and I was thinking you should come out east with me."

"Not sure about that, Av," he says almost tentatively, looking back to his food like it has all the answers. But I decide to keep going; the request is already out there at this point.

"Come on. It will help all my grandmother's questions about who I'm living with." Giving him my sweetest smile, I bat my eyelashes at him.

That makes him chuckle, shaking his head at my antics. "I don't know. I'll think on it."

I nod. Okay, at least it's not a hell no.

Parker asks me meaningful questions throughout the rest of our meal, and because I know he has no problem sitting in comfortable silence with me, I know they are out of genuine curiosity. He asks what my aunt does over in Paris, more about my grandparents, and what my first job as an interior designer was like. The rapt attention and intrigue for me seems different from before our trip to Hudson Valley, or maybe even before the twins' birthday party. I'm not sure when things started to change, but there is no denying they certainly have. I try not to analyze it too much and just soak up being in his orb for the time being.

I'll save the overanalyzing for tomorrow... because apparently, Parker lets nothing go.

BABES GROUP CHAT

SLOAN

Blossom just called! Her and Dalton are in the city on business this week, so they are extending their trip to come to the game with all of us!

QUINN

That's even better! I bet you miss having her around. Seriously can't wait to see you guys.

SLOAN

I tempt her weekly to move to NY and come work for me again at Masqued... Dalton is not so keen on the idea.

ME

Haha... there's no way he's letting her out of his sight. But yay for getting to see all my girls!

QUINN

How's Parker?

ME

Confusing AF

SLOAN

Why??

ME

I told him I tweaked my back at dance last night and he just called to let me know he has his personal masseuse setting up an in-home massage for me tonight.

QUINN

Aw but that's really sweet.

ME

Exactly!!! All kinds of mixed signals are being sent at this point.

SLOAN

First off, enjoy the massage, sounds like you need it. Second off, if he keeps sending you mixed signals, I think you should talk to him.

SLOAN

If it's too much you know you can stay with Wes and me.

QUINN

Yes, and as much as I want to hear about you two giving in and banging again, you know you're always welcome to go stay over at our place. We're rarely there, so you are welcome there with plenty of privacy.

ME

Thank you both. But full transparency, I don't want to leave. We have finally broken new ground as friends and it's not his fault I'm a horny slut attracted to a man with more baggage than JFK.

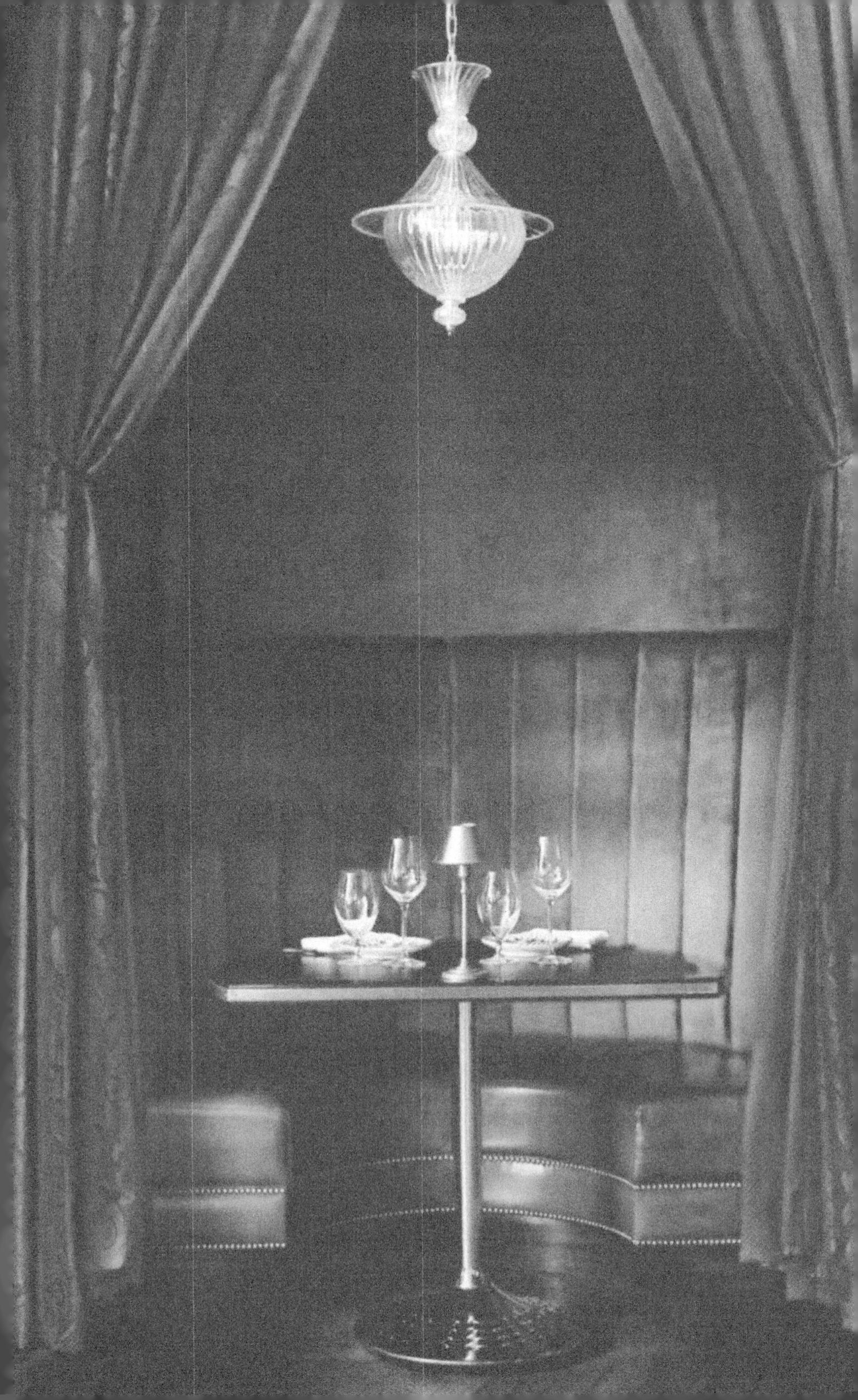

Fifteen

Ava

When I say Parker lets nothing go, that means the second I mentioned my aching body to him last night, he was already making a plan to have a masseuse meet me at his place the next day.

Stepping out of the elevator doors, I'm greeted by a tall, handsome man, and I should be excited. Instead, I'm wishful thinking of ulterior motives and Parker being the one standing here waiting on me.

The massage therapist, Bennett, allows me privacy to undress and settle onto the table in the living room area. And when his hands start caressing my neck and back, I can't help but want them to be different hands leading to tattooed forearms. His smell all around us in his home.

Eventually, I relax into a daze-like state because, while his hands might not be the ones I'm dreaming of, they are an absolute expert in relaxation and soothing.

When Bennett rubs my back gently, letting me know he is finished, I feel the drool on the corner of my mouth from dozing off.

"Miss Ava, you are all set. Can I grab you a cold-water bottle from the refrigerator?"

"Bennett, you can head out. I'll grab her one."

Parker's voice has my head snapping up to attention.

He's sitting in a chair over in the corner of the room, his ankle resting on his knee, reminding me of our last time at Masqued. His stormy eyes meet mine, and a zing of electricity sparks to life between us.

How long has he been there watching? And why the fuck does that turn me on so much?

I thank Bennett before he leaves, and my eyes stalk Parker grabbing me a bottle of water from the refrigerator before walking back toward me.

"How was it?"

I lean up on my elbows, perching my head up, the sheet still laying over my back. "It was amazing. Not nearly long enough, but they never are."

He twists the top and extends the water bottle out to me. I see his eyes trail down my neck to my partially exposed breasts. I love the way his eyes darken and his tongue peeks out to lick his lips at the sight. His reaction makes me feel brazen. Swallowing the water, I let the sheet fall a little more with no attempt to cover myself.

"Not nearly long enough, huh?" Parker asks, his voice huskier than before.

He reaches out for the water. "Lie back down."

Parker grabs the oil, and I do as he says. I would do just about anything in this moment to have his hands on me.

My clit pulses in anticipation. My body wants this man so bad, it's unreal.

But his next words are what really have me panting with need.

"What's aching, little brat?"

Parker

My hands twitch with the need to touch her. I was just moments away from pulling Bennett's hands off her. Luckily, he finished…or he felt my death glares and was a smart enough man to step away.

"What's aching, little brat?" I ask while pouring some of the massage oil into my hands.

"Everything," she says with a devious smirk over her shoulder. The look in her eyes tells me all I need to know. She's desperate for me…exactly how I want her.

I lower the sheet that's draped over her body to just above her perfectly plump ass, exposing her long, lean back. My finger drags along her spine, causing goosebumps to erupt all over her skin. Ava quakes beneath my touch, and I've barely begun my exploration of her.

My oil-slicked hands smooth up her back, and I swear a low moan escapes her mouth. I smile inwardly as something inside me stirs. She wasn't making these noises before when Bennett's hands were on her.

"Feel good, Angel?"

"Yes… Mmm, please don't stop," she begs, and my cock twitches.

Ava's body is absolutely incredible, and I let my hands roam as they please. Touching every inch of her exposed back and savoring every sound that leaves her lips. When I feel like her back has had enough attention, I slowly slide the sheet over, revealing one of her gorgeous fucking legs.

Starting with her calf, my fingers knead and caress her. When I'm mere inches from her ass, I let my thumb wander and lightly stroke. Then they travel back down to her ankle, repeating the same process on the next leg. She releases a sigh when my thumbs graze the wetness coating her inner thighs, then trail back down again. As if she was holding her breath in anticipation.

I notice that Ava has shifted her legs apart ever-so slightly. As if I need more of an invitation. I'm moments away from fucking her right on this damn massage table.

Folding up the sheet so it is only covering her ass, I apply more oil to my hands and steadily work my way up both her legs. When I reach the slickness of her inner thighs, I pause. Ava lets out a groan of frustration, and I chuckle.

"What's wrong?" I ask in a smooth tone. Trying hard not to reveal my overwhelming desire to have her.

"I need—I… Fuck," she curses when I run my knuckle through her sex.

"Hmm?" I prod. For some reason, I need her to tell me she wants more. Tell me she wants this as much as I do.

"Please touch me, Sir." A sense of relief hits me with those words, and I reward her by sinking my finger into her drenched cunt.

"Is this all for me?" I ask when another wave of wetness coats my hand.

"Yes… all for you," she pants and raises her hips, bracing herself on her elbows. Giving me the perfect view of her pussy.

I have to taste her.

Walking to the end of the table, I grip her waist, lifting her hips even more. Without hesitation, I lean in and drag my tongue through her sex, eliciting a feral groan from Ava. Fuck, she tastes amazing.

An unexplainable growl erupts from my throat as I devour her. I'm desperate to hear her scream my name, to beg me for sweet release.

"Yes, yesss…" she moans when I pause on her clit, sucking softly. Her body tenses and her legs tremble.

I pull away for just a moment, breathing my command against her. "Break for me, Angel. Come all over my face."

As if needing my permission, she lets go as soon as my tongue circles around her clit. Detonating like a firework on the Fourth of July as I keep up my ministrations. Her body shudders through it, and she moans from deep in her chest, gripping onto the sheet beneath her. With a groan, I fist my cock, which is longing to be inside of this woman.

Right.

Fucking.

Now.

Standing abruptly, I pull her legs down the table until her ass is leaning over the edge. She gasps at the sudden movement, earning her a swift little smack on her butt cheek.

Ava arches her back with a greedy whimper, pushing herself

against my thick cock that's barely contained behind my pants zipper. Fuck, I want her.

I undo my belt and my pants in a hurry. We lock eyes as she peers at me from over her shoulder, her beautiful gaze pleading for me.

Dragging my tip through her soaked pussy is a sensation I don't think I could articulate. I tease her entrance, pressing in just the tiniest bit before pulling out. Then I do it again, a little farther this time, feeling her stretch around me.

"Please," Ava begs.

Shit, what am I doing? I pull out suddenly, and Ava sags in defeat.

"Parker?" she questions, her voice filled with emotion.

She probably thinks I changed my mind. Little does she know how long I've dreamt of having her again, and I'm tired of fighting it. I want to claim her body, owning every inch of her. See her submit to my every whim and command.

"Shh, it's okay. I'm grabbing a condom," I say as I pull one out of my wallet.

Her body perks up at my words, even giving her butt a little wiggle. As if egging me on, and it does. I rip the wrapper and sheath my cock in record time.

"Is this what you want?" I ask, smacking my cock against her ass cheek.

"God, yes. Please, Parker," she pleads. But that's not what I want to hear.

My hand swats at the other cheek, and she mewls in response. "Please, Sir. I need you," she moans, realizing what I was waiting for. I needed her to be the one to jump first, to take us over this edge.

I sink inside her, relishing the feel of her around my cock once more. I knew we'd end up like this again. The pull I have toward her is something I never thought I would find in my lifetime. But fuck if it doesn't feel good to be here.

"You're so perfect, Av," I say as I thrust my hips into her, hard. At this point, I know I'm not going to last. It's been too long, and I have been aching to be inside of her.

"Ah, fuck…you feel so good," she groans. Fisting her hair, I pull her chest off the massage table, my grip firmly in place as I continue to fuck her. Beads of sweat trail down her back, and I lean over and lick up her spine.

Her pussy convulses from the sensation, and I can feel her orgasm approaching.

"Such a needy little brat you are," I taunt, while her body quakes beneath me. Squeezing my cock as I thrust into her.

My hand wraps around her front, fingers finding her clit while continuing deep strokes that have her moans on a constant loop.

"Come for me again," I demand, and she whimpers in response, but her body listens. Ava writhes under my touch as her release flows through her. The sound of my name from her lips as she breaks is like music to my ears.

I'm so fucking close.

Pulling myself out of her, I rip off the condom. She turns, stunned by my sudden retreat. But her lust-filled stare focuses in on my hand wrapped around my cock.

"On your knees, Angel. I'm going to come down that gorgeous throat of yours," I command, and she drops to her knees. Sitting impeccably still with her mouth open and tongue out, her eyes latch onto mine.

Fucking hell, she's absolutely perfect.

Within seconds, I'm coming on her tongue, moaning when her lips close around my cock and she sucks me dry. She eagerly swallows me down before popping off my length with a dazed and satisfied look on her face that makes me groan.

"That was…" I blow out a heavy breath, unable to put it into words. Staring at her as she remains on the floor in front of me, I'm in awe. My hand cups her cheek, trying to convey how amazing that truly was. I hope she can see what my eyes are trying to convey.

Ava smiles. "Thank you, Sir."

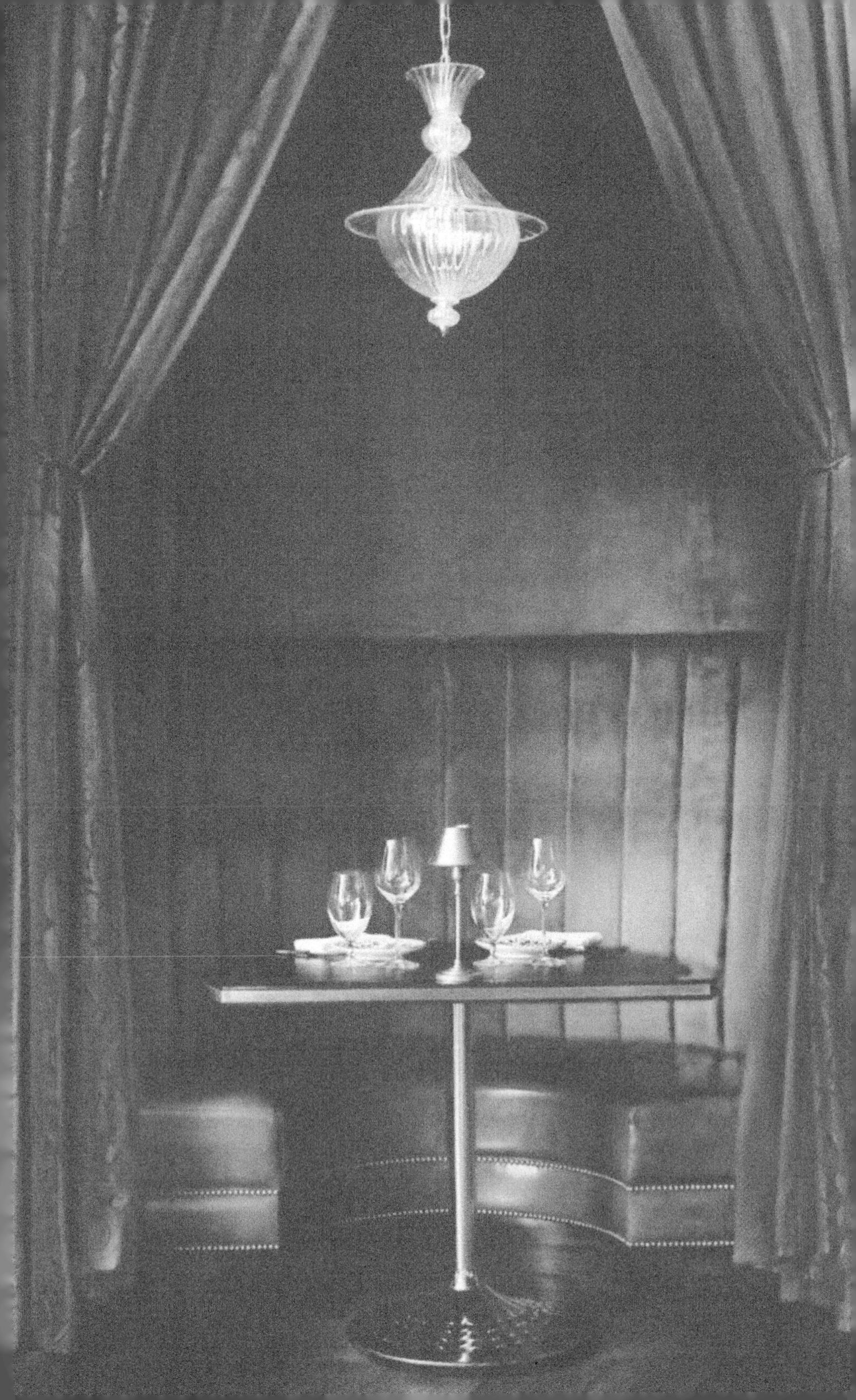

Sixteen

Ava

I run a brush through my wet hair while I peek around Parker's room. My heart warms when I see one picture on display of a young Parker and what I assume to be his parents. I was right; he does look so much like his mother, but his dad has those unmistakable grey eyes. My chest clenches at how happy they all appear in this picture. Parker knows greater loss than anyone else I've ever known, and my soul aches at the thought of what he feels when he looks at this picture.

His footsteps sound from the hallway, and I hop back into his bed, not wanting to trigger his mind to those memories tonight.

"Good thing I ordered a big box of these yesterday." Parker smirks, tossing my latest snack obsession on his bed.

I let out a little squeal. "How did you know?"

Heart-shield, activate immediately.

"Kinda hard to miss when you are always crunching on them."

"Oh, shut up…. And just admit you are sweet sometimes," I say, taking a bite into a Bare cinnamon apple crisp, exaggerating the crunching noise.

"Only sometimes?" he teases, getting back into his bed beside me.

"Yup, and other times, you're an arrogant asshole. Who turns me on way too much." Pretty apparent when we just finished round three of the night in his shower and decided we needed a midnight snack since we barely ate dinner.

He growls, pulling me into his rock-hard cock. There's only the thin pair of boxer briefs between us and his possessive hold on me.

"Oh, and possessive…which, speaking of, you didn't seem too jealous of your massage therapist's hands all over me. I was pretty shocked when I walked in and saw a male."

He lets out a low chuckle. "I don't think I realized how jealous of a person I was until you came to work for me."

I try analyzing that statement, wondering if he means he wasn't that way with his ex. Or maybe her infidelity caused him to be that way.

Rightfully so.

Parker places a mind-melting kiss on my lips before pulling back. "You are one hundred percent right that I would not want another straight man's hands on you, even if he was someone I trusted."

He may have never known he was jealous, but I didn't realize how hot that could be. I love knowing even though I may never fully have Parker, I have that piece of him. A piece that wants all of me to himself.

"Good thing I know without a doubt that you are not Bennett's type. I've known him for many years. He's actually married to my barber, Jeff."

Oh… ohhh, that makes so much sense.

A comfortable silence settles between us as we both eat our snacks. It starts to sink in that maybe I should get up now and go to my room. That way, he doesn't get all weird on me. For my own self-preservation, I'd rather be the one to kick myself out.

Placing my empty snack bag on the side table, I roll onto him, kissing his cheek, forehead, and then his lips. "Thank you for everything tonight. It's always amazing with you."

But when I go to pull away, he does the opposite, holding me close. "Wait, are you trying to leave right now?"

"Well, kinda. I figured it was what you would want, and I'm okay with that too. Less complicated." I swallow thickly, trying to make myself believe everything I'm saying.

He seems to think about that for a minute. "But I wanted to make you come again," Parker says, grinding up into me.

"I'll never say no to that." I swivel my own hips and feel him still hard beneath me. "One more round, and then I'll return to my bed."

His cloudy eyes trail to my lips. "Sounds perfect." Parker's tone is questionable, but I don't read too much into it as he squeezes my ass and our tongues meld together.

The chemistry and desire never waver between us. His lips and hands on me are all it takes to have me soaking wet against his boxers.

I bite his bottom lip. "Can I ride your cock, Sir?"

Parker doesn't respond with words. Instead, he reaches between us, pushing his boxers down enough to let his cock free. My mouth salivates at the sight. I'm more than eager to have him raw again. We had the condom discussion earlier before round three in the shower.

Birth control… check.

Both clean… check.

I slide my already dripping wet pussy along his hard length, teasing the tip, but never letting it slip too far in. Grinding my clit against him, I let out a moan.

Parker growls as he grabs his cock in his hand, pushing inside of me. I groan at the stretch of him filling me up. Every time he is inside of me, it's an unexplainable euphoria I've never felt before. And each time, it's becoming more and more evident that it's not going away any time soon.

"There he is," I whimper as his hips move in tandem with mine. "I knew you wouldn't let me have control for too long."

He reaches up, tweaking my nipple, causing my body to ripple with more pleasure. "Don't worry, if I was your Dom, I'd give you permission to ride my cock whenever you want."

That only spurs me on. I bounce up and down on his cock, and his thumb finds my clit, pressing into it with just the right amount of pressure. Running my fingers through the longer strands of hair on top his head, I tug as my mouth finds his. I lose all control when my orgasm hits, and he drinks in my every moan.

Gripping my hips, he kisses me through each wave of bliss. Only when my body comes back down from its high does he break away.

"Spin around. I want to see that ass now," he demands.

Yes, Sir.

I flip around, straddling his lap. When I look back, I see Parker's cock wet with my cum in his hand, his other squeezing my ass. He rubs the tip against the tight untouched hole, and I reach back, spreading myself apart for him to see.

"I can't wait to fucking take you here."

I can't either.

"When?" My voice is so low, I barely recognize the sound.

"We need to work up to it, but I promise you, I'm going to. No need to worry, little brat. I'll have my cock in every part of you." I want that, I want him…everywhere.

I whimper, and he slides into me, causing me to moan even louder.

"Fuck, that pussy is already clenching me again."

"Yes, yes. I want it so bad," I say, pushing back into, my fingertips gripping his muscular thighs as I move up and down on his thick length.

He smacks my ass, caressing the sting as I whimper. "Yes, Angel, bounce that ass up and down. You are fucking killing me right now."

"Look at me," he commands, and I peek over my right shoulder, meeting his dark gaze.

Parker lifts his thumb to his mouth, wetting it, and I don't stop grinding down onto him, so close to my next release.

He presses the tip of his thumb into my ass, and my whole-body shudders. The intrusion feels so dirty yet so fucking right, and I know without a doubt I will be begging this man to take me there when he thinks I'm ready.

"Now apply that same pressure to your clit. I want to feel you quivering around my cock again."

I do as he says, riding his dick like a madwoman. I'm scared this will be my last fix and worried I'll never have enough of it. Of him.

"Come for me," he growls with another smack to my ass, and I completely fall apart, my eyes watering from the force of my release. Parker follows behind, and I swear his moans push me to the brink again as my body shakes and tingles.

And just like every other time tonight, he places a gentle kiss to my lips when we finish. It gives me butterflies unlike anything else. Which is exactly why a few minutes later, I'm searching his room for my clothes, knowing it's what's best for me.

"Your clothes are in the living room from your massage," he says, tossing me one of his black undershirts. "Here, wear this."

I know this is fucking dangerous for my mental sanity. It may just be a piece of clothing, but every female on this planet knows it's so much more than that. But that doesn't stop me from letting him tug it down over my body. And it sure as hell doesn't stop me from taking in the way he devours me in it.

"Thank you for tonight. I better get some sleep or else my boss will be very unhappy with me tomorrow."

He laughs at that, and with a smirk, he says, "I'm pretty sure your boss will be anything but unhappy with you."

I'm so thrilled he isn't freaking out or acting weird. Maybe some of that armor clad wall may finally be coming down.

"How will I ever repay you for the guest room full of black cat hair and all these orgasms?" I tease, before I walk out of his room.

Parker seems to think about something, and then he says, "Well, I do have a favor to ask of you."

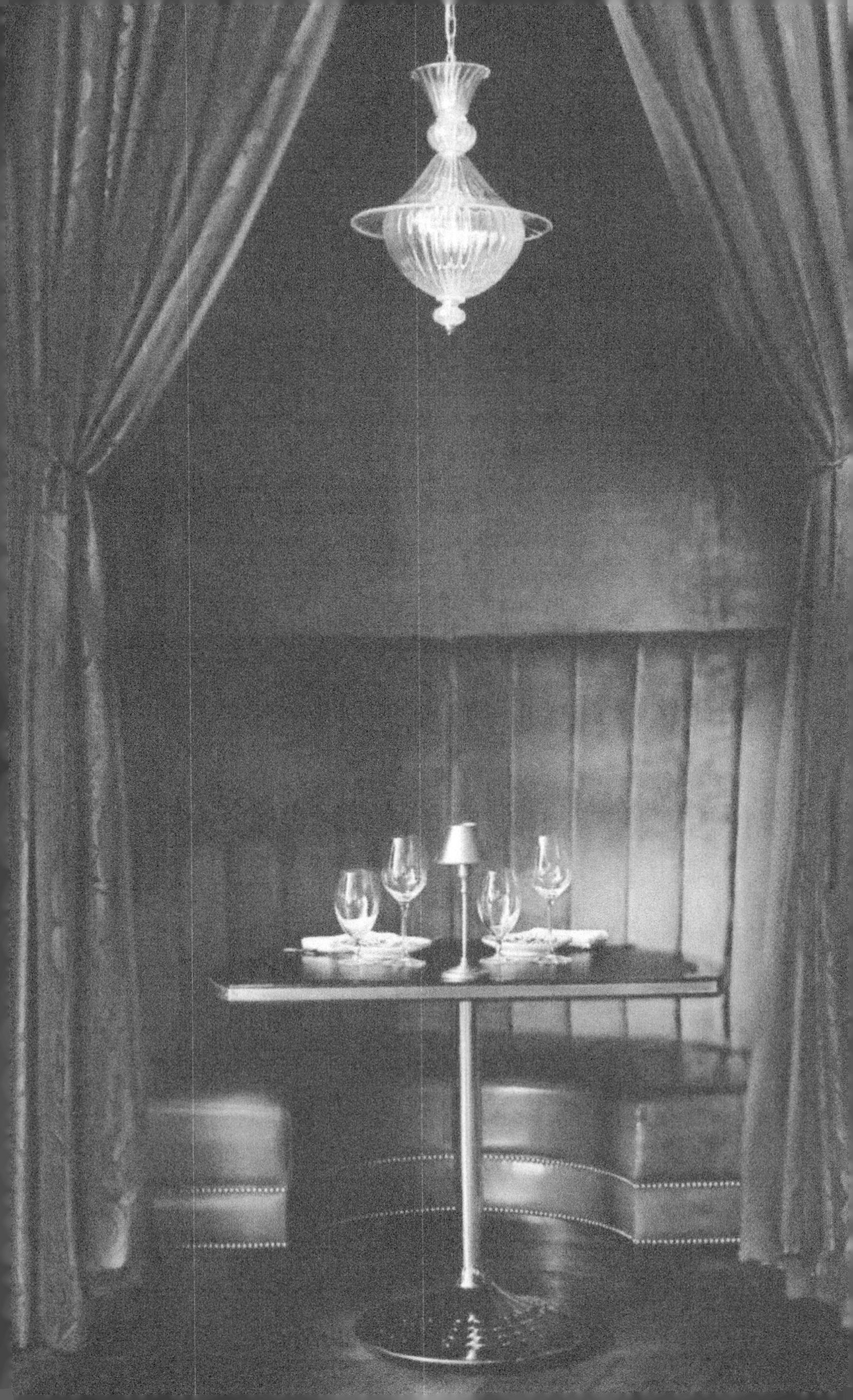

Seventeen

Parker

I peek at my opened office door every few seconds, waiting for her arrival. I knew the minute I truly gave in to my desire for Ava, this would happen. I'd want her every second of every day.

Her asking me to join her at her grandparents' house was just another step in the direction I thought I would never head again. I haven't given her my answer just yet, but I know damn well I will. I'm honored to meet the people she holds so dear. Not only was it a shock that she wanted me to go, but the fact that the idea of meeting her family didn't have me running for the hills is something I still need to digest.

After our first encounter at Masqued, she made me feel so out of control that it was a reckless decision to allow myself to have her again.

Too many negative things have happened in my life that I wasn't in control of involving people I care about, and I refuse to let that ever happen again. Which is exactly why I played the asshole card for so long with Ava. But the more and more our lives have tangled together, the harder it's become to stay away.

I've never been so attracted to another person. Our chemistry and the way we read the other's desires are unexplainable and incomparable to anything I've ever experienced. She has also become an unlikely friend over the past month, and I know that will make it even harder when she moves on from whatever this is.

I was so fucking stupid to not give in to this long ago. She made it clear she understood it would just be sex between us, but I couldn't believe it back then. Couldn't see past my own fucked-up issues.

Speaking of issues; she's even agreed to be my date to the wedding with my distant family as a favor to me. Even though she owes me absolutely nothing, already giving me more than I probably deserve from her. I know it's going to be one hell of a day being amongst all of them, but having her beside me might be the crutch I need to get through it all.

The past couple of weeks, she's been in my bed more than her own. Although every morning, I wake up to cold sheets beside me. I'm choosing to ignore the fact she feels the need to escape in the middle of the night, along with the disappointment that fills me.

My ears perk up when I hear her voice in the lobby of my office.

"He isn't expecting you," I hear Tasha's distant voice snark.

"He is the one who called me," Ava clips back, and I am on my feet, not liking Tasha's tone with her.

"I don't believe you, Ava. You need to know your place. Sit down, and I'll go check with Mr. Cole to see if he even has time to talk to you. Next time, follow the correct protocol, which is contacting me ahead of time."

Ava's gaze zones in, and I see her contemplating the venom she wants to spew in my assistant's direction, but I speak first.

"No, Tasha, you need to know your place. I don't expect you to talk like that to anyone coming into this office to see me, much less Miss Pierce. Do you understand me?" I ask, loud and clear, feeling Ava's attention land on me.

Tasha nods.

"If that's an issue for you, then we've got a problem, so tell me now, because she will be treated with nothing but respect from you. Clear?"

She nods again. "Yes, sir."

I see the way Ava's eyes narrow at her, her lips twisting, trying to hold back what she wants to say, so I say it for her.

"Don't call me sir. Mr. Cole will do for you, Tasha."

She lowers her gaze, sitting back down as Ava smiles a big, satisfied grin and walks toward me.

I wave for her to enter my office, shutting the door behind us, thankful for the automatic locking mechanism.

Ava's hazel eyes, dark with lust, find mine. She's turned on by the way I stood up for her.

"Put your hands on my desk," I command, and like the good little brat she is, she listens.

"Now you're really trying to make her hate me," she says, looking over her shoulder.

I move to stand beside her. "I don't give a fuck about her, and neither should you."

"So, you haven't fucked her?"

My eyebrows pinch together. "Why would you think that?"

"She just seems awfully jealous of me for no reason."

I trail my finger down the spine of her dress. "There are so many *reasons*, Ava, and none of them having to do with me fucking her. I've never even considered it."

Smacking her ass, she whimpers.

"Are you ready to shut up and let me make you come?"

She nods quickly, biting her lip as she tries to hold back a smile. Standing behind her, I push the black dress she's wearing over her hips. I have thought about nothing but this since I saw her parading around the hotel in this dress earlier today.

Fuck, what a sight.

She looks like an angel and acts like a brat… The definition of sexy as sin.

Slowly pulling her thong down, my fingers trace gently over the inside of her thighs.

"Step out," I demand. And stuff her thong into my pocket.

I tap the inside of her thigh, already feeling her wetness spreading there. My hard cock twitches against my zipper. "Now spread your legs apart."

"Do you want to come, Av?" I ask, adjusting myself, my cock so ready to take her. Once I felt her raw, the obsession only grew, and my dick knows what it wants. *What I want.*

She mewls in anticipation, pushing back into me.

I run my nose up her neck. Barely licking the shell of her ear, I whisper, "You know what I want to hear."

"Yes, Sir. Please make me come."

I drop to my knees behind her, gripping her ankles and spreading her legs wider. Burying my nose in her sweet cunt, I take a long, slow taste of her that has her gasping. My fingertips dig into her cheeks, putting her ass and pussy on full display for me.

"I see your pussy clenching; she wants more so bad." I groan at the sight, swearing I could come from just looking at her like this, with her essence lingering on my lips.

"So bad," she says breathily, wiggling her ass in my face. My tongue goes back to her slit, desperate for another taste. She grinds back into me, trying to find that relief she so desperately wants.

Losing my grip on her ass cheeks, I reach up, sticking two of my fingers in her mouth. "I know my little brat likes her mouth full of cock when she comes… Next time."

She moans around my fingers, the sounds spurring me on as I pull in and out of her mouth, letting my other fingers slide inside of her soaking-wet pussy. Rubbing on her G-spot, I get her closer to seeing stars.

"Fuck, that's so good. I'm about to come." She whimpers as I retract my fingers, moving my face back between her legs. My tongue finds her clit, applying the perfect amount of pressure as I flick and swirl until she's trembling.

"Yessss. Right there, baby."

It's the first time she's ever called me that, and fuck, if I don't love the slip-up.

A knock at the door startles us both, interrupting the fantasy in my head of her calling me that daily.

"Parker, I'm here a little early." The familiar male voice is muffled.

"Seriously? Is that Logan?" Ava asks, her head whipping toward the door.

"Yes," I growl, pushing her back down. "But he can wait. You aren't leaving until you come all over my face."

"I'm finishing my lunch. I'll be out to get you in a few," I shout.

"Okay," he says, but I don't give a fuck if it's okay or not.

I go back to her cunt, pressing my tongue onto her swollen nub, my nose wet from her juices. She swivels her hips in the same motion my tongue moves against her, creating the perfect friction she needs to come.

Ava feels her orgasm approaching and attempts to cover her mouth. Moving my thumb to apply the same pressure as my tongue, I reach for her elbow, pulling it away with my other hand, "Let him hear what he will never fucking have," I say, my breath blowing over her pussy before I start licking again. My thumb and tongue move in tandem until she falls completely over the edge. *And that she does.* So fucking hard and beautiful, like always.

Her torso collapses onto my desk, and I place a kiss on her ass cheek. "You are perfect, Angel."

Tugging her dress back down over her hips, I help Ava stand on shaky legs, running my fingers through her hair. I want him to know what just happened in this room, but I know it would embarrass her, which is the only reason I help her look less freshly fucked.

"What about my panties?" she asks, reaching for where a sliver of the lace peeks out of my pocket. I wave my index finger at her. "Nope, these are mine now. Since you are done for the day, you don't need them anyways."

She laughs lightly, giving me a playful smack on the chest.

I want to pack up and leave with her, but I have things I need to handle here at the office. One of them just interrupted my favorite meal.

I kiss her on the top of her head, apparently a new habit of mine. Her hand goes to my belt loop, and she whispers, "I promise to take care of you later, Sir."

Fucking hell. I didn't think my cock could get any harder. "I'll see you at home," I say, walking her out before I fuck her right against this door for him to hear.

Ava acknowledges Logan quickly, and he watches her strut toward the elevator. I take a minute to get myself together, let him stare, because I know he'll never have her.

I address Tasha first. "So you have an issue with Ava coming up here when she isn't on my calendar, but you allow Logan to attempt to interrupt my meeting with her when you know he isn't scheduled for another thirty minutes?"

She looks to Logan with a grimace before answering me. "I told him you were in there with Miss Pierce, but he insisted."

"I'm sure he did," I say, leveling Logan with my gaze.

I head back into my office without a word, and after a few moments, he walks through the open door speaking before I even have a chance to sit down. "I knew you wanted her from the minute you walked into the bar that night after we hired her."

"First off, *we* didn't hire her. *I* did," I say, pointing to my chest.

"And you are wrong. I wanted her long before then. But I stood back and let you have your chance with her. You are the one who fucked that up all by yourself."

Logan's quiet, pondering how to respond to what we both know is the truth.

A huge part of me wants to tell him he never stood a chance with Ava. There's no way he could please her the way I can, but contrary to what most think, I'm not that much of an asshole. Even if it's facts. Period.

"And since I hear you like Tasha so much, I'm sending her with you on this new project in Jersey."

"What?" Fear flashes in his eyes. He doesn't want to date Tasha; he just wants to get his dick wet, and he knows them working this closely won't allow him to lie and blow her off so easily.

"Yup, it appears I don't need her services as my assistant anymore, and you will need some extra hands down in Jersey."

"This is bullshit and all because of Ava."

"I'd shut your mouth. I don't care who your grandfather is; I would tread lightly with me, Logan. Jersey is a good opportunity for you, so take what you get."

Logan doesn't say anything else, and I excuse him so I can finish up my work for the day.

I type up a formal email, letting Tasha and HR know of her future assignment. When I press send, Ava is my first thought because, somehow, I know she will be happy with this decision.

A text comes through from her. The thrill seeing her name

causes me should be highly concerning, but the image on my screen has me completely ignoring that thought.

Her in my bathtub, bubbles to the brim. The suds hiding most of her breasts, showcasing enough to tease me. Her beautiful face with that mischievous, bratty grin has my cock hardening against my slacks.

> **BRAT**
> Have I told you lately how much I love being your roomie? There are so many perks... this bathtub being the BIGGEST one.

Suddenly, work can wait. I'm going home.

Babes Group Chat

QUINN

Listen to your voicemail... The girls helped me babble the happy birthday song and it was so cute! Hope you have a great day. Only two more years till thirty!

SLOAN

Happy Birthday to our beautiful blonde bestie! Love you times a million babe! Have the best day, Aves!

SLOAN

Don't forget to let me know a night you are free for margs next week, it doesn't have to be Friday.

ME

Love you girls so much! Thank you! And Q, 30 doesn't scare me

ME

I will look at my schedule asap Lo. I may recruit you to help me find a dress for that wedding I agreed to go to with Parker. I'll call you once we get back in the city.

QUINN

Shit it certainly scares me! Give Grandma a big squeeze from me and tell Grandpa he still owes me that dance.

SLOAN

Aw yes tell them hello and we miss them. I still can't believe you are taking Parker out east to meet them.

QUINN

You know your grandma is going to be planning the wedding right??

ME

I know but he doesn't have family like you all do. He needs this. They will be good for his soul.

SLOAN

You sound very invested in his soul.

QUINN

Yeah Av... what happened to this being a dick investment??

ME

It's still a dick investment but he's my friend too.

ME

Never thought I'd say that but it's true.

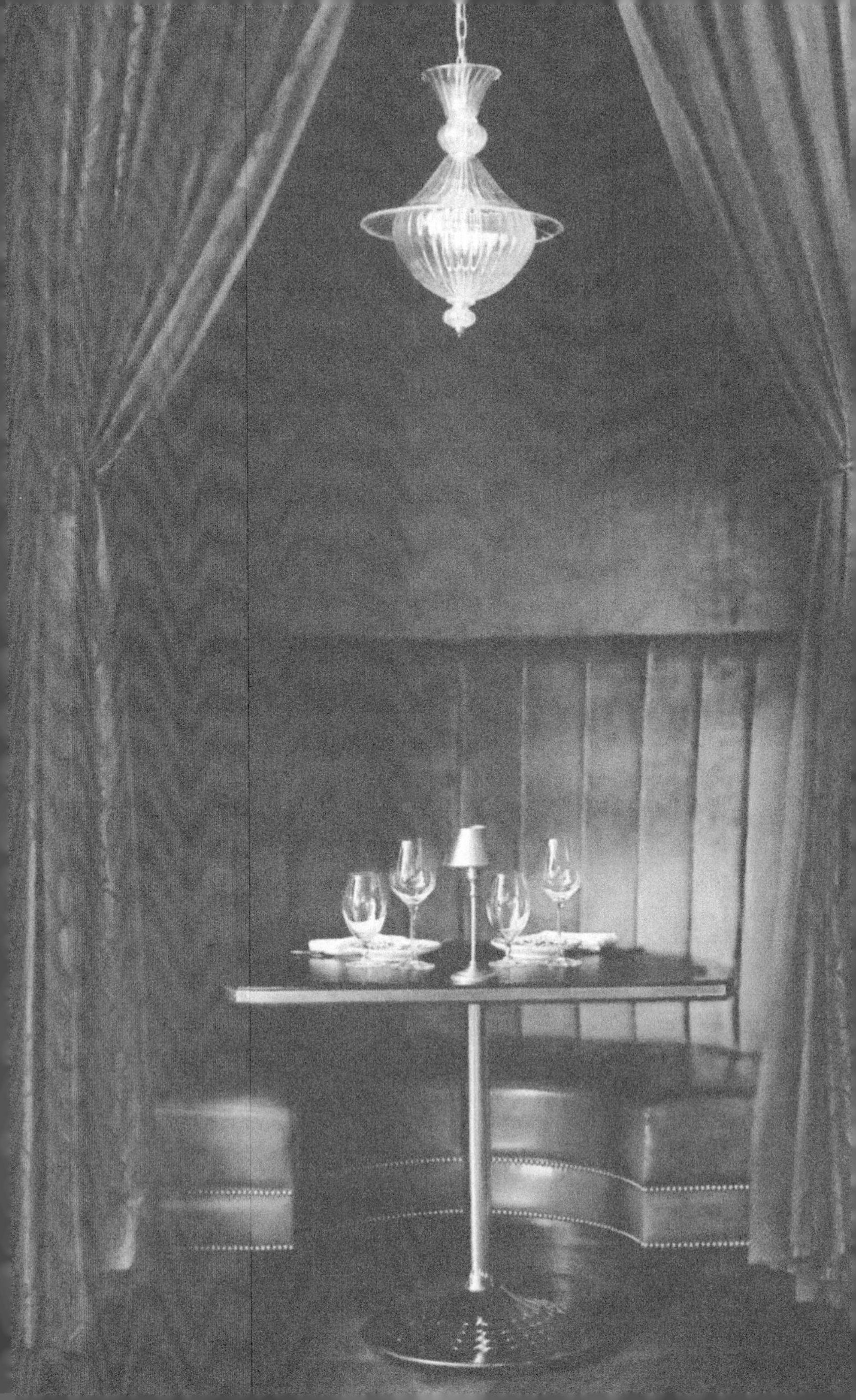

Eighteen

Ava

"So that..." my grandma whispers, pointing from the kitchen toward the den where Parker and my grandfather are sitting, "is your boss? And the man you've been living with?"

"Yes, Grandma, now pick your jaw up off the floor." I rub my thumb over her chin. "I think you've got some drool right there."

"Ava Marie Pierce. He's beautiful, I can't help it. I'm old, not dead," she says, swatting me with a kitchen towel she used to pull the freshly baked cake out of the oven.

"There is no way that man is only your friend."

I blush at her accusation. I've always been very close with my grandmother, but telling her he bangs me six ways to Sunday on the daily isn't quite the type of conversation I want to have with her.

"Don't get your hopes up, Grandma. You are correct, we aren't just friends, but we also won't ever be more. So don't go picking out great grandkids' names or anything."

"Hmmm. No wonder you didn't want your parents to know where you were staying." Her eyes are still narrowed in on me, trying to read me like she's always been able to do so easily.

I feel bad that I asked her to lie to my mom about my current living situation, but I didn't want their intrusive questions and accusations. Especially not when I'm having my own dreadful thoughts about what me moving out of Parker's penthouse in a few weeks will mean for us.

"You'd be proud of me. I did answer her call earlier," I offer with a shrug.

"I'm glad, love. How was the call?"

"Typical. She wished me a happy birthday and brought up letting them throw me a big party full of all their associates. I politely declined, said thank you, and that was that." Basically, she loves to use any excuse to show off all their money, even if that means using her daughter who she barely knows anymore.

She shakes her head. "I'm not sure where your grandfather and I went wrong with her. She was always shown affection as a child, but at some point, money replaced love, and the change in her was irrevocable."

I'll never understand either. It's hard to believe she and my aunt grew up in the same household. But I've come to terms with the fact I'll never get that type of unconditional love from my parents. I think deep down, they are okay with it too. Sometimes I wonder if they even wanted a child.

"Aunt Samantha called and screamed happy birthday at the top of her lungs." I think back to Parker's face when he heard that on the car ride over here. He was so upset with me that I hadn't told him today was my birthday.

Grandma chuckles. "Of course she did. I miss her so much. Did she tell you she's planning a trip home later this summer?"

"She did, and I can't wait," I beam.

"We better go save your *friend*. There is no telling what crazy stories your grandfather is telling him."

We both take a few steps, and I stop her. "Don't ask him about his family, okay?"

I see the sadness cast over her face as she takes in my words. "His parents both passed away years back. He's an only child."

She clutches her chest. "That breaks my heart." I nod because it breaks mine too, and I find myself constantly wanting to protect him from the hurt.

"But thank you for telling me. I would never want to bring up something that would cause him pain."

"I know," I say, squeezing her hand.

We find them both on the couch, legs spread, leaning toward the TV, watching as the Carolina Bulls play the Red Sox.

Boston's third baseman hits a double, and my grandfather, a die-hard Yankees' fan, cusses at the screen. When the Yankees aren't playing, he's an anybody-but-Boston fan. Especially when it's Eli's team.

You see a lot more Carolina Bulls jerseys roaming around Long Island these days.

"He wouldn't have gotten that hit on Eli," Parker says. "We played him in the college world series and Eli struck him out twice in game three... The guy's a prick. Next-level shit-talker."

My grandpa looks to him with wide eyes. "Wait, you played?"

"Yes, that's actually how I know Ava, through Eli."

I had explained all that to my grandma, but either she didn't tell him or, more than likely, he wasn't actually listening to her when she did.

"Oh, I thought you were her boss."

"He is." I speak up, making our presence known, walking around to sit on the opposite couch.

"Well shit, you should have started with him being Eli's friend, Av," he says to me before turning his attention back to Parker. "I've got a soft spot for that man's soon-to-be wife. Quinnie is my sweetheart. Love her like a granddaughter. Eli's sister, Sloan too. Those girls always look out for my Ava Marie."

I smile at his sentiment over my best friends. Just like I fell in love with their families, they bonded with my grandparents throughout college. Especially Quinn when she and I moved into their apartment after Sloan moved to Cali.

"Yes, that whole crew is one of a kind. And there is no doubt they all adore Ava. They are all lucky to have each other." My belly dips as he looks over to me with a soft smile.

"What position did you play?" my grandfather asks him.

"I played first base, but my senior year when I was rounding second, trying to beat the throw to third, my Achilles popped. A career-ending injury." I trace Parker's expressions as he tells my grandfather this. I think out of all the painful things in his life, this one seems to hurt the least. Maybe not physically, but definitely emotionally.

My grandfather's grimace turns into a smile. "Sorry to hear that, but sounds like you've found a successful career in the big city."

Parker nods before responding. "It's been a hell of a ride to get here, but I'm thankful for the success."

My grandfather isn't one to pry, but just in case, I interrupt the conversation before he proves me wrong. "Since the game's almost over and Eli isn't pitching, how about that walk?"

"Sure," Parker says, standing as I do.

"Parker, do you smoke cigars?" my grandpa asks.

"Of course. Cigars and whiskey are the way to my heart," he teases, and my grandpa smiles proudly.

"Well, meet me in the humidor after dinner. You'll fit right in."

"Speaking of dinner, what time are we eating?" I look to my grandma, who I'm sure has that all planned out.

"I was thinking seven. Sound good?"

Pssh, she was not thinking anything. She has all her i's dotted and all her t's crossed. My grandmother is a hostess extraordinaire. It may be for four people or four hundred, but she's got it handled either way.

"Perfect."

"Oh, and just so you know, I am having Chef Erika come out tonight. I just wanted everything to be perfect and these old hands aren't as quick anymore." *See, planned to perfection.*

I pull her in for a hug. "Anything is good with me. You know how much I love Chef Erika. But you will always be the yummiest cook in my eyes. So tonight, I get the best of both worlds since you baked me a cake." I give her a big kiss on the cheek.

"You guys enjoy your walk. Parker, be sure to bring me back a piece of sea glass. All my special guests have to leave one behind for me to remember them by." She points to the beautiful vases she has on display with lots of blues and greens… only one piece of sacred orange.

"I actually have some of these in storage that were my mom's. I'm sure she would love for someone to have them on display. I'll have to get them out and let Ava take a look." I wonder who helped him store all their belongings. I wonder if he has ever gone through everything. Did he keep only certain items? I want to know it all. I want to be the one sitting beside him as we sift through the items that bring him joy and he can tell me about all the happy memories.

My grandma smiles brightly. "I'd love that."

We step out onto their back patio, and he takes my hand, leading me down the steps onto the sand. Both of us are already dressed for a summer day outdoors.

I almost sputtered my coffee this morning when he walked out of his room, leg tat on full display in his shorts, navy linen shirt, and flip-flops. Something I didn't even think the man owned, but was utterly dreamy in, nonetheless.

To top it all off, right before we walked out the door, he ran his fingers through his hair, pushing the longer strands on the top back and slid a baseball hat on…*backwards.*

Parker's deep voice drags me from my thoughts. "They were exactly how you described them."

Wait, who? Oh yeah, my grandparents he just met. That damn backwards hat and leg tat.

"And how was that?" I manage to ask.

"Filthy rich, but so laid back they'd make a homeless man feel welcome at their table."

That honestly fits them to a tee.

I smile, nodding, thankful for them and the fact I'm more like them than my own parents. Money doesn't make you better, being a good human does.

"I can see why you have so many fond memories here. I'm really glad you convinced me to come out east with you, even though your tactics were completely unfair."

I giggle. "So you did or didn't enjoy the road head?"

He levels me with a stare. "You know I did."

Me too. Making him lose control is my new favorite thing.

It's hot out today, but the breeze coming off the ocean gives us the perfect summer temperature. We continue walking along in silence, meeting a few other beachcombers along the way. Parker picks up a few pieces of glass, examining them before tossing them back. Apparently, they aren't up to his standards.

We pass a couple with a beautiful German shepherd. "Aw, I wish Binx was here."

"Ava, you can't be serious, the cat would drown."

"Ugh! Don't say that," I say, smacking his arm. "He's come out to my grandparents for the weekend before with me."

"Please tell me you didn't try to bring him for a walk on the beach." He chuckles.

Parker tries to talk a lot of shit about my cat, but deep down, I think he loves him and just doesn't want to admit it. He even told me he'd have someone come check on Binx for the weekend, so I didn't have to pack him up and bring him out here, saying all these changes were probably stressful on him.

Now, does that sound like someone who hates my so-called demon cat?

"Of course not, but he did gain three pounds in one weekend from all the treats my grandma gave him."

"That will probably be me this weekend," he says, patting his sickening washboard abs. "That cake smelled delicious."

"I didn't say you could have any of my cake," I taunt, and his narrowed eyes flick to me.

"It's the least you can do since you didn't tell me today was your fucking birthday. I still can't believe that. I wouldn't have made you work so hard to get me out here. I was already going to say yes anyways."

"Well, I didn't want you to feel some type of weird obligation to get me something."

He stops, peering at me for a second with a look I can't decipher, and before I know it, he's tossing me over his shoulder. "I'll get you something, alright. I should throw your ass in this water for not telling me," Parker says, running ankle-deep into the water.

"No, Parker, please! No!"

I hate the feeling of wet clothes against my skin; it's a major cringe of mine.

A deep chuckle leaves his chest. "Those are words I never thought I'd hear from you, Av."

"Oh, shut up and put me down," I say with a huff, smacking his ass.

"Okay," he says, and I let out a squeal as he pretends to let me slip from his grasp again.

Slapping my ass, he says, "And I'm the one who does the ass-smacking around here, brat."

"Yeah, yeah…"

"Holy shit, that's what I've been searching for." He stands me upright in the shallow water beside him.

"What, what?" I ask as I look around, confused by the sudden shift.

Parker bends down, grabbing something, and I see it right as the water washes the sand away from it again and he picks it up.

"Orange sea glass," he whispers, like he's truly respecting the holy grail of sea glass.

"It's beautiful and unique." Stepping closer, I trace my finger across the slick surface. "Is that why all the others weren't good enough?"

Parker glances from me to the piece of glass in his hands and emotion passes over his features, like he's realizing something for the first time. The way he looks at me is enough to have my stomach fluttering every damn time.

He swallows thickly. "Yes, exactly." His voice sounds huskier than it should over sea glass, and now I'm wondering if this is about the shiny orange treasure at all.

Looking back to the glass, he clears his throat, regaining his footing. "I didn't want to be like all the others. I wanted my piece to stand out like the single orange piece in the vase with all the blues and greens."

I love that he wants this small token to always serve as a reminder of him in my grandparents' house. A little pang in my chest fires off at the fact it will also be a constant memento of my time with Parker, but in all reality, he won't be easy to forget, no matter how brief we are.

"My grandmother is going to be ecstatic with this find. You'll be her new favorite." I smile, remembering the day she added the first, and before now, the only piece of orange glass to her collection.

"I feel like I'm about to get brownie points." He smiles at me, and I love how carefree he appears right now, toes in the sand, linen shirt opened and blowing in the breeze. "Better yet, I bet she'll make you share your cake with me."

I reach up and twist his nipple. "We will see about that."

"You little brat," I hear him growl, and I take off running down the beach. He catches up to me way too easily. "You are lucky I have this prized possession in my hand, or I'd really toss you in that ocean."

"Whatever," I say playfully, rolling my eyes.

"Be glad their house is big; I'd hate for them to hear their sweet little granddaughter getting her ass spanked tonight… because it's guaranteed to happen."

"Promise?" I bite my lip as I smirk up at him.

He leans down, tugging my lip from between my teeth with his own. His bite sinks into me just slightly, but then his lips are on mine, kissing me thoroughly, making my body hotter than any summer sun ever could.

When we finally pull back for air, he whispers, "Is that promise enough?"

"Yeah, P," I whisper, and he takes my hand in his, interlocking our fingers. My toes tingle with the thought that he just full-on kissed me in public.

What would a life with Parker outside of closed doors be like?

Too good to be true.

"Parker," my grandmother gasps. "You sweet, sweet man. You outdid yourself with this." Taking the orange sea glass into her hands gently, she examines its uniqueness.

"It's my new favorite!" she declares, shrugging her shoulders toward me. "Sorry, Ava. I'll always love yours too."

"Wait, you are the one who found the other piece of orange she has?" He grins, eyes searching mine as my lips twist to the side.

I'm not sure why I didn't tell him on the beach. Maybe my stupid little heart was whispering it was cosmic, and I was scared he would ruin that thought for me.

"I will admit, I have a few others in my bedroom, but they were all found by Frederick and I. Ava was the first person to ever find one and gift it to me for my vase," Grandma says, placing his in the vase next to mine. The bright orange pops against the turquoise beside it.

"She was about seventeen and had a rough week, so she came to spend some time with us. She took lots of walks that weekend. I assumed she was meeting up with one of the boys down the beach who she used to hang out with. Until she brought home that piece of orange sea glass with tears in her eyes."

I remember that day like it was yesterday. That was the week I truly realized my parents had no care in the world for my wants and dreams in life. At that time, I wasn't even sure they loved me. Now I know their love just comes with terms and conditions.

"Again, at first, I thought she was crying over the young boy she had spent some time with earlier that summer."

Ew, heck no. That only consisted of about three dates, which were beyond ick, and I haven't seen him since. I can't believe I am sitting here, letting her tell Parker all this.

"But that was the weekend I took my blinders off and came to terms with the fact my daughter wasn't the mother my sweet Ava needed," she says, pulling me in for a hug. "Ava has a huge heart, and she deserved so much more than she got from them growing up."

I swallow the emotion threatening to surface from how vulnerable I felt at that time of my life.

"Why did the sea glass make you cry?"

Parker's question surprises me, but I answer honestly. "That little piece of washed-up glass brought me so much happiness during a time of turmoil when I felt so unloved by two people who were supposed to love me always. And that's when it hit me. Money doesn't buy you love; it doesn't buy you happiness." And right then, at seventeen years old, I knew that was a motto I would live by. "So I came in, told my grandmother everything, even that I didn't care what my parents said; I was going to NYU when I graduated at the end of that year and I wasn't going to do what gave me prestige. I was going to do what made me happy."

Parker doesn't say anything as his eyes trace my face in wonder, almost like he is trying to imagine that upset seventeen-year-old girl having her teenage epiphany.

The doorbell rings, breaking the spell.

"Ahh, that must be Chef Erika. Parker, prepare to be wowed tonight."

His eyes stay locked on mine. "I've already been wowed," he says so low, I almost don't hear it. My stomach flips and I find myself hoping this isn't the last time he looks at me like this.

"Thank you both for dinner. The seafood pasta was phenomenal. She truly is a talent," I say to both my grandparents, who, as always, went above and beyond to make sure my birthday was very special.

"Erika is doing bigger events, even weddings now. I was so glad we were able to get her here tonight," Grandma says, just as she sets my strawberry cake in front of me.

It smells impeccable.

"That's awesome for her! And speaking of weddings, we will be out here in a few weeks for a wedding, so maybe I can twist Parker's arm to stop by and see you guys again."

"There will be no twisting. I'll be sad if we don't stop," he responds genuinely, and my chest warms at the smile he sends my way.

"So, you are going as Parker's date?" Of course, that's all she would focus on.

"Somehow I convinced her to take pity on me," Parker teases, squeezing my thigh under the table, and I rub my thumb over his hand.

"This is all so exciting. And you better stop by, or I will hunt both of you down," my grandma says, beaming at us.

"Yes, you two should stay with us. We have enjoyed having you both. Trust me, Parker, once I show you the humidor room, you'll want to come back. I have a special reserve I am going to pull out just for you," my grandpa says. I love how welcoming they have both been to Parker.

"We will definitely be back. Even if Ava doesn't invite me, I'll stop by." Parker laughs, but somehow, I believe him.

My grandmother starts lighting my candles. "Let's sing this

birthday girl her song so you boys can get to your smokes and whiskey."

I blow out my candles, making a wish with one person in mind. One I'm not sure I knew I wanted so badly until today.

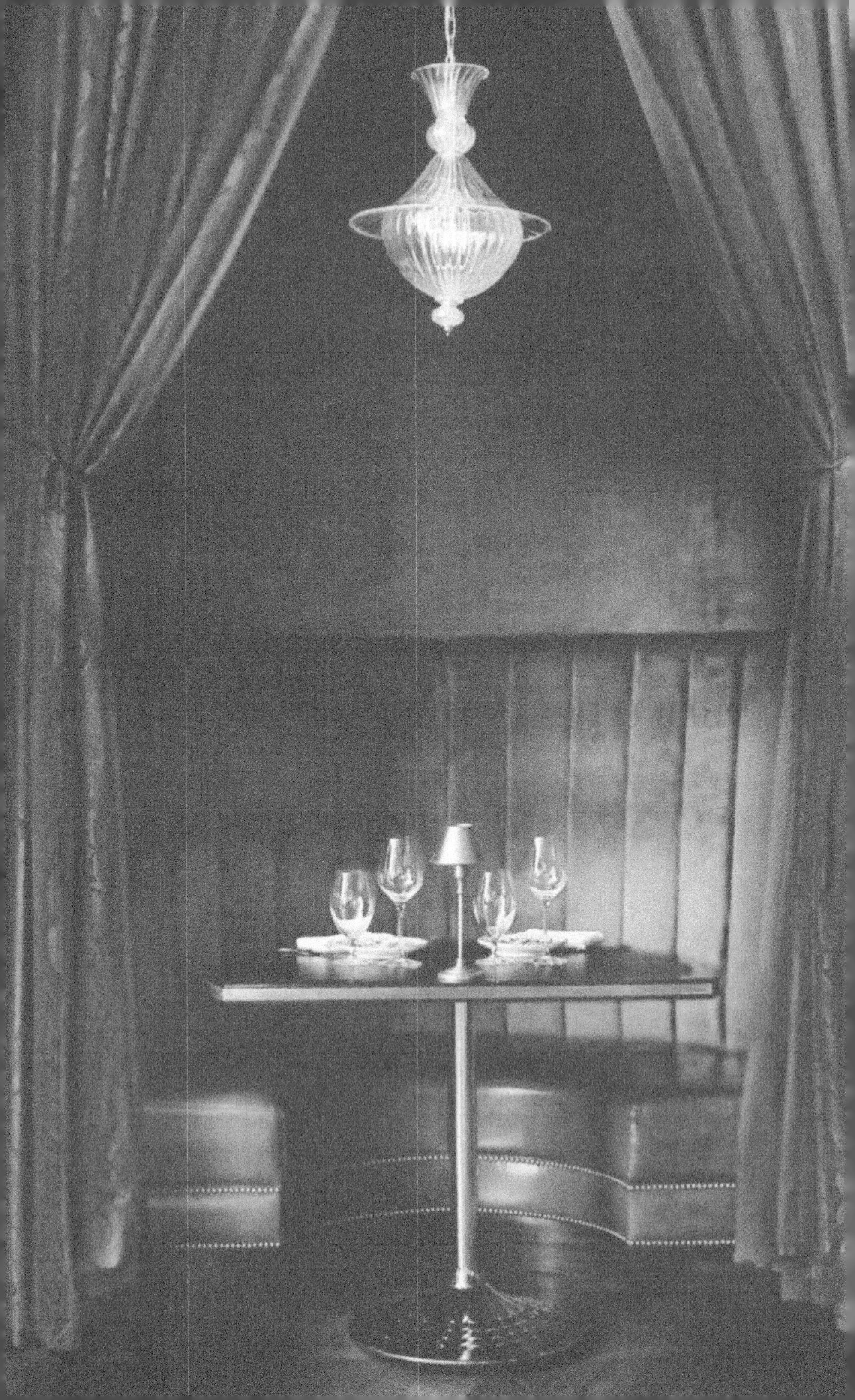

Nineteen

Parker

"Now this is how you watch a baseball game," Blossom says while bouncing Addy on her lap, with her boyfriend Dalton seated next to her.

It's been a while since the girls have been able to spend time with her. You should have heard the squeals when Blossom and Dalton walked into the suite. She used to be Sloan's PA before she moved back to New York. So like me, they have become an extension of their friendship group over the years.

"It really is," Wes agrees, handing me a beer.

"Yeah, thanks again for doing all this," Sloan adds from behind us in the private sky box.

"Of course. I can't wait to watch Eli kill it out there," I say with a smile.

"Pshhh. Some Yankees fan you are," Ava chides from beside me. My little brat, always trying to get a rise from me.

I raise my hand to my heart. "I am forever a Yankees fan, but I'm also a huge fan of my best friend. I think one trumps the other."

"Hell yeah! That's what I'm talking about," Quinn cheers with Sophie in her arms. She then turns her gaze to Ava. "See, he can compromise… I don't know what you're talking about."

Ava's eyes go wide in shock, and a devious smirk spreads across Quinn's face. As if knowing what she just did.

Turning my body to face her, I quirk an eyebrow in question. "Uncompromising, huh?"

A gorgeous blush creeps up her cheeks as I feel our friends discretely watching our exchange. She licks her lips and tilts her defiant chin.

I lean in closer so only she can hear me. "I thought you like it when I take control, Angel. I might have to remind you of such things tonight." Backing away, I watch as her breathing becomes heavier, and her pupils dilate with the knowledge of what I'm going to do to her body later.

Changing the subject quickly, Ava directs her attention to Blossom. "I'm so glad you guys were able to make it. Feels like forever since I've seen you."

"I know! When Quinn mentioned the Bulls coming to New York and all of you were going to be together, I knew we had to get our asses to the East Coast. Bummed about the parentals not being here this weekend, though. I was looking forward to their shenanigans."

"Ugh, I know, they were totally bummed too. They booked this Mediterranean cruise over a year ago. When they heard we were all doing this, my mom was literally about to cancel their trip," Quinn says.

"Oh, that's crazy. I'm sure they're having the time of their lives there. I can picture it now," Blossom adds with a bright smile and a wink.

"I'd rather not picture it…" Sloan teases her former assistant. "But I'm glad you both decided to make New York one of your destinations during your travels. Feels like you have been everywhere but here these last six months."

"I wouldn't miss this reunion for the life of me. Besides, I've been dying to squish these little munchkins," Blossom says, pulling Addy in for a tight squeeze.

Addy squeaks, and then climbs over into Dalton's lap, seemingly fixated on his shiny watch.

It's still early in the game, so we have the time to catch up and just relax before Eli is sent in. Quinn eventually sets up a pop-up pen for the girls to play in while we eat and have a few beers.

"Thank you," Ava whispers to me as she leans in.

"For what?" I ask, hoping she means the three orgasms from this morning. Although she already proved how thankful she was.

"For setting this all up. I miss them all. Seems like life is moving so fast. I miss these moments," Ava responds honestly.

I place a reassuring hand on her leg and squeeze gently. "I agree. Need to make time for the important things in life." And I know without a doubt her brain will be dissecting my every word, but I mean it. Having Ava around has opened my eyes to how much I've been missing out on… How little I've actually been living, as opposed to just going through the motions.

Once again, I feel the eyes of our friends observing our every move, and quite frankly, I don't give a shit. I'm not sure what Ava told her friends of our situationship, but if I know these girls like I think I do, she's told them everything…down to every orgasm.

As she places her hand on top of mine, I whisper to her, "Not sure if you noticed, but we have an audience."

"Oh, I've noticed." She chuckles, and I observe the way her face lights up with her smile. My eyes linger on her lips for a moment too long before my attention is being pulled to where little Sophie is using my pant leg to get herself into a standing position.

"How did you get out?" I ask the toddler, then bend down to pick her up, walking toward the back of the skybox where she and her sister were playing.

Sophie's giggles fill the room when I toss her into the air and catch her. Addy, not wanting to miss out on the action, makes her way over for a turn. Before I know it, I'm being attacked by two hysterical toddlers.

"Oh, you think that's funny?" I ask Addy as she steals the hat off my head and places it on hers. Sophie is koala-hugging my leg while sitting on my foot, waiting for me to take her on a ride around the space. I scan the room, searching for reinforcements, but everyone seems to be enjoying the spectacle.

I freeze when I take in the look of pure admiration in Ava's eyes. It has never been aimed in my direction before, and I want to find every opportunity to earn it again.

Lifting my chin to her, she snaps out of the daze she was in. Setting aside her wandering thoughts for another day, she comes to my rescue, scooping Sophie off my foot. Ava nuzzles her neck, earning her a belly laugh.

"Didn't realize you were the fun uncle," she teases.

"I guess there're still things for you to learn about me." I wink, granting me another genuine smile from Ava.

"Come on, you two. Eli is warming up in the bullpen," Quinn says, and I pass her a squirming Addy.

"Do you know how sexy you look with babies in your arms?" Ava finally says when we take our seats, just moments before our section bursts into cheers as number Forty-One jogs across the field to the mound.

"You think I'm sexy?" I prod, nudging her with my elbow.

"You know damn well you're fucking sexy. But seeing you with babies like that…" she trails off as she bites her knuckle in exaggeration, but I can see the lingering desire shining in her hazel eyes.

Who would have thought that babies would turn her on so much? Not me, that's for sure. To be honest, I haven't given the idea of kids much thought. With the things I've been through in life, I've often thought the heartache that comes with having a family may not be worth the happiness. But I'm not so sure living that way is really living anymore.

I must be staring, because Ava waves her hand in front of my face, breaking my trance-like state.

"You okay? I thought I lost you there for a minute," she says, grabbing her beer and taking a sip.

I clear my throat, pushing away those foreign ideas. "Yeah, yeah. I'm good."

She side-eyes me for a moment longer, then focuses back on the game, where Eli has already struck out two batters.

The next half hour flies by, with Eli crushing it on the mound, and leading the Bulls to a 4 to 3 win over the Yankees.

We stay in the box and wait for Eli's arrival. In the meantime, the girls are busy planning their summer visits.

"I guess you knew what you were doing," Wes says, throwing his words from the first night at Masqued back at me while we hang out by the ice bucket filled with beer.

Chuckling to myself, I take a sip of my beer, shrugging my shoulders. "Does anyone truly know what they're doing?"

"I sure as fuck did. Might have taken me a while, but I got what I wanted," he replies, and his eyes laser in on where Sloan is laughing with her girls.

"We're just having fun. I enjoy hanging out with her." I cringe slightly as soon as the words leave my mouth. Even though they're the truth, there's more to it…to us, than just that. But both of us are too stubborn to admit it.

"Ha! I've heard those words before," Dalton chimes in.

"Just don't fuck it up," Wes says. Not only for Ava's sake, but for his wife's.

I raise my beer to his. "Wasn't planning on it."

Cheers erupt from the girls' circle, and they turn to face us all at once. "Uh oh, here comes trouble," Wes jokes.

"Oh stop, no trouble." Sloan comes over and bats Wes in the chest playfully.

Quinn comes to stand in front of us. "We just figured out our family trip weekend. And you and Ava are both coming… No excuses." Ah yes, their annual family trip, a tradition they've upheld since their childhood. I've been invited to tag along before but never wanted to impose even though they're always more than welcoming.

Ava comes to stand in front of me, hazel eyes searching my face. "We're thinking the weekend after Thanksgiving," she says to me, but also to the group. I can't help but feel a sense of relief that Ava wants me there too.

"We're thinking of going back to that ski resort in Vermont," Quinn says, just as Eli comes through the suite doors.

"Dada!" the littles scream and set off to attack him. He picks them both up, one in each arm, and showers them in love.

"So, what did I walk into? Where we going?" Eli asks as he leans in to kiss Quinn.

"Skiing!" the ladies cheer in practical unison.

"Eep! So excited we were able to figure out a weekend. Been hearing about this trip for years!" Blossom exclaims with a little dance.

"This is going to be so much fun. Even though I'm not much of a skier, I love tubing," Ava says cheerfully, then turns to me. "The cabins there are amazing, with cozy living rooms and big fireplaces. Plus they are huge, so we will have all the privacy we'll need." She adds that last bit just above a whisper.

I don't think she realizes that she's making plans for us six months from now. Surprisingly, the thought doesn't make me want to run. Instead, I wrap my arms around her, pulling her body into me, and place a light kiss on the top of her head.

"We will get you on those slopes this year," Quinn says to Ava.

"Like hell you will. I am perfectly fine riding my ass down the tubing hill." Ava laughs, and the girls all break into their own conversation once more.

"Great game, man," Wes says to Eli. The three guys start talking stats, and I'm trying my best to listen, but I'm too distracted.

My gaze is set on Ava and every move she makes. I stare at her in awe. It astounds me how easily our lives have meshed together. But I know from experience to never get your hopes up.

It's like they say, no expectations, no disappointments. Unfortunately, I've learned to live my life that way.

Babes Group Chat

SLOAN

We found Ava a dress yesterday. 🔥😭

QUINN

I'm sorry to say but I feel bad for that bride because all eyes are going to be on you.

SLOAN

You better watch it, you're going to be a bride too one day.

QUINN

And???

QUINN

There is only one set of eyes I care about being on me and I know without a doubt they will be.

ME

I mean, where's the lie?

SLOAN

Touché... but he'll probably be unable to see from all the tears he'll be shedding.

QUINN

Oh gosh I'm going to cry just thinking about it.

ME

I seriously can't wait. When do we get to start planning?

QUINN

Lol maybe wait till he asks me first.

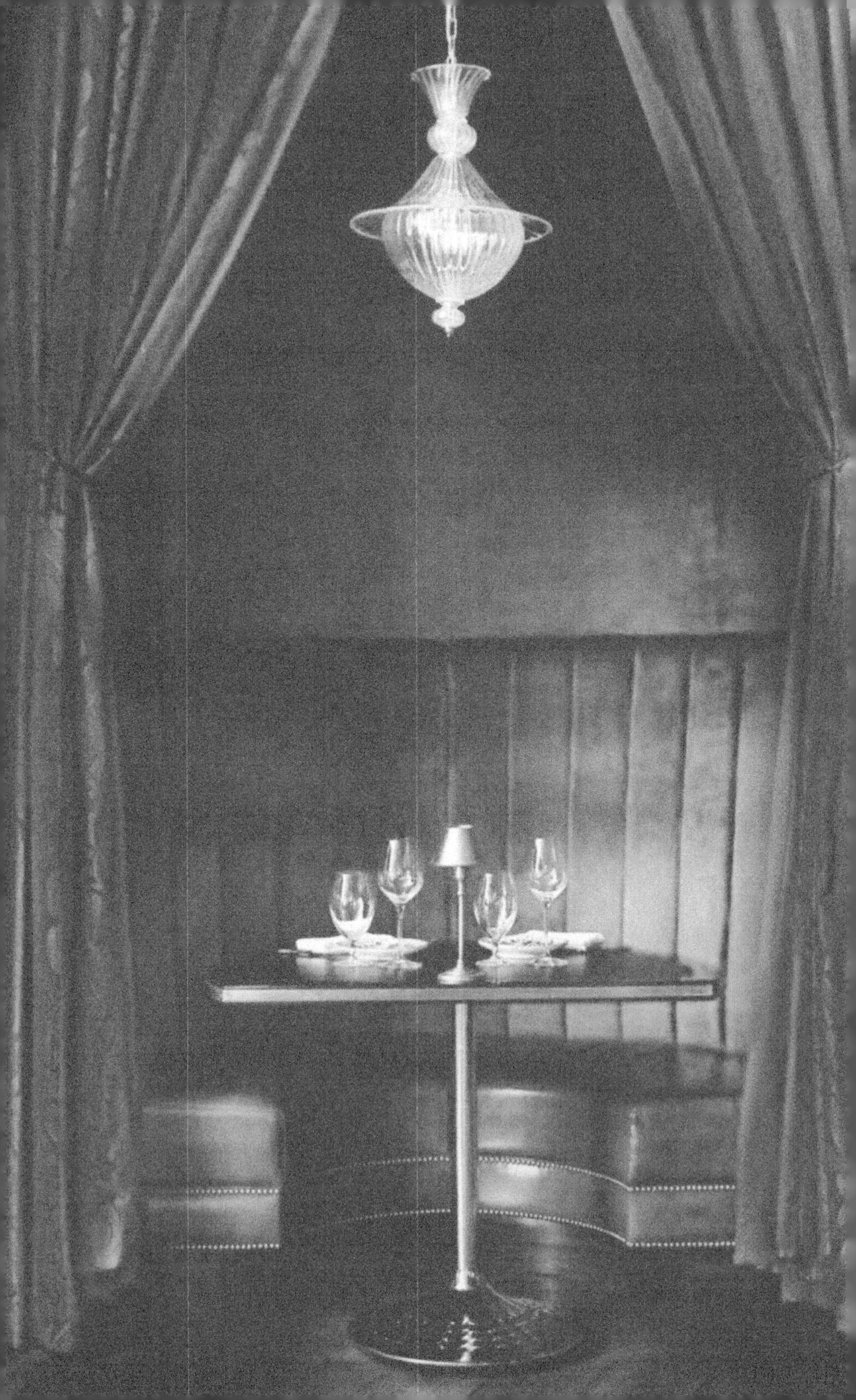

Twenty

Ava

After living with this man for about a month, I thought I had seen a lot of sexy sights, but this might be my favorite.

Parker lounges on the couch, book in one hand, while his other rests on top of a curled-up Binx lying on his shirtless chest.

"I knew it!" I exclaim, setting down the boba tea I was craving this morning.

He slowly lifts his head to acknowledge my presence. Looking back to my cat, and then up at me, Parker shrugs. "Binx and I have bonded recently."

"Oh yeah, over what exactly?"

"Well, you, of course," he says, giving Binx a gentle rub. He just sits there purring, making no moves to come greet me.

Traitor.

"He appreciates me keeping you so busy in my room all the time that he gets your whole bed to himself so it's a win-win relationship." Parker smirks, and I try holding back my smile, fighting not to give in to his charm. "Actually, Binx even mentioned he thinks you should start sleeping in my bed all night because he really hates when you disturb him in the middle of the night."

A thrill runs through me at the thought of Parker wanting me in his bed for more than just sex. I try playing it cool as I walk over toward them, scratching behind Binx's little black ear. "Is that right, Binxy boy? Maybe I'll give it a try tonight," I say, then meet Parker's grey stare, and that's when I notice the book he's reading.

"Learning anything new?" I giggle. I have been waiting for him to notice the new reading material I slipped onto his shelf earlier this week.

"Yes, first thing's first. We need a safe word."

"That sounds like a doable first task on our Dom/sub journey." My heart races at what that would mean for us. Could he be considering this as more than temporary, or is he simply playing along?

"So, what will it be?"

I ponder on that, but it comes to me quickly.

"Balloon."

His brow furrows before a big grin spreads from corner to corner of his lips.

"Because I would never touch another balloon in your presence again."

Parker chuckles, deep and smooth. "Not going to lie…that's fucking perfect."

"I need to study some more before we use it. BDSM can be dangerous, and all jokes aside, if you are serious about it, it's something I'd love for us to explore together."

My belly swoops. He is genuinely considering this.

"I'll get you some annotation stickers so I can go back and read the important pieces and the ones you think you want to try," I say, confirming how serious I am.

I told myself I bought the book as a joke, but deep down the possibility that we may actually do this sends an unreasonable amount of excitement coursing through my body.

I SPENT some time out on the patio sipping my tea and sketching new design ideas that I haven't been able to get out of my head since our trip up to Hudson Valley. It was the perfect chill morning, but as I come inside, I feel the energy shift in the penthouse.

Long gone is the charming Parker from earlier, and in his place is an asshole I haven't seen in a while. One I almost forgot existed. Maybe I needed this reminder.

"Where is my damn blender bottle?" he asks, slamming yet another cabinet door.

"I have no idea. I unloaded all the dishes last night, but I didn't see it in there or the sink."

"Well, I certainly didn't move it, or I'd know where the fuck it is right now."

I brush him off, not about to entertain him acting pissy to me for no reason.

"I'm about to head out to dance. I could bring home a late lunch."

"No," he practically growls before changing his tone. "I'm good. I have lunch plans, so don't worry about me."

"Oookaaay. I guess I'll see you later, then." I don't attempt a goodbye kiss because I refuse to address whatever has crawled up his ass until he can realize his actions and apologize for being a d-bag.

As the elevator door opens, Parker finally acknowledges me. "Ava…"

I turn toward him, unable to control the hope I feel from my name on his lips.

"I'll see you later, okay?" His words seem forced and emotionless.

Unsure if he's really asking me or reminding himself, I nod in response, which must satisfy him because he turns toward his room. And that small bit of hope I felt is quickly replaced by a sense of trepidation.

Dance class was not its normal reprieve. It took me till almost the end of the class to get Parker's mood change out of my head.

At least I worked up an appetite, so I head to my favorite deli not too far from Parker's office. When I pass the door to his place, I can't help but wonder what type of meeting he had today. It seemed to come up suddenly, and it certainly changed his whole demeanor. I saw a shell of the man I've known lately when I looked into his eyes before leaving his penthouse.

I don't know whether to be worried for him…or me.

A few more blocks into my walk, I see one of the cafés Olivia's always gushing over. I'm tempted to go in and grab a coffee, but instead, I'm stopping in my tracks at the sight of Parker through the window. He stands at the same time the beautiful brunette sitting across from him does.

They step toward the door, and I quickly move past the storefront, so they don't see me on their way out. They don't kiss, they don't hug, and he doesn't even wait for her to get into the black sedan waiting on her, but I watch her as she stares after him.

It's a stare full of desire, longing, and maybe even regret.

My stomach sours at the thought, and I suddenly have no appetite. *Who is this woman?*

Is he seeing someone, or maybe I'm completely overthinking and there is nothing to this. But his attitude from earlier is what really has me questioning it all.

I analyze everything about the woman on my walk home. Maybe I'm overreacting, but how can I not when I'm in an uncommitted situationship?

If I didn't want to admit it before today, there is no more lying to myself. My heart is completely on the line where Parker is concerned, and it's hitting me just how scary that is when it comes to a man who doesn't want someone with relationship expectations. *He tried to warn me.*

From the beginning, he has been weary of anything more with me. But his words from that night at Quinn and Eli's constantly flash back into my mind, making me question if he even knows what his heart is capable of.

When I get back to his house, I hear him in his bedroom, but I won't be the one seeking him out.

I curl up on my bed beside Binx, and his gentle purr eventually lures me to sleep.

THE OTHER SIDE of my mattress dips, waking me up. Binx hops over me to greet his new favorite person, but I lie there pretending to still be asleep. Maybe it's the unshed tears in my eyes from fear of what he's going to say.

For some reason, today has triggered so many thoughts about how things will change once I move back to my own apartment, or even worse, when Luxure is finished. I hate feeling so fucking vulnerable.

"Ava?" He whispers my name like it's a question.

I don't answer at first, and he moves to cuddle behind me. I want to protest, but his body wrapped around mine gives me the reprieve I've been seeking all day. "Av…"

"Hmmm?" I finally say, keeping my eyes closed.

His tattooed hand pushes my hair out of my face. "Would you be willing to go out to dinner with this asshole tonight? I know I don't deserve it after the way I acted earlier."

Oh, good for you… Two dates in one day. I still don't answer him.

"Angel, I am so sorry." The sincerity in his voice has me turning to face him.

I give him a weak smile, and he continues. "I'm embarrassed by how I acted earlier. It's no excuse, but I was annoyed I had to go out on a Saturday for a last-minute lunch meeting that I didn't even want to have in the first place."

I know a rational human would be most thankful he realized his behavior earlier and apologized for it. But right now, all I care about is the bit of relief he's giving me about what I witnessed earlier.

I bite my tongue from asking who his meeting was with and what it was about because I'd be lying if I said I still wasn't curious after seeing the way she looked at him. But I believe Parker when he says he didn't want to go, and I try holding on to that thought.

Realizing he's waiting for my response, I look him in the eye. "We all have bad days, thanks for apologizing. Just make sure it doesn't happen again, or I'm going to start calling you a big brat," I tease, the unease in my chest from earlier finally leaving as he holds me tighter in his arms.

I feel him release the breath he must have been holding, and then he places a kiss on my forehead. "Does that mean you'll go on a date with me tonight? Or I can cook us something here."

"Well, if we stay here, less clothing is required." I run my fingertips down the front of his t-shirt.

"I like the sound of that." He smirks, and I bite my bottom lip.

"I know exactly how you can make me forget all about earlier."

Parker raises his eyebrow. "How?"

"You can cook me tacos…naked." I wiggle my eyebrows suggestively.

"And what would it take to have you watch me while I cooked…naked?"

His husky voice has me swallowing thickly before I answer, "Margaritas."

"Deal… I'll Instacart everything I need and have it within the hour." He pulls me into him, pressing a chaste kiss to my lips. "I say we get naked now."

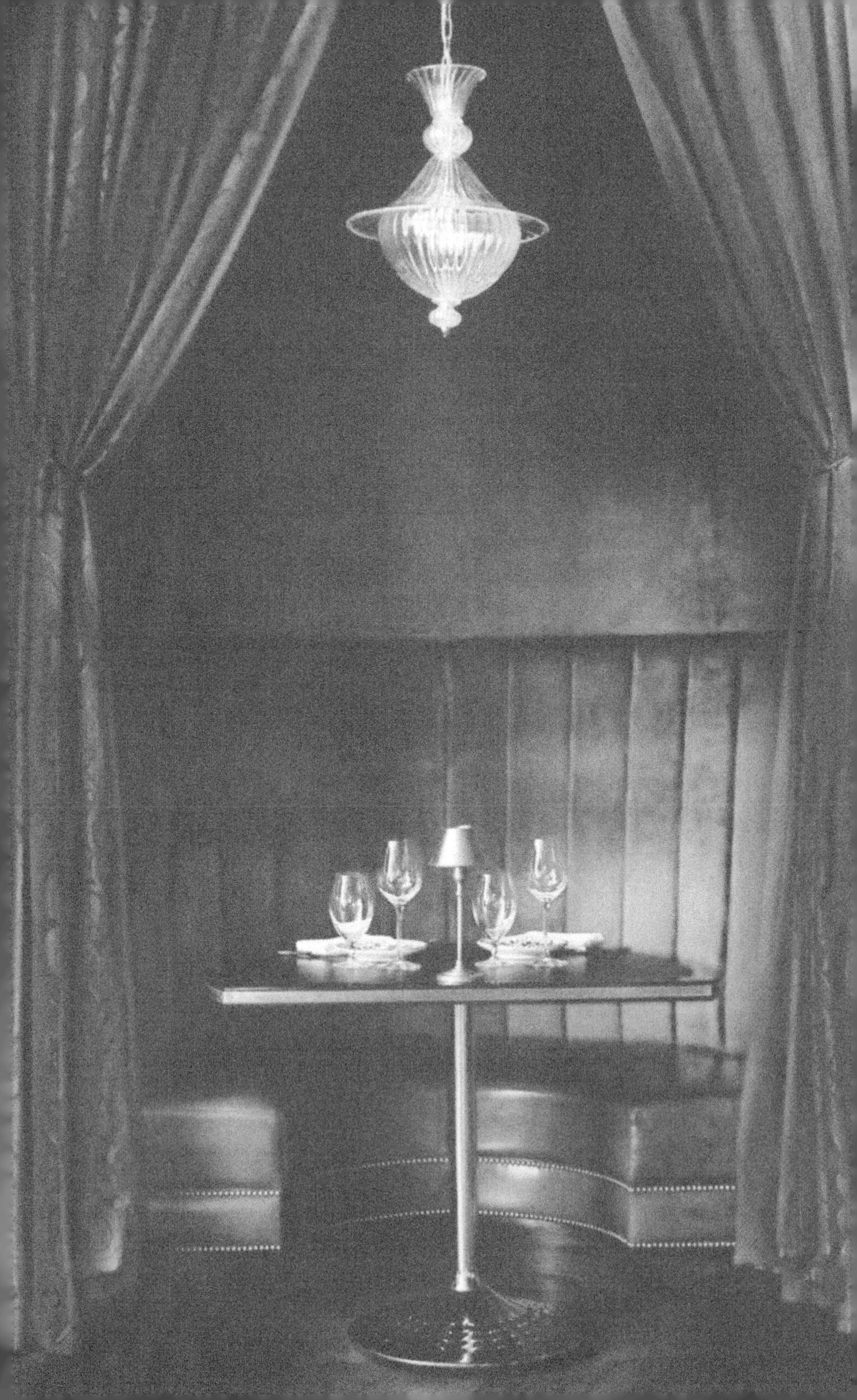

Twenty-One

Parker

Fuck, I don't want to be here surrounded by these fake ass people. Why did I agree to this?

Because you wanted to prove to them you made it…without any of their help.

I take another sip of my whiskey as I watch the crowd of my supposed family members mill about during the pre-ceremony lunch. I can't help the disgust permanently etched onto my face today. My only saving grace is having Ava here with me. Her presence is the strength I need to make it through this wedding.

I filled her in further on my fucked-up family situation on the ride out here. How they practically ignored my dad and me after my mom passed, then abandoned me when I had no one else. Not once did my aunt or uncle invite me over for dinner or the holidays. I was alone, left to figure out this thing we call life on my own. Now, all of a sudden, I'm invited to a wedding. Even though I know exactly why I was truly invited today… But joke's on them, I really don't give a fuck. By the time I finished explaining what we're walking into, my girl was about ready to start throwing down.

My girl. Scarily enough, those words don't fuel my desire to run as far away as possible. A smile spreads across my face at the thought of how I'm going to reward her later back at our hotel.

We opted to stay in a hotel this evening as opposed to her grandparents' place. Although the offer was much appreciated, I'm going to need to let some of my aggression out tonight. I don't think Grandma and Grandpa Pierce want to be privy to how loud Ava can scream my name. We compromised with a lunch tomorrow before we head back to the city. It's an unfamiliar feeling to be so welcomed into a home. I can honestly say they're everything Ava exclaims them to be.

The smile I'm sporting quickly disappears when the groom, my cousin, Jason, comes to sit beside me.

"Glad you could make it, Parks," he says, clinking his glass to mine. *Parks.* I hate that fucking nickname.

"Congrats on the big day," I say through a tight-lipped smile.

"Thanks, man. Julianna is something else," he says, seemingly forgetting our past. *What an idiot.*

"She sure is… So, you planning on taking over for Uncle Ted soon? Seems like he's almost ready for retirement," I ask, trying to change the subject.

"Yeah, I'm working my way up to it. He's still keeping me at bay. Not sure he's ready to relinquish the control yet."

"Ahh, yeah. I get that," I reply. Small talk has never been my thing, so I look out to the crowd to see if my distraction is back from the drink line.

"Oh, damn. Is that Ava Pierce over there?" Jason says as Ava makes her way through the crowd. I'm distracted by the way her hips sway in the body-hugging olive-green dress she's wearing.

Wait, what did he say?

"How do you know Ava?" I ask abruptly. My temper flares at the thought of him knowing her intimately.

"Oh...growing up, her grandparents had a place not far from my house. We used to hang out all the time when we were younger," he replies, oblivious to the change in my mood. "Damn, she is fucking sex—"

"Aren't you getting married today?" I interrupt, not wanting to hear one more word about her from his mouth.

"Yeah, man." He nudges my shoulder. "You know how it is."

"No, I don't," I say flatly. Does this dude have memory loss or something...acting all nonchalant.

Ava reaches our table and hands me a fresh drink. My mood must be written all over my face because her eyes warily slide to my cousin. She takes him in for a minute.

"Jason?" she questions.

"I thought that was you!" he exclaims, then stands to pull her in for hug. My grip on my tumbler tightens.

"Guess there's no need to introduce you to the groom," I mumble.

"I didn't realize you were the groom...or Parker's cousin, for that matter. Congratulations!" she says.

Jason eyes the annoyed expression on my face, then looks back at Ava. "Oh shit, you're here with Parks. What are the chances?"

"Guess not that slim," I say, standing abruptly.

"Well, I'd hate to keep you. I'm sure you have a ton of people to catch up with before the ceremony. I'll see you later. Can't wait to meet your bride." Ava plasters on one of her practiced smiles, subsequently dismissing him from our table without him realizing it.

When his back is to our table, I finally feel like I can breathe again. Ava watches me carefully with a raised eyebrow. "Are you alright?"

"Peachy," I grumble, then down the rest of my glass.

"Is it because I know your cousin?" she asks, hurt etched in her expression. Fuck, I'm an asshole. This has nothing to do with her, and everything to do with him. *Slimy fuck that he is.*

Wrapping my arms around her, I pull her in close and give her a gentle kiss on the head. I close my eyes and calm my mind for a moment. Disappointed I let Jason's presence disrupt my peace so easily.

"No, that's not it…" I go to explain more, but the staff announces that it is time we head to the ceremony space, effectively ending our conversation.

"You'll tell me later?" she asks, and I nod.

Her fingers lace with mine as we make our way to the shuttles, my mind reeling on how she'll react to my embarrassing truth.

Ava

I can't believe Jason Lannister, who I haven't seen in over ten years, is Parker's cousin. There is absolutely no resemblance, and they couldn't be any more different. His cousin is still the definition of an ick wrapped up in a bow tie.

I hate the way this family has treated Parker over the years, and what little I know of Jason from all those summers ago fits that narrative. His family is exactly like my parents.

The longer we sit here as the bridal party walks down the aisle, the more I wonder why Parker is even giving these people the time of day by being here.

The harpist changes the melody, and the officiant directs everyone to stand. The beautiful white dress comes into view, and I look up to find a stunning yet familiar face.

OH MY... No fucking way.

She starts her walk down the aisle, and there is no doubt in my mind it is *her*. My eyes bounce between the bride and Parker, trying to see if his facial expression gives anything a way.

His never wavers, but I don't miss hers.

Just like last weekend.

Her gaze lands on Parker in the crowd, and I notice she lingers on his face longer than any other. There is no denying the regret that washes over her before she regains composure.

I don't even know what to think in this moment. Is Parker not who I thought he was?

Parker's fingertips trace circles over my knee as I sit there, wondering if she's the reason he finally decided he wanted to come around his family.

It's obvious they have motivated him to prove himself to them, but how far did he take that? Was that lunch a goodbye before the wedding?

No part of me thinks he was with her while we've been together this past month, but it's obvious they have some sort of history.

Was his hurt so deep that he took it as far as to have an affair with his cousin's soon-to-be wife?

And if so, how would I feel about that?

A SEEMINGLY UNAFFECTED Parker takes my hand in his, following the crowd away from the ceremony area.

I let my hand slip from his grip, stepping in front of him. I don't follow the crowd toward the cocktail and hors d'oeuvres; instead, I head for the empty gardens off to our left.

Whether it's selfish or not, I need answers, and I need them right now.

"Ava, this way?" Parker nods in the direction of the pavilion, but I keep walking.

Most likely reading the look on my face, he is behind me in seconds. "What's wrong?"

I continue walking, wanting to get well away from everyone, but Parker grabs my elbow. "Hey…what's going on?" The concern in his voice and the way his eyebrows pinch together makes me feel guilty, but *what. The. Fuck.*

"I saw you with her. Who is she to you?" I feel the tears threatening to spill from my eyes.

"Angel…who?" Parker asks, stepping toward me. "There hasn't been anyone else since you came to work for me. What are you talking—"

"Your lunch meeting last Saturday." I use air quotes for emphasis.

He closes his eyes, shaking his head. "How?"

"That's not important. Tell me the truth, Parker. What the fuck have you brought me to today? Did we come to watch your cousin get married or your ex fuck-buddy?"

There is no doubt in my mind she has been with Parker just by the way she looks at him. I know, because he isn't easy to forget.

His next words feel like they slam into me, rocking me to the core.

"My ex-fiancée," he whispers.

"Wh...what?" I manage to say.

"You asked who she was?"

My head shakes, trying my best to process what he is saying.

"The bride...the one who just walked down the aisle to your cousin, the one you met for lunch last Saturday, is your fucking ex-fiancée?" I say the last part a little too loudly.

He hangs his head, almost in embarrassment, and that's when it hits me.

"It was him she was cheating on you with, wasn't it?"

Nodding, Parker barely lifts his head to peer at me.

My whole demeanor changes in an instant. I'm ready to fight every motherfucker at this wedding. The way each of them has dismissed him his whole life until now that he has more money than most of them. The bride, the groom, his freaking family. Hell, her family too. They have to know who Jason is to Parker unless she lied to hide her actions.

Rage ripples through me like I've never felt.

That dumb bitch. I let out an evil laugh. "Well, joke's on her… First off, have you seen you? And second off, all Jason had to do was try to stick his tongue down my throat one time for me to never speak to him again until today."

He looks at me incredulously, most likely having whiplash from my personality changes.

Then his nose snarls up in disgust. "He touched you?"

"Don't worry, I kneed him in the balls and told him to lose my number."

Now it's his turn to laugh. "I hate that he even knows your name."

There's my possessive P.

"The bride knows your dick size, so I think you have me beat today, Sir… Which again, she must be fucking crazy."

He grins at that, holding his head a little higher. "No, she's just money hungry. He promised her lots of shiny things and big trips. And she fell right into the trap. Or maybe he did. Put it this way, they deserve each other, though."

"So why did you meet her last weekend?"

"I should have just explained all this to you that day, but for some reason, I revert to that same embarrassed, vulnerable twenty-three-year-old guy when it comes to Julianna and Jason." He runs his hands through his hair. "Being broke back then allowed me to see her true colors and I'm thankful for that, but it doesn't mean it didn't hurt."

I take his hand, lifting it to my lips, and press a kiss to his fingertips.

"Plus, I was trying to grieve the loss of the most important person in my life." The way his voice breaks almost does me in.

Yeah, and fuck Julianna for that too. I swear, if it wasn't her wedding day, I would go in there and sucker punch her pretty little face.

"But that Saturday, she called me, saying she was in town and begging me to come meet her. It had been a long time since she had asked me to do that, so of course I said no at first, but then she told me it was really important and it needed to be discussed before this weekend." He pauses for a second, shaking his head like he can't believe her, or maybe himself.

"I figured she was bullshitting me, but my conscience got the best of me, worried for her wellbeing. I know how powerful my uncle is, and even though no part of me wanted her again, I didn't want her to be stuck in a situation she couldn't get out of. But it wasn't anything like that. It was the same as the other times she's tried contacting me over the years."

"Let me guess, she begged you to take her back. Said she would call everything off if you would."

His nostrils flare with a heavy breath. "Yep."

"I can only imagine how hard that was. I'm sure you still have some sort of feelings for her. I mean, you were engaged..." Every part of me wants him to correct me. It has my heart beating faster.

"No, it wasn't hard at all. There was only one person who was on my mind at that moment, and it wasn't her."

Is he saying what I think he is?

Gently grabbing my chin, he leans down, staring into my eyes. "I was thinking about you."

I swallow roughly and whisper, "You were thinking about me?"

"I think about you twenty-four-seven, Angel," he says boldly, specks of blue shining in his grey eyes. His words sending a tidal wave of feelings through me… Relief, excitement, hope, joy, desire.

"And you know what I've realized standing here talking to you… There is only one person's opinion I care about here today, and she's leaving with me anyways. I'm not sure why I felt such a need to show up and prove to all of them they were wrong about me, my dad, my family, but fuck them and fuck this wedding."

"Yes, seriously…"

I'm interrupted by none other than the bride herself. "Parker," she says, holding her dress off the ground, the photographer behind her.

Julianna turns toward the camera. "Do you mind giving me a second? Let Jason know I'll meet him on the other side of the gardens. Those blooms are better for our pictures."

Then turning back to us, she smiles, sweetly addressing me, "Can you give us a minute of privacy?"

Parker goes to say something, but I press my hand to his chest.

"No, I can't. You got that last Saturday, and I think he made himself pretty clear then." I take a step toward her. "Matter of fact, you didn't even deserve that. I would take pity on you, but since it's your wedding day, and you are begging another man for his time, let me put it to you like this…"

My glare is menacing, and there is no denying the bite in my tone.

"You had a man who would have given you so much more than money ever could, but you fucked that up. Personally, I'd like to thank you for that part. But on the other hand, I hope you know how disgusting you are for doing that to him, especially right after his mom passed away."

I almost feel bad for the tears forming in her eyes.

Grabbing Parker's hand in mine, I storm past her, not stopping until we almost make it to the valet.

"Does this mean we get to leave now?" Parker's question draws my attention up to him.

His beautiful face graces me with the biggest smile I think I've ever seen from him.

Seconds later, his mouth is crashing onto mine, and he's pulling my body flush with his. We both moan in what feels like relief at the contact. One hand cups the back of my head and the other grips my ass as his tongue devours mine. If I wasn't ready to leave before, I sure as hell am now.

"My little brat, standing up for me more than anyone ever has. You have no idea what that means to me," he breathes over my lips.

Parker stands to his full height again, and I place my hands on his chest. "I'd do it again in a heartbeat if I had the chance. And yes, we are definitely leaving."

I lean up on my tippy toes. "I'm feeling extra bratty right now." Watching his pupils dilate, I move to the shell of his ear. "I think you need to fuck it out of me, Sir."

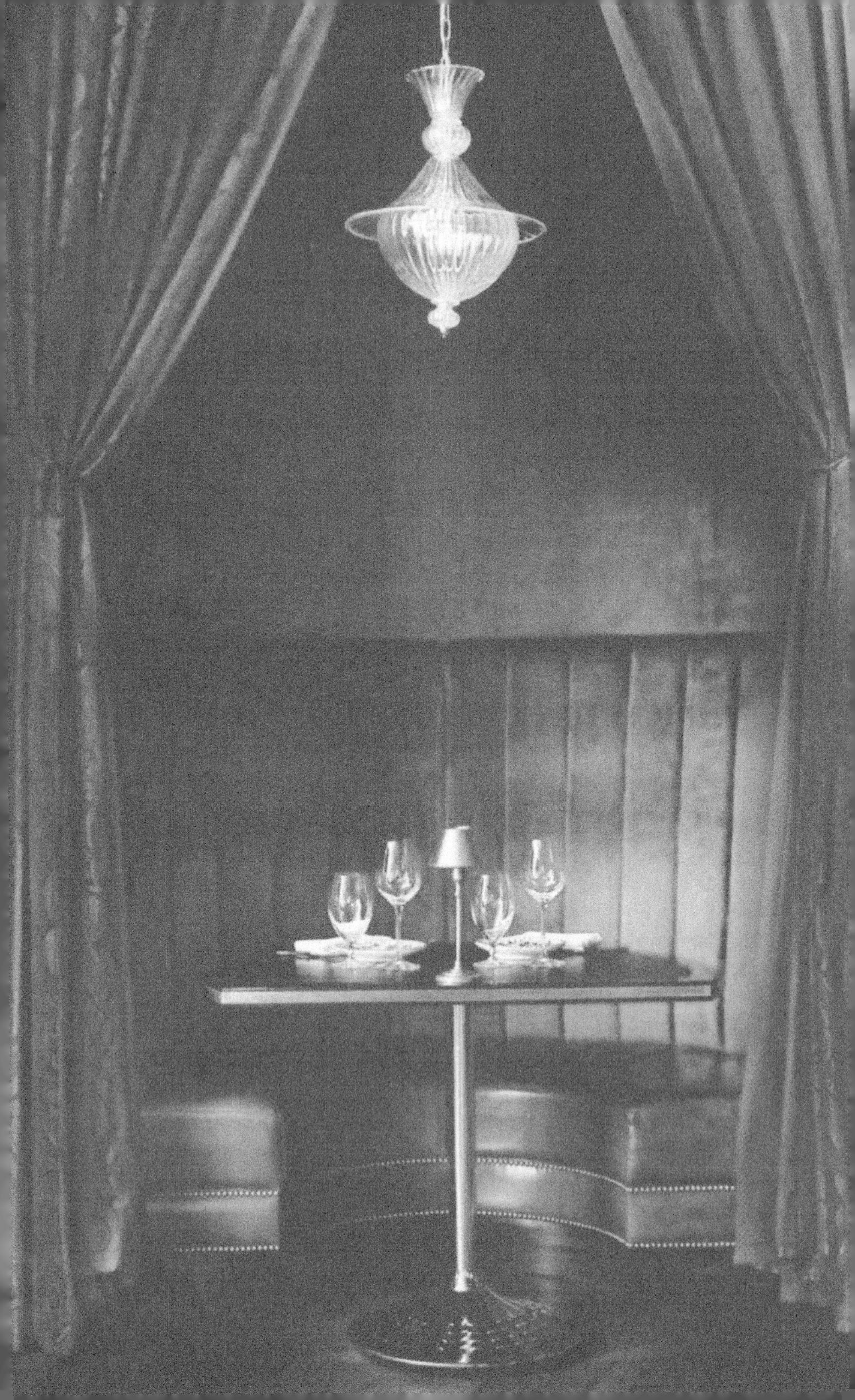

Twenty-Two

Parker

"Glad to see that smile, Mr. Cole," Stuart says as I practically skip into the apartment building.

"Thanks, Stuart!" I reply over my shoulder, heading straight to the elevator.

I'm so fucking excited to show Ava. When those papers came across my desk earlier today, there was no other person I wanted to share the news with other than her. It was exceptional timing, honestly. Ever since we came home from the wedding the other day, I have been looking for the perfect way to tell her I want more… I need more.

I wanted to make it special, so I picked up two strawberry shortcakes from the bakery she's always raving about. I hope she's as thrilled about this as I am.

The elevator doors can't move fast enough, so I press the close button over and over.

"Av, I'm home!" I say, the excitement evident in my tone. I find Ava on the couch with a sketchbook in her lap, Binx curled up along her side. With the hotel project nearing its end, she's been sketching a lot more. Building her portfolio for upcoming opportunities, but little does she know, I have the best one yet.

I'm grinning from ear to ear when I approach her, papers tucked carefully under my arm. She sets the book aside and leans up, but something is off. Her expression seems less than happy to see me, let alone hear what news I want to share.

Taking a seat next to her, I grab her hand in mine. Nerves crawl up my spine. Did I fuck up somehow?

"Is everything alright?" Praying to God I'm not the cause of her mood. I couldn't imagine being the reason for the sad expression on her face when every day I try my hardest to be the reason she smiles.

"No, everything is not alright," she says through a shaky breath, wiping away a stray tear.

"Angel, what's going on?" I brace myself for the other shoe to drop. Everything has been going so perfectly. Almost too perfect.

She wraps her arms around my middle and nestles into me. Holding on for dear life, as if afraid to let go. *Fuck, is she letting go?*

"What happened?" I ask, pulling her in closer.

Ava remains silent, and then slowly uncurls herself from my chest. My stomach drops with the space she's created. *This is it, isn't it?*

"It's silly… I think I'm PMSing. I'm sorry for being so emotional." But the tear trailing down her cheek tells a different story.

"Don't ever apologize for how you feel. Tell me what's running through that mind of yours," I say, bringing my knuckle to her lips, which are currently pulled to the side. A tell-tale sign she has something she wants to say.

"Forget it... It's not important. You came in here all happy about something. What did you want to say?" Ava asks, trying to change the subject.

"Angel, everything you have to say is important. From the minute you wake up to the minute we fall asleep, I want to know it all. I live for your random thoughts and the little things that make you smile. I love the way your eyes light up when you taste something delicious, and the way they darken when you're thinking of the next bratty thing you can do to get my attention. The way you get a satisfied grin when you get your latest sketch just right. I want all of it... So please, tell me."

She eyes me cautiously, like what she's about to say might scare me.

"Myapartmentisready..." she rushes out on an exhale. But I can see the disappointment in her expression.

"Is that a bad thing?" My heart swells at the thought of her being upset about leaving. If I'm being honest, I don't want her to go. I've never felt as alive as I have with her being here.

Ava gnaws on her lip. She doesn't want to be the one to break, the one to take the leap. I don't blame her; I always told her not to.

So, I'll do it for her.

"Would I be selfish if I said I don't want you to leave?"

Her eyes shine as a sweet grin spreads across her face. "What are you saying, P?"

"I want you to stay here, permanently." As if knowing his

name wasn't included, Binx rubs up on me with a meow. "Him too, I guess," I add with a chuckle.

"Are you serious?" she questions, biting her lips to contain her excitement.

"Yes, Ava Marie Pierce, I want you to live here, and not in the guest room. In my room, with me."

Within the next second, she's tackling me onto the couch and showering me with kisses. My hands grab hold of her ass and pull her body closer to mine. I need to feel her everywhere, all the time. I don't want this feeling to ever fade, because I finally realize what this is… *It's love.*

I am head over heels in love with this woman.

"The thought of moving out made me so sad. I didn't want to leave. I—" I place a finger over her lips, stopping her from robbing me of this moment. One I knew was coming. From the moment she opened that sassy ass mouth of hers, I knew she was something special, something to cherish.

"I love you, Angel. There isn't a day that goes by that I don't yearn to be by your side," I tell her, my gaze locked onto her emotion-filled hazel eyes. "I was stupid to ever push you away. I think deep down I knew how easily I could fall for you, and that's why I acted the way I did…trying to keep you at arm's length. Too afraid of what would happen if I let someone new in. Thank you for seeing past that, for seeing me."

Her eyes shine with emotion.

"Oh, Parker… I love you too. I was just so afraid to tell you. Terrified that hearing those words would scare you away." She wraps her arms around me, and I hold on tight. Savoring the feel of this moment. One I never believed would happen for me.

"The first night I saw you, I felt an immediate attraction. I know you did too. I remember an excitement I had never experienced, but then your last name and my assumptions about people who grew up with money had my guard fully up. Even after that, I was insanely attracted to you, hence why I gave in so quickly at Masqued. I hated myself for how badly I continued to want you after that night. How much I thought about you. Then I saw you catch the bouquet at Wes and Sloan's wedding, and I knew you had your sights set on a fairytale, one I could never give you... Or at least, that's what I thought. Now I know that couldn't be further from the truth. The only thing I'm scared about is losing you."

She pulls away slowly, placing her hand on my chest. Her eyes bounce between mine, shining with love and affection. Everything I've yearned for all these years. Leaning in, I kiss her, hard. Letting our connection run free as we wrap ourselves around each other.

"Wait, what did you have to tell me before?"

"It can wait. Right now, I need to show my girl how much I love her."

She cups my face in her hands as I stand with her body around mine, my palms holding her up by her ass.

"I don't think I'll ever tire of hearing those words come out of your mouth," she says against my neck, dragging her lips up my jaw before kissing me deeply. I stand up with her wrapped around me and head toward my room. Hastily stripping off our clothes on our way. My body physically aching to be with her...right now. As if my soul is anxiously awaiting to connect to its counterpart.

This right here...

These feelings coursing through me.

It's better than I ever imagined.

I don't know if I ever truly made love before. But that's exactly what this is, and now I know she feels it too.

She loves me… This beautiful, smart, amazing woman loves me.

Lifting her leg to wrap around me, I slide into her. Ava's back arches with every thrust of my hips. Her soft moans are like the sweetest melody… A new soundtrack to add to my playlist.

I can feel her heartbeat where our bodies are connected, and I place my hand over it. Cherishing it, because it's mine…she is mine and I am hers.

The possessiveness that overtakes me at that acknowledgment has me thrusting deep inside of her. Filling every inch of her repeatedly.

"Please don't stop," she pleads.

Ava's hair has fallen across her face, blocking my favorite view. My hand reaches up and gently pushes the strands away. While cupping her cheek with my palm, her hazel eyes lock onto mine, conveying the words I feel with every fiber of my being.

Leaning down, I kiss her deeply. Needing to be connected to her in every way possible. She opens instantly and our tongues tangle, stroking softly against one another.

I feel her body tense below me, and I know my girl is almost there.

"Let go, baby… I'll be here to catch you."

A stream of unintelligible words flies from her lips as she comes around me.

"That's it... Fuck, you're so beautiful," I croon when her eyes lock onto mine in pure ecstasy. My mouth sealing with hers, I swallow every moan.

My thrusts become erratic, and I know I'm about to come, but I want to make this last. To savor every moment.

Her hands reach for my hair, threading into the long strands as she pants through her aftershocks.

"Please come inside me," she begs, and I'm a goner. Unable to withhold my release any longer.

The way we tangle in each other as we fall onto my bed is pure bliss. Our labored breaths return to normal as we lie together. My hand slowly strokes the soft skin of her shoulder, and her head rests on my tattooed chest.

"Thank you for loving me," I whisper into her hair before placing a kiss on top of her head.

"How could I not?" she replies, nuzzling closer.

"I didn't make it easy, I'm sure."

"You're worth it... Now you're stuck with me." She grins as she peers up at me, and I smile like a love-sick fool right back.

This... this right here, is exactly where I'm meant to be. All the pain and strife I've felt in my life has led me right here... To her.

"Okay, okay...can you please tell me now," Ava pleads while taking a bite of her pizza.

"Is the suspense killing you?" I tease, bopping her on the nose.

"Uh duh!" she says like the little brat she is, and I can't help but laugh.

"Well…I know you're anxiously trying to figure out what your next project will be…"

She sits up a little taller at my prolonged answer.

"I was hoping you'd be interested in this one," I say, passing the signed contract to the Hudson Valley property to her.

Ava studies the paper for a minute, skimming over the words. I know the minute she realizes because her eyes go wide, then dart to mine. A gleeful smile spreads across her face.

"You got the property!" she squeals.

"I did."

"Oh my gosh. Parker, this is amazing. Wait, you said next project… Do you mean…" she questions, her hand going to cover her mouth in shock.

I chuckle. "Yes, Av. I want you to take the lead on this. I want you to design it."

"Are you serious? This is huge! I don't know—" Her expression changes, as if self-doubt has taken over my talented girl's mind.

"I'm going to stop you right there," I say, effectively pausing her negative train of thought. "You are one of the brightest, most talented designers I've ever worked with. I'm not going to let you sit here and doubt yourself. I want you on this project… I want to do this together."

"Damn, I love you," she says, climbing across the couch to get closer to me. Those words from her lips light me up more than I thought possible.

"Is that a yes, Miss Pierce?"

"That's a definite yes, but I have one condition."

"What's that?" I question with a quirked eyebrow, dragging her body till she's pressed against my side.

"That we keep the old farmhouse... Renovate it. Make it something special for us and our families to use."

I'm nodding before she's even finished. "I think that would be perfect."

Part of me knew that when I took her to Hudson Valley, it would somehow end up being something special to the both of us. I just wasn't ready to admit it then. And now as Ava sits next to me, all starry-eyed, with her sketchbook already in her lap, I couldn't think of anything better.

With a look of pure determination, she peers up at me and asks, "When do we start?"

I chuckle. "We will start soon enough, but for now, I have one more surprise for you."

She follows behind me, and with our fingers interlocked, we walk up the stairs. I can see her mind racing with thoughts of what else I could be showing her until the reflection of the chrome comes into view.

Her mouth falls open as we breach the top of the loft, letting out an audible gasp. "Parker, you didn't!"

"Oh, but I did." I smirk.

She takes a few steps to the center of the room, trailing her hand up the stainless-steel beauty. Gripping the pole, she does one small twirl that's sexy as hell, letting her head dip back before meeting my stare.

"I freaking love it." She smiles widely. It may be a stripper pole to most, but to her, it's an escape after a long day, her favorite hobby, and now it's another symbol of how permanent I feel about her in my life.

Biting her lip, she shakes her head in disbelief. "I just can't believe you actually had this installed."

I step over to the pole, and she grabs my arm, pulling me closer.

"I can't believe I didn't think of it sooner."

Searing my lips to hers, I whisper,, "Let's be honest, I'm the one who will benefit from this the most."

"I've been fantasizing about giving you your own private show since opening night at Masqued."

Groaning, I'm already rock hard as I walk across the room toward a black chest. Opening the dresser doors, I look back over my shoulder with a sly grin. "You have no idea."

She flushes at my admission, even more so when I turn to her with a small leather paddle in my grip. I watch her thighs clench as I slap it against my palm gently.

"I also stocked us up with a few things to try out."

She peers past me into the small open door, able to see restraints and a whip among several other similar items.

Taking another step back to her, I command, "Turn around and put both your hands on the pole."

She swallows thickly and does exactly as I ask, arching her back in the process.

I glide the leather over the back of her oversized T-shirt, relishing how she shivers. Using the tip of it, I push the shirt up, exposing her thong-covered ass.

"Good girl, now do you remember your safe word?"

"Yes, Sir. I promise, I'll use it if I need to." A moan escapes as this fantasy comes to life.

"I know my brat loves getting her ass spanked," I say in a low, husky tone, running the paddle over her perky bottom. "If I give you five smacks, will you dance for me?"

She whimpers on a plea, nodding eagerly.

"Okay, Angel. This is just a small dip in the water. I plan to take us to much greater depths within the future. Are you ready?"

While rubbing her thighs together in anticipation, she speaks the words I'm waiting to hear.

"Please, Sir. I'm ready."

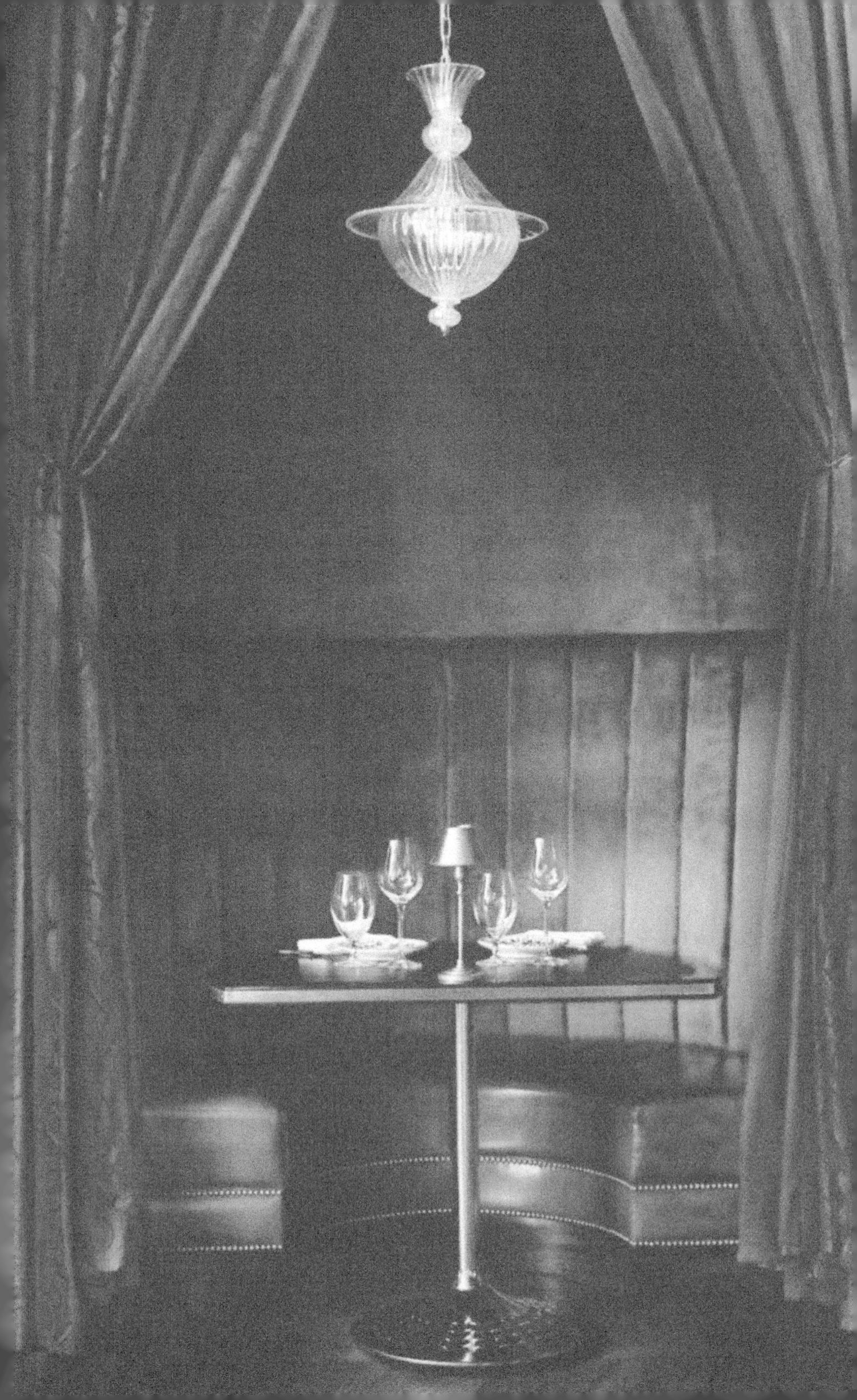

Twenty-Three

Ava

Four months later

Our car pulls up to the Luxure, and my heart flutters with pride. Tonight's party is to celebrate the grand opening next week. It's so wild to think about how far Parker and I have come since that first day I walked through those doors.

My hand finds Parker's before we step out. "Have I told you how thankful I am you gave me this opportunity?"

His eyes trace my face, before trailing down my body. "*Have I told you* how stunning you are tonight?"

Parker's hand lifts the sea glass around my neck. "And seeing you in this." He shakes his head, his eyes full of emotion. "I swear, I think she sent you to me. To test me, to love me…to utterly complete me."

His words make me feel like the most special person in the world. Bending my head, I place a kiss to his knuckles.

I had the honor of helping Parker go through the storage unit he has containing his parents' belongings. When his dad passed away, he said it was just too much, so his parents' best friends boxed up anything they thought could be important to Parker one day, and for the last five years, it has been sitting untouched.

I almost couldn't believe my eyes when we stumbled across the bubble-wrapped vase full of his mother's sea glass.

With a few new pictures of his parents, the vase sits perfectly on his bookshelf. Just missing a single piece, which now rests perfectly on a chain around my neck, thanks to Parker.

The most unique one, small in size, and the only orange one in the collection.

I place my hand over his, leaning up to kiss him. "There is no doubt in my mind, she had a hand in your happiness." I am beyond grateful that happiness included me.

He kisses me one more time before stepping out of the car and offering me his hand.

"And back to your original comment. You were the best one for the job, and it shows in every detail of this place. I may have made you sweat a little bit that day, but there was no question the job was yours."

I beam up at him. I wouldn't have believed him six months ago, but knowing now what I know about Parker, I absolutely do.

"I love you. Now let's go celebrate."

OUR WHOLE CREW IS HERE, and it means the world to me. To us.

The excitement on Parker's face when he saw all of them almost gutted me, but in the best way. Especially hearing my grandfather tell him how proud of his accomplishments he should be.

Parker has a lot of things in life, but seeing him find his true place and feel comfortable among our friends and my family melts my heart. He admitted to me that in the past he had avoided the Barton and King family trips because being surrounded by a big family was awesome in the moment, but then he'd come home to his empty place and feel so down.

But he doesn't feel like that anymore.

And as far as my grandparents go, I'm pretty sure they call his phone now more than mine. According to my grandma, *"Parker never misses her calls."* I give them a hard time, but I love it more than I could ever say. We are all going to Paris for Thanksgiving to celebrate with my Aunt Samantha, and I can't wait for Parker to meet her.

So far tonight, my grandpa finally got the dance Quinn has been promising him, and the guys are all talking shit about who is going to bust their ass snowboarding in Vermont next month.

"It's official, Wes and I are going to see Braxton for another tattoo next week," Sloan says, and Quinn pipes up.

"I love his girlfriend. Can we invite her to the next girls' night when I'm in town?"

I look over to where Olivia stands, talking to Mr. Bryant. She's been on cloud nine all week, finding out that Parker gave her the promotion she deserved, as his attention is going to be in Hudson Valley for a while to come.

"Yes, absolutely. She kept me sane when I first started working here. I adore her."

"Speaking of staying sane…don't turn around. But did you know your parents were coming tonight?" Sloan has me freezing in place.

What??

"Like, you are sure it's them?" I ask in disbelief. When I called to invite them a few weeks ago, I never even received a call back.

"No doubt, and they are approaching quickly," Quinn mumbles under her breath.

"Darling, there you are." I hear my mother's high-pitched voice as her hand lands on my back.

"Hi, Mom… Dad. What are you guys doing here?" I try my best to sound welcoming, even though my hackles are up, wondering what they are truly doing here.

"We were over on this side of town for a business meeting and wanted to come see the cute little hotel you are working at now."

I practically hear Quinn grinding her teeth behind me from the cocktail table she and Sloan are leaning against. I guess it had nothing to do with the voicemail I left inviting them to tonight, or the phone call I'm sure my grandmother made on my behalf.

Holding my head high, I respond proudly, "Actually, I designed this whole hotel with the help of the investor and project managers."

"Oh, that's right, and we are so happy to hear you are dating the investor now. Mother told me," my mom says, and I instantly hate she makes it about his money.

"You two should come to the event we are hosting next

month." My dad's voice sounds almost unfamiliar to me at this point in my life.

I know I should be kind in this moment, but I've taken the high road a lot with my parents. More than anything, I want them to understand.

"Honestly, Dad, I would if it wasn't for the fact this is the first time I've heard from either of you in weeks. Any conversation we have is about money or social events. I just want my parents to check in on me from time to time and not have another agenda."

I can tell I have shocked both of them, but it was time I said it.

"But I do appreciate you stopping by tonight, and I would love for you to stay. Meet Parker, have a drink with Grandma and Grandpa, and look around at all the design details I am so proud of here in this hotel."

I feel Parker approach as his hand finds my lower back.

"Hello," he says, and I can tell by his voice he is trying to read the room.

"Parker Cole, these are my parents. Russell and Elizabeth Pierce."

Parker reaches out his tattooed hand, shaking both of theirs.

"Thank you for coming. You should be so proud of Ava. She put such a special touch on this hotel. And it's all everyone can talk about tonight." His arm pulls me into his side, pressing a kiss to the top of my head.

Apparently, he read the room very well.

My mother speaks up this time. "We are proud of her. It's beautiful in here."

I hope she means it, and a big part of me will always wish for that from my parents, but then I think about all the others surrounding me who support me without question and that's what truly makes all the difference to me.

Olivia's voice sounds over the microphone. "Thank you, ladies and gentlemen, for attending the reveal of Luxure. We are beyond thrilled to have you all here for our special night. The rooftop garden and restaurant are now open for cocktail hour."

Parker turns his attention back to my parents. "Well, please enjoy yourselves. The rooftop was all your daughter's doing and it will be a major highlight for our guests, it's impeccable." He squeezes my hand before continuing, "I'm sorry, but I do need to steal Ava for just a few."

"Of course, and it was nice to meet you, Mr. Cole," my mom responds.

I lean in to give each of them a hug. "Just in case you guys head out before I'm back, thank you again for stopping by."

My mom grabs my hand as I turn to walk away. "Ava, we really are happy for you."

I give her a genuine smile, hoping my honesty with them tonight can help us turn a new leaf. But either way, my hand in Parker's as I walk away fills my soul with so much love and adoration.

"So those were my parents," I say as we walk down the corridor.

"Exactly what I expected. But good thing I have something that will take your mind off them."

"Oh yeah?" I ask, narrowing my eyes as I look up at him.

His voice grows husky as he pushes the door open to the conference room. "My little brat has been such a good girl, so of course she gets rewarded."

Parker

Locking the conference door behind me, I stalk over to where Ava stands in front of the long table, eying the bouquet and note I left for her there.

My fingertips trace over the smooth skin of her arms when I reach her. She leans farther into my touch, pressing her ass into me.

"I'm so proud of you. None of this could have happened without you," I say, kissing up the column of her neck. Distracting her from the present in front of her.

"Mmm. How proud are you?" she teases, shaking her ass slightly. She loves taunting me with one of my favorite things.

"So. Fucking. Proud."

Ava spins around and wraps her arms around my shoulders. Shimmying her skirt up to her hips, I lift her onto the conference table, making her yelp.

Her eyes go wide. "Here?" she questions me with a giggle.

"Do you know how long I've waited to take you on this table?" I pause, dragging my fingers over her exposed thighs. "Since that very first day you waltzed through those doors to interview, and every day since." My cock thickens at the reminder.

I step in between her spread legs, cupping the back of her neck. She moans as I lean down and kiss her deeply, then pull away.

"Hands on the table behind you, Av," I demand, stunning her at first, but she snaps into action.

Unzipping my suit pants, I free my cock. Then I grab hold of her legs and spread them wider until she's almost in a split. Thank fuck for those pole dancing classes.

My mouth waters at her perfect pussy on full display for me. With a groan, I hover above her and spit, watching as it coats her cunt.

"Holy fuck, that's so hot," Ava whimpers, and I waste no time sliding inside her. Our bodies move in unison, her hips matching every thrust of mine.

I shudder as I feel her pussy clench around me.

"That's it, Angel... Milk my cock," I growl as I calm my movements to a torturously slow pace.

"Oh fuck, Parker I... Oh fuck!" Her breath hitches as I grind my hips and my thumb finds her clit. As soon as I start to rub the bundle of nerves, her body vibrates below me, her hands grabbing for my shoulders.

"Nuh uh... not yet." I thrust harder to feel her body teeter on the edge of no return. If she comes, I won't be able to stop myself from following, and I'm not ready to have this end just yet.

In one swift move, I flip her, so her chest is pressed against the conference table and her perfectly round ass perched for me to play with. I can't help it when my hand connects with her ass cheek, and then again on the other. They redden instantly, and my dick twitches at the sight. She lets out a loud throaty moan, and I wrap my hand around her mouth to stifle the sound.

"Shhh..." I say teasingly. "We wouldn't want anyone to hear you now, would we?" I enter her again in one fluid motion. "Fuck, you feel so good." Biting her shoulder, I pick up my pace.

She groans as my cock fills her over and over again. Her body begins to tremble, her moans quiet but consistent, and I don't think I can hold off much longer.

"Parker, I'm going to come," she gasps, earning her another swat on her ass.

"Oh my God," breathes out as she pushes herself farther onto my cock, taking all that I can give and clenching around me.

She's getting louder by the second, and I want to make sure no one catches us. I know this floor of the building should be empty, considering the party has moved to the rooftop garden, but that doesn't mean someone hasn't gone perusing around to check out the place.

Thinking quickly, I grab my loosened tie from around my neck and string it through her half-opened mouth, holding on to each of the ends in one hand. I feel an instant flush of juices flow from Ava's sweet pussy. My girl likes it rough and dirty.

"If you need me to loosen my grip on the tie, you tap three times on the table," I tell her, knowing she will be unable to use her safe word if she needs to.

She pushes herself onto me farther in response, her wetness coating her thighs and mine.

Fuck yes. I don't think I'll ever get tired of the way her body melts for me.

I bend over her, getting close to her ear and nipping at her skin on my way. "Tonight, you will ask for my permission to come, and you will ask properly. When I decide you're ready, then, and only then, will you get your release. Do you understand?"

She quivers, nodding frantically in understanding.

Lifting her chin all the way up, so we make eye contact, I add, "You look so fucking beautiful right now...taking my cock like the good little brat you are."

Her eyes roll back in her head as she lets out the sexiest fucking sound. My thrusts quicken when I feel her body begin to quake.

"Do you need to come, Angel?" I let up on the tie, allowing her to speak.

"Fuck yes, Parker, please," she gasps.

"Ask correctly." I tsk, watching her pupils blaze in lust as they lock onto mine.

"Please, Sir, can I come? Please, please, please," she begs, hands nails digging into the desk below her.

"Come all over my cock, Av. I want to feel that pussy clench all around me."

Just as the permission leaves my lips, I tighten my hold on the tie and fuck her harder.

Her body breaks under me, and as always, it's the most euphoric feeling. She never ceases to amaze me with what she's willing to try, and lately, that's been a hell of a lot.

There is no denying our connection. She was made for me, and I her.

I feel my cock twitch, her orgasm pulsing around me as I empty myself deep inside of her with a barely restrained roar.

"Holy shit, that was perfect," I breathe out as I kiss a trail up her shoulders. She is slumped over the table, thoroughly fucked. Her cheeks are flushed, and she has the most adorable smile on her face as her mind returns to her body.

"Thank you, Sir."

Ah, those words are like music to my ears. And I intend on hearing them for the rest of my life, if she'll have me.

Because she's it for me.

She is my forever.

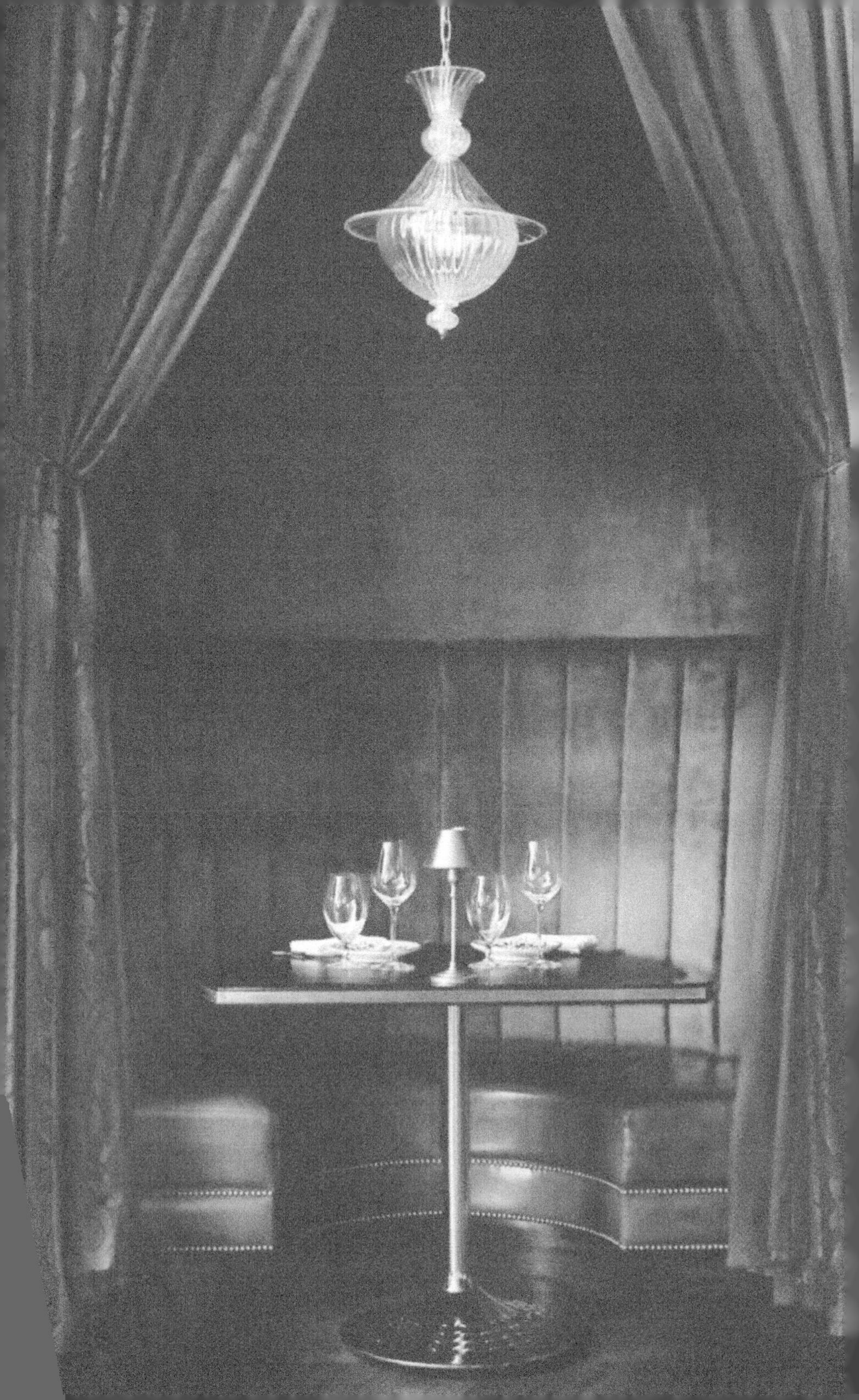

Epilogue

Ava

A little over a month later

I plop down on the couch beside Parker, who is currently deep in conversation with Dalton.

Today was so fun. I don't think I've ever seen Parker laugh so much as he has on this trip. Even though I was the butt of his jokes most of the day. *Literally.* My ass hurts from falling over and over as I attempted to snowboard with him. Needless to say, I'm exhausted.

I stuff my feet under his warm thigh. Even though he's mid-sentence, he pulls me in, and I snuggle up to him as close as possible.

The snow falls all around the home we've rented for the weekend. Floor-to-ceiling glass surrounds the living room space, giving us the perfect view of the snowy Vermont night.

"Well, I know a great designer," I hear Parker say, causing me to zone in on the conversation. "But you can't borrow her right now. She's busy creating the oasis of everyone's dreams with me in Hudson Valley." His attention shifts to me, and I smile up at him.

The Hudson Valley project is just getting started, and it's already breathing life into Parker that I think he's been missing for a long time. He isn't the same man I met two years ago. Now he's one who smiles more than he scowls. A man who laughs and jokes. A man who is a cat lover. A man who shows me with his actions every day just how much I mean to him.

I'm so thankful he treats me like a complete partner on this project, asking my opinion and input on every little detail. The property has become extremely important to me…to us.

I was even able to pull off a little surprise of my own for once. Tears glossed his eyes when we drove up to the property and the landscapers were planting the rose garden in honor of his mom. It was simply a priceless moment and the perfect start to the special project.

Just thinking about his reaction has emotions threatening to choke me up until I'm pulled from my thoughts. Blossom and Sloan are getting out some games from the chest in the living room.

"I think we should play, boys against girls," Sloan says in Wes's direction.

"You don't want any of this," Wes teases her, and she playfully sticks out her tongue.

"What are we celebrating?" Wes asks Eli, who is carrying a bottle of champagne as he and Quinn walk back into the kitchen from putting the girls down. They are staying next door to us with Quinn and Eli's parents in the house they are sharing with Wes's mom and dad. Even though they all typically party harder than us, they offered to keep them at night so we didn't have to worry about being too quiet. I think it was just their excuse to get some extra grandparent time.

"Me whooping you and Eli's ass on the slopes today," Quinn quips in her true competitive fashion. Even though I have no doubt she put them to shame. Sloan wasn't feeling her best, so she offered to stay back at the chalet with the twins so that Quinn and Eli could both enjoy the slopes, since the grandparents were on nighttime duty.

"Ignore her. We are celebrating Q and I setting a date for the wedding," Eli says proudly as he passes around glasses of champagne.

"Oh my gosh, when?" I ask at the same time Sloan and Blossom blurt the same.

Quinn looks at us with that *don't kill me* wince on her face. "Before baseball season starts."

Why doesn't this surprise me? I knew these two wouldn't wait long. And honestly, why should they? They've been through enough; they deserve this.

"Well, we better get busy planning," I say, my mind already running with lists and ideas based off things she has told me she wanted in the past.

"That is so exciting... It feels like we were picking out Sloan's dress just yesterday," Blossom chimes in, and I notice the way Sloan is looking at Wes before she speaks up. "I'll make some calls tomorrow. We need to get you a dress fitting ASAP."

Quinn looks to Sloan and me, most likely shocked at how calm we are.

"Why aren't you two freaking out?"

"Because we will make it work... I have a whole-ass Pinterest board with everything I know you like already," I say proudly.

Not admitting that I recently started one for myself as well. For the first time ever, a wedding is on my own radar. *One day.*

She whips her head to Sloan. "And you?"

"When it comes to you two, I learned to expect the unexpected. I figured it was coming," Sloan says calmly, and Eli interrupts, holding his flute in the air.

"To my good luck charm and the woman of my dreams… I can't wait to see you coming down that aisle toward me, Queenie girl." He leans in, kissing her, and we all cheer, so happy for them and their love story.

I stand up, clinking my glasses with the girls. Sloan brings the champagne to her lips, but doesn't take a sip. *Hmmm…that's strange.*

"Drink up, babes… Also, can we please do the bachelorette in Mexico for old times' sake?" Quinn asks, taking another swig of her champagne, and I follow suit.

Sloan stands there, smiling, and it's so obvious she's hiding something from us. I see Quinn's eyes narrow in on her, and then Sloan's hand goes protectively to her belly.

I gasp, right as Quinn shouts, "Bitch, are you pregnant?"

"Wait, what? Who's pregnant?" Eli asks, and Wes must catch on to what's going on because he moves quickly to Lo's side. "We are… Surprise!"

Pandemonium ensues with everyone hugging and congratulating them.

I look over to Parker, happy I have my person here to experience all these highs with. I trail my finger over the new collar around my neck. It's delicate, all gold, and looks beautiful above the sea glass pendant I still wear often.

We have officially started our exploration into our Dom/sub relationship, and let's just say, so far, it has been nothing but amazing. I didn't think our connection could get any deeper, but this commitment has taken us to another level of intimacy.

I feel so entwined with every piece of Parker. That thought would have terrified me before, but now I have complete confidence in our relationship and devotion to one another.

Smiling on at my friends and all their exciting news, it feels amazing to know I will have this one day with the man I love.

For now, we're going to keep exploring all aspects of life and building our dreams together.

Parker sees me watching him from across the room, and I trace his every move as he makes his way toward me. He leans down, whispering in my ear, "Is now a good time to announce our news?"

I stare up at him in confusion, until understanding hits and a big smile takes over my face.

The big softy wanted Binx to have a friend when we are gone, so we are getting another cat.

Holding in my laugh at the fact he thinks this is big news, I say, "We will let them have their moment."

He smiles, kissing my forehead, and whispers, "I love you, Angel."

"I love you more, P."

"I don't think that's possible."

The End

Afterword

Thank you so much for reading Reckless Encounters. It means the world to us to have your support.

Reviews are everything to us authors. So, if you enjoyed reading, please consider leaving a review!

Acknowledgments

First and foremost, we want to thank our readers. From the bottom of our hearts, we thank you for taking a chance on us.

Thank you to my ride or die, LOML, my husband, for always supporting me and loving me through everything. Also, for the writing inspo :)

Shout out to my best girl for entertaining herself when I needed to fit in some writing and for inspiring me to be the best version of myself. I love you both forever and ever.

Thank you to my book bestie now co-author for riding this wild roller coaster with me and being the other part of my brain. Let's keep making magic together, babe! -A

I want to thank my husband for dealing with my many late nights filled with writing and half-watched shows. Thank you for encouraging and supporting this crazy dream of mine.

Thank you to my two little ladies for understanding that "I need just a few more minutes" really means "until I get this scene finished." You two are the reason I'm shooting for the stars. I want to make you proud.

Eeep! My other half, thank you for doing this with me. We make one kick-ass team and I'm so proud of what we've accomplished so far. With every book I grow more and more excited to see how far we can go! xox – L

We also want to thank those closest to us for their support and love throughout this dream of ours.

Sara, our sweet friend, PA, and BETA reader. Thank you for all that you do for us. You have been a true blessing. We appreciate you!

To our editor Mackenzie, we adore you. Thank you so much for the time spent on our babies and for helping make it the best version it could be. It is such a pleasure working with you. Your suggestions are always so on point and exactly what we need, forever grateful for your flexibility as well.

To our Beta team — Thank you to Melissa B, Mackenzie, Anna, Melissa W, Jessica, Kelsey, Adrian, Kazia, and Ashley for being betas. Your feedback, ideas, and support helped make these characters even better. All of you helped us truly develop Ava and Parker's story and give everyone the HEA they wanted for these two.

Thank you to our ARC/Street team. We appreciate each and every one of you for taking the time to give us honest reviews and promote our book. Reviews help authors more than people realize and we are so appreciative.

We especially love our street team group chats… when it pops off in there, it's the best. You babes are so fun, and your encouragement has been the best part of our busy days in the writing cave.

TL Swan, not only would we not have met because of your readers' group, but we also wouldn't have been encouraged to be authors. Thank you to Tee and the fellow cygnets for all the advice and constant motivation to go for it!! We love having the group for a listening ear or some sound advice. Special thank you to our author friend JR Gale with this one and all your advice.

Last but certainly not least, we want to shout out to our Book Obsessed Babes community...

Each of you inspires us to continue this crazy journey.

Thank you all for being a part of something that we cherish. We're truly grateful.

About the Author

A New Yorker and a Southern Belle.
Two Book Obsessed Babes that became lifelong best friends over their love for a good romance novel.

When they're not writing, they're devouring a good book or spending time with their family and friends.

Total opposites in some ways and exactly the same in others, making them a dynamic author duo.

Keep in touch with us... Follow our Socials

Also by L.A. Shaw

Make You Series

#0.5 Make You Miss Me (Trent & Ashley)

#1 Make You Love Me (Greyson & Lottie)

#2 Make You Want Me (Nox & Emerson- Book 1)

#3 Make You Keep Me (Nox & Emerson- Book 2)

#4 Fall 2024 (Trent & Ashley)

Reckless Hearts Series

#1 Reckless Abandon (Sloan & Wesley)

#2 Reckless Impulse (Eli & Quinn)

#3 Reckless Encounters (Ava & Parker)

Wild Blooms Series

Blossom & Bliss (Blossom & Dalton)

Made in the USA
Las Vegas, NV
30 June 2024